"Whatever you want to do with me, do it."

At Swan's words, Rob's mouth pressed to hers. Then she felt a sharp sensation and cried out in surprise. He had nipped her lip, the inner edge where it was plump and tender.

"You taste good," he whispered. "Like sex and deep, shuddering sighs. I want to drink you to the last drop."

He tasted like sex, too. Powerful male-on-the-hunt sex. It was intoxicating.

His lips found the side of her neck. Instinctively he seemed to know the sweet spot at the base of her throat. Hot kisses there made her arch her back as she rocked against his pelvis. The hard flesh encased in his jeans caused her to moan in anticipation.

"We can still stop," he told her. "It's not too late."

Stop? Swan had never heard anything more ridiculous in her life.

Blaze™

Dear Reader,

Every once in a while, if we're lucky, we get a chance to revisit something that has brought us great joy and satisfaction. This is one of those times for me. When the opportunity to write for Blaze came my way, I felt very lucky, and not just because it's an exciting, innovative and no-holds-barred line. It was my chance to revisit series romance.

I started my career at Harlequin-Silhouette, and what a great way to start. The books were fun, sexy, challenging and intensely satisfying to write. I hope they were as satisfying to read. But things have changed a little since then. Blaze has broken new ground, not to mention a few rules, and they continue to shake things up, which makes them irresistible to writers— and readers—who love to live on the edge.

When the idea for *Brief Encounters* came to me, I knew it was a series romance, and I suspected it was a Blaze book. So I was delighted when my editor agreed and invited me to write not one, but three, Blaze books. The prospect of writing about a heroine who designed men's underwear seemed to have limitless possibilities for racy fun and games. Swan McKenna doesn't just fantasize about whether men are wearing briefs or boxers, she gets to go there!

I hope you enjoy Swan's "encounters" with FBI agent Rob Gaines, whose turn as an underwear model was about as much steamy fun as I've ever had writing about a hero. I also hope you'll look for *Beyond Suspicion,* a two-in-one collection that features the reissue of my top-selling series romance, *The Man at Ivy Bridge,* available in January 2004.

It's good to be back!

Suzanne Forster

BRIEF ENCOUNTERS

Suzanne Forster

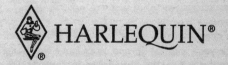

HARLEQUIN®

TORONTO • NEW YORK • LONDON
AMSTERDAM • PARIS • SYDNEY • HAMBURG
STOCKHOLM • ATHENS • TOKYO • MILAN • MADRID
PRAGUE • WARSAW • BUDAPEST • AUCKLAND

Long overdue thanks to my intrepid plot group: Olga Bicos, Lori Herter, Lou Kaku, Jill Marie Landis and Meryl Sawyer. For the group therapy as much as for the brainstorming. Your support makes work— and life—a pleasure!

ISBN 0-373-79105-4

BRIEF ENCOUNTERS

1

SWAN MCKENNA had been inspecting half-naked men for the better part of the afternoon. And she still hadn't found Mr. Right. Watching men strip down to their underwear was a job most women would have loved. And Swan should have loved it more than most. It was her underwear they were stripping down to. Well, not *her* underwear. She was wearing that. This was underwear she'd designed.

Now she needed a guy who could *sell* it.

"I need a man who can bump and grind!" she implored.

Swan was speaking on her cell phone to her assistant, Gerard Nichols, who was acting as host for the auditioning models. Swan's partner, Lynne Carmichael, who normally dealt with this sort of thing, was on the road doing advance work for their upcoming boutique tour. Her departure had left Swan and Gerard scrambling to get ready for the launch party tomorrow night. This was their first real show and L.A.'s fashion press had been invited for an exclusive sneak peek at the "cheeky" new line of male undergarments.

If Swan wasn't a bundle of naked nerve endings, she should have been. She and Lynne had worked for years to get to this place, against staggering odds. The fashion world regularly feasted on its own young and Swan felt a little like a chicken wing right now. One scathing review could crush them.

*A couple of guys who can striptease without getting all
tangled up in their army camouflage thongs. Is that too
much to ask?*

"It's a Village People revival out here," Gerard replied
in theatrical whispers. "We've got a Native American
chieftain, complete with headdress, a fireman with an ax,
a pistol-packin' cowboy. And, oh, my, call 9-1-1! The
telephone repairman who just walked in is to die for,
Swan. To *die* for."

Gerard was stationed in the foyer and Swan was in the
spacious music room of the Italianate villa that had recently become the operating headquarters for Brief Encounters, Swan and Lynne's design company.

"Oh, oh, oh, and there's a Marquis de Sade." Gerard
let out a little squeak. "He has a *whip,* Swan! An honest-
to-goodness whip! Shall I send him in?"

Swan's only response was a tiny jet of air through her
nostrils. Laughter took too much energy. Gerard was in
his element right now, she supposed. From the moment
she'd first met him, Swan had known that Gerard was gay.
She knew because he'd told her. *Hello, my name is Gerard Nichols, and I'm gay.* At the time Swan had wondered if that was how he introduced himself to everyone.
She discovered later that, generally, it was.

When he'd walked into her tiny Manhattan Beach, California, office that day, he'd also informed her that he was
answering her Assistant Wanted ad and she need look no
further. Sure, he'd grown up wanting to be an underwear
model like Mark Whalberg, but, at thirty-something, he
was a little too fond of strawberry-cheesecake ice cream.
Design was his second choice, but he couldn't draw. So
he was content to be indispensable.

And he was. Swan would have been lost without him.

"Let's try the telephone repairman," she said. "He
sounds safer. That fire-swallowing Adonis you just sent

in here dropped his baton and nearly set the place ablaze. No more of that, okay? And no more live animals, especially snakes.''

Swan didn't like snakes and this one had actually fallen from its handler's bare shoulders and slithered under the sofa Swan was sitting on. She still had goose bumps over that. It was a wonder it hadn't sent her running to the bathroom to relieve herself. For as long as she could remember, she'd suffered with a high-strung bladder. Some people got hives when they were nervous. Swan McKenna had to pee.

''But, Swaaaan—''

''No way, Gerard. Nothing creepy crawly, nothing with more than two legs, nothing flammable and nothing that is going to explode. This is a fashion show, not a demolition derby. Besides, I'm late with the insurance premium this quarter. I'm not even sure we're covered.''

She heard him sigh into the phone. Gerard enjoyed bells and whistles and had been arguing that the party's fashion show needed more special effects. Since Swan and Lynne couldn't afford pyrotechnics and laser lights, Gerard had suggested they let the models provide the runway pizzazz. Swan had finally agreed that he could invite some of his more exotic friends to audition, but this was ridiculous.

''The marquis looks like fun, Swan. Are you sure?''

''I've never been more sure, Gerard. Do *not* send in the guy with the whip.''

Gerard clicked off, and Swan went back to work on the growing stack of portfolios provided by the models. Résumés and glossy head shots were strewn across the glass-topped coffee table she was using as a work surface. Most of the guys were wanna-bes rather than professional models, which was lucky because Brief Encounters was currently too broke to pay modeling fees. The party food and decorations were largely donated, thanks to Gerard's ingenuity, and the men who'd shown up to audition were volunteering their time, hoping to get some exposure, probably—which shouldn't be a problem in her underwear.

Swan held the back of her hand to her forehead and felt the stickiness. August was typically the hottest month of the summer, even at the beach, and the fifty-year-old villa wasn't air-conditioned. Swan had dressed defensively, in capris and a tank top, but naked would have been too warm in this place.

The kicker was that she wasn't even supposed to be doing this task. Lynne had cooked up the impromptu launch party idea, hoping it would generate some publicity. It was a good idea and Swan had gone along with it; but Lynne was the gregarious one, the free spirit who had a flair for this sort of thing, which was why she worked sales, marketing and PR. Swan was the organizer and the bean counter. She also did most of the actual designing, but other than a few fittings and alterations, she rarely worked with the models.

Lynne was supposed to have come back to run the auditions, but she'd left a message from San Francisco, saying that something big was up and she would call back later to explain. She'd also dropped the name of a huge international designer. Lynne loved being mysterious, but this wasn't the time, not when they were facing their first-ever tour. At least Lynne had finalized all the details of their first runway show in Los Angeles, including the models, but Swan still had the launch party to deal with.

The music room door opened and the telephone repairman was all but pushed inside by Gerard, who grinned and waggled his fingers at Swan before leaving. The new model looked around as if he had no idea where he was or why he was there. A bad sign. Swan waved him into the room, but he didn't budge.

"I'm here to—"

"Yes, I know," she said brightly. "Great outfit. You're my first repairman, and I must say, it works."

And *how* it worked. This guy could have installed her phone any day of the week. Gerard hadn't done him justice, she realized. If Lynne had been there, she would have given him the compliment she reserved for lifeguards and the Olympic water polo team: *studly.*

Of course, Swan was trained to notice such things, but the man's legs were so long he must have had his blue jeans specially made. And who could miss the way he'd planted himself, his hips canted at an angle that emphasized their narrowness *and* the wide rake of his shoulders. The expression on his face was priceless, too. Bemused and quizzical, faintly suspicious. Male.

Swan felt heat stealing up the back of her neck and realized she was having a physical reaction right here in the music room. Was that possible? Something was tingling, and it wasn't her bladder!

"Ma'am...?"

His voice snapped her out of her trance. What in the world was she doing? Fantasizing in broad daylight? The only question that should have been on her mind at that moment was, can he dance?

"The CD player's over there," she said, pointing at the boom box that Gerard had set up on an antique tea cart. The regal old piece sat by a wall of cherry bookcases that housed the room's music library, and Swan wondered if the cart was appalled at the noisy machine that was vibrating its brass knobs and handles. She wondered if the whole house was appalled.

"Go ahead and put your music in," she told him.

The heat had now spread to her face, but she resisted the impulse to fan herself as she sorted through photos. She found one she planned to call back, but now she needed a pencil to make a note of it. Of course, every pencil she owned was missing in action. When the August weather had started to get to her, she'd pulled her long auburn hair up into a loose bun to cool her neck. Patting around, she found a No. 2 Ticonderoga stuck in the waves. Her hair probably resembled a floor mop by now, but there wasn't time to repair it. She tugged the pencil free, her hair miraculously staying in its knot, and her gaze drifted toward the model.

He was standing right where she'd left him.

"You didn't bring any music, right?" Some of the guys had brought their own CDs and some hadn't. "That's okay," she said as she hurried over to the boom box, popped in a disc and pushed the Play button. Hot, pulsing music filled the room. If you could dance, "Disco Inferno" was your song.

The music was too loud to talk over, so she gave the model a directorial point of her finger. "You're on," it said. She moved to the music herself, shaking her shoulders and nodding encouragingly. She'd actually had to dance with one of the guys to get him going, and it looked as if she had another shy one on her hands.

Maybe that was the secret of this one's appeal. Not just studly, but shy.

He *was* heart attack material, she admitted, wondering what she was going to have to do to inspire him. It was just plain hot the way his blue work shirt fell open at the neck and his tool belt hung on his hips. His hands were braced on the worn leather and he'd cocked his head, as if to say he wasn't making a move until he was good and ready. But, boy, when he did. All he would have to do was to shake those shoulders and women everywhere would fall on their noses. Swan was teetering already. He could have sold underwear to a nudist colony.

This was the best raw material she'd seen all day, so

to speak. She had to get him dancing. *Okay, what would Lynne do?* she asked herself—and not for the first time. Her partner had a bold, carefree manner that Swan had always admired. Lynne knew how to keep men guessing, which seemed to make them want her all the more. She was flirty and provocative, but whenever Swan tried that, she got into trouble. Maybe this was her chance to practice.

Swan walked briskly over to the model. To hesitate was death. As she approached, he gave her a searching look and a lazy smile that said he might be checking her out, as well. Not as shy as she thought? She felt an instant's unease but dismissed it. Her mission was to find men with happy feet. Sure he looked good, but could he move? Could he dance and undress at the same time? Could he make a woman hot, maybe even her, who hadn't been above 98.6 in years? And, more important, could he sell the thongs, briefs and tank tops that were going to be Brief Encounters's showcase products?

"Maybe I can help," she said. "Just relax and go with me."

She braced her legs and rotated her hips, only to see his brows flatten skeptically. "Come on," she coaxed. "You can do it."

She began to sing along with the music and shake her shoulders, but still nothing. What? Was he practicing to be a palace guard?

With a sigh, she placed her hands on his hips and began rocking them back and forth, encouraging him to rotate. This was exactly what Lynne would have done, but it was so *not* Swan McKenna. Her heart was pounding as fast as the music.

"Yes, that's it!" she said, thinking she'd felt him move. "Work with me. That's right, work with me, baby."

Work with me, baby?

She didn't dare look up, or he would have seen the flush creeping up her neck. She gripped him harder, rotating wider. "Shake it one time for me," she croaked.

What was happening to her voice?

"Ma'am?"

"No, keep moving," she insisted. "I think you're getting the idea."

Swan was staring at the man's rotating pelvis so hard she could have counted the teeth on his zipper. It didn't take X-ray vision to know what was lovingly cradled inside those beautifully worn jeans. She could see the telltale bulge. It ran nearly the length of his fly, and as much as she didn't want to be guilty of ogling him, there was nowhere else to look.

"You are so hired," she said under her breath.

She wasn't quite sure what happened next. Either her hands slipped or he suddenly mastered Bump and Grind 101, because his rotating pelvis came into brief heated contact with her thigh.

"You mean, like that?" he asked.

Swan gave out a little squeal and jumped back. She sounded like Gerard, but the unexpected contact had startled her. Had he actually brushed her leg with his crotch? Obviously this guy didn't need any more help. He had the idea.

"Oookay," she said, "that was progress."

Swan was now red to her scalp. Nevertheless she ordered herself to meet his gaze and to hold it until she'd calmed down. He still looked a little perplexed, rather like a stag in headlights, but she wasn't buying the innocent act. This was a business and she had a show to put on. Her entire future was riding on it and the futures of others, as well. She'd had to let their seamstresses go until things picked up, and that had been far harder to do than this.

Besides, Lynne would never have been playing coy games with one of these guys. She might have coaxed him along with a few dancing lessons, but if he hadn't caught on, he would have been sent on his way.

"Nice move," she said, trying to sound faintly sardonic. "Now drop those jeans and show me what you got."

Her partner would have been proud.

But the repairman was still hesitant and something in Swan took over again. This was where all the other models had balked, too. Not that she blamed them. She couldn't have stripped for an audience, either. With her nerves she would have had to wear diapers!

Business, she reminded herself. *You're not asking him to expose state secrets, just the underwear you designed.* All the models were supposed to be wearing Brief Encounters under their costumes.

"All right, I'll help," she told him, "but this is the last time."

She walked back to him, snappily undid the tool belt that hung around his trim waist and let it drop. It landed on the floor with a heavy metallic thud.

Whoa. The ladies were going to scream when that happened. Swan could guarantee it. If he had anywhere near the effect on them he was having on her, Brief Encounters was going to sell out their stock at the first show.

"Disco Inferno" blared into its chorus and the repairman lifted his hands as if he were either surrendering the fort or waiting for her to do the honors. Swan quickly obliged, wondering what alien organism had taken control of her brain. She undid the brass button on his jeans and lowered his zipper.

"I can't do this for you on the runway," she said.

But then again, maybe she could. What a video clip that would be. *It's the middle of the fashion show and* one of the models can't get his costume off, so the designer goes up to help him? That could be a showstopper. *Oh, my God, Lynne, come back. I've either had a flash of brilliance or I'm losing my mind.*

His jeans were undone, but she still had the challenge of getting them over his tightly locked gluts. It took some tugging, but finally the denim material gave way and dropped to the floor. Unfortunately the stubborn jeans took her with them. Suddenly she found herself squatting right in front of him, staring at the bulge in person. But there was just one problem.

He wasn't wearing her underwear. He wasn't wearing *anyone's* underwear!

It was a penis, Swan realized to her horror. The very thing she was trying to cover with her designs. No one should ever see a penis in one of her shows, especially one that looked suspiciously…alert?

Swan was just inches away from said organ, but she was still too shocked to do much of anything but gape. Worse, *much* worse, for some inexplicable reason, she was intrigued. Her whole body vibrated with a wild, unfamiliar emotion and for one crazy second in time she fought off a terrible impulse to touch it. Only to see how it felt. She wasn't going to run a finger up and down the entire length of it or fondle it, for heaven's sake. She was just curious.

The object of Swan's fantasy suddenly twitched and a strangled sound slipped from her throat. Worse, her valiant attempts to speak resulted in nothing but helpless gurgles and groans. At that very moment the music room door opened and as if summoned by the Devil himself, Gerard poked his head in.

"Are you finished? Oh, I guess not!" He swiftly shut the door.

Swan knew how it must have looked. And sounded,

given the obscene noises she'd been making. She would never hear the end of this. At least the music had stopped. She wasn't sure when that had happened. Now she needed to get up off her knees so she could climb to the top floor of the mansion and jump out the window.

The model offered a hand, but Swan didn't dare. He was bottomless and parts of him were still winking at her. What in the world was wrong with him? Did his privates have some neurological disorder?

"Ma'am? Are you all right?"

"I'm fine," she said, turning away from him to get to her feet. Once she'd managed that, she slapped smooth her bunched-up capris and straightened her top.

Without turning around she said, "I guess there's no point in getting you some underwear and starting this audition over?"

"No, probably not. I don't dance."

"You don't wear underwear, either. So then, why exactly are you here?"

"To fix the phone?"

She glanced over her shoulder at the decidedly virile specimen with his jeans around his ankles. "You really are a telephone repairman?"

"Afraid so," he said.

"Oh, my God."

"Can I put my pants on now?" he asked.

What had she done? Swan had no idea what the correct etiquette was in a situation such as this. Should she go back and pull his pants up for him? Should she beg his forgiveness? Luckily, the repairman wasn't concerned about manners. He bent down, grabbed his jeans and shimmied back into them. As he retrieved his tool belt, a flood of apologies began pouring forth from Swan's mouth. She wondered if she and Lynne could be sued for something like this! That was all she needed. A sexual harassment charge.

"Could I give you some underwear?" she offered. "A lifetime supply?" Now she was bribing him. Were there laws against that?

"What fun would that be?" he replied in a tone that was wickedly soft.

She searched his handsome face, looking for signs of mercy and compassion. "Fun? Oh, right! That wouldn't be any fun at all."

Was that a flicker of amusement in his cool blue eyes? She couldn't tell. She was momentarily distracted by the striking contrast of the dark hair falling onto his forehead and his faintly arched brows. She would have given anything to know if he was attracted to her. His body seemed to like her well enough, but maybe that was an aberration. She didn't usually have that effect on men.

He picked up his tool belt and draped it over his shoulder. "Maybe you should point me to your office," he said, "and I'll make myself useful. Someone reported a phone problem."

Swan wasn't aware of any such problem, but Lynne or Gerard could have called it in. "Through that door and down the hall to your right," she said. "You can't miss it. There's a life-size poster of a local lifeguard in Brief Encounters. We wanted Vin Diesel, but—"

He was already heading for the door. "I am so sorry," she called after him. "I thought you were one of the models. Really, I did! Sir?"

He hesitated, and she immediately thought better of the question that had been in her head since she'd been on the floor in front of him. *Is that normal for you? I mean, in a resting state, is that normal?*

"Never mind," she said, waving him on. "I just, uh,

well—I'm sorry about that twitching problem. I have a nervous condition myself."

He turned around with a glint in his eye that was positively demonic. "Nerves don't make me twitch," he said. "Women do—and you *should* be sorry."

His voice was dangerously low and husky, and she had the feeling he didn't often give women the once-over quite so boldly. His hot gaze brushed her body, lingering here and there—especially *there*, as if he were imagining *her* with her pants down and him on his knees. Her belly clutched deeply. Her skin had begun to flush and tingle, and by the time his eyes returned to hers she was actually trembling inside. It was a sensation she hadn't felt in a very long time.

Swiftly another sensation came upon her. She had to pee! She crossed her ankles and smiled as best she could under the circumstances.

He must have noticed because he snorted low laughter. "Maybe we had both better get back to work?" he suggested. And with that he was gone.

Swan groaned and headed for the bathroom, which was just off the music room, fortunately. Her face was still ablaze with embarrassment, but at least she would get a moment alone to collect herself.

From behind she heard Gerard call out, "Oh, Swa-aan…"

She stopped dead in her tracks, whirled around and pointed her finger at him. "Not a word, Gerard. Not one word from you."

"Whatever you say," he murmured.

Swan thought she heard a reference to "Deep Throat" as she dashed into her sanctuary and shut the door. She didn't have to see her beastly assistant to know that he was grinning from ear to ear.

ROB GAINES should not have been smiling. He had work to do. He shouldn't have been thinking about her, either, but short of a drug-induced coma, he didn't see that happening. How often did an incredibly hot redhead sidle up to a man, pull down his pants and drop to her knees in front of him? At a moment like that there wasn't a whole lot else to think about except what she was planning to do next, with her breath so steamy hot and her gorgeous mouth just inches from his—

The twinge of near pain in his groin brought him back to his senses.

Gaines, stop smiling or you're going to permanently injure yourself.

He pulled a pair of needle-nose pliers and went to work. But as he played with the phone, his thoughts veered back to her. Too bad he couldn't sign up for dance lessons. She could teach him how to dip and he could teach her what happens when curious little girls play games with big boys.

He could imagine reaching around to undo all that wild redness she kept piled on top of her head and letting it fall loose around her shoulders. He could also imagine kissing her gorgeous lips until they were wet with desire.

He could imagine a few other things, too, but his jeans were getting crowded again—and he had work to do. A mission to accomplish. Quickly. Before anyone had a chance to walk in and interrupt him.

2

SWAN HAD ALL OF NINETY seconds to herself in the bathroom before her cell phone rang. She considered ignoring it but remembered Lynne had promised to call, and she needed to talk to her partner. If it turned out to be someone else, they would just have to listen to her tinkle.

Swan hit the talk button, but didn't even get to say hello.

"Can you spell yacht?" Lynne Carmichael sang out. "I'm on his yacht, Swan! Gvon Marcello's yacht! We're heading out to sea in a matter of minutes."

"I can't even spell Gvon," Swan admitted. "What are you doing on his yacht? I need you here!"

And that was an understatement. She and Lynne weren't just business partners, they'd been all but inseparable since childhood, sharing everything, especially their problems. They'd gone to the same schools right up until they graduated high school, when Swan had received a scholarship to study design at Brooks College, and Lynne had pursued a business degree at U.S.C.

"Swan, this is big. *Big*. I showed Gvon our stuff, and he loves it. He's dropping hints that he might give us our own label. We'd design for him, but it would be our name on the clothes. And he doesn't want just underwear. He wants loungewear, too, and maybe eventually, sportswear, men's *and* women's. Think about it, Swan. This is a dream come true."

Swan had thought their tour was a dream come true,

but she could hear Lynne's excitement. "How did you meet him and why are you on his yacht?"

"It was that fund-raiser fashion show I told you about. One of the models introduced me to Gvon, and I had my suitcase of samples with me. Now he wants to talk business, and he said we could do that on his boat—I mean, yacht, *excuse* me!"

Swan's sense of urgency grew and it wasn't just physical. "Lynne, is this what we want to do? Team up with someone else?" They'd worked so hard for this chance to have their own line and they'd always seemed equally driven to succeed. Lynne came from money and Swan didn't, but that had never mattered to either of them. Swan sometimes wondered if they each needed to prove themselves *because* of their very different stations in life— Lynne because she'd been given so much and Swan because she'd been given so little.

"It's not someone else. It's Gvon Marcello! How many pipsqueak designers like us ever get this chance? Just to be near him is golden."

Lynne was not going to be talked out of this opportunity. That much was clear, and Swan didn't necessarily want to pass it up, either. Big breaks came rarely in their business.

"Okay, okay, do what you can," Swan said, "and then get yourself back here. The party's tomorrow night."

There was a distinct gulp on the other end. "I'll never make it back for the party, Swan. We're heading out for some secret destination, and even I don't know where we're going. Gvon's destinations are always secret, so the press won't find out."

"And you'll be back *when?*"

"Two days, three at the most. I know this is crazy and unexpected, but think of the chance to bond with a couture designer."

"Bond? It sounds like you're being kidnapped."

"Oops, we're leaving. Hear that horn? Now, listen to me, Swan, this is important. Art Long called me, and our loan's come through. You need to go to the bank at ten tomorrow and pick up the check. Art will be waiting for you."

The check, thank God! They'd had to mass produce their line to supply the boutiques, and the cost was staggering. Without this money, they wouldn't be able to handle the mounting bills or pay their share of the tour expenses.

"You're going to have to sign for it," Lynne was saying, "and you may have to sign my name, as well, but don't worry. You've done that before on business stuff. Besides, Art's the loan officer, and he'll push it through."

Swan winced at the pressure, both from Lynne's news and her own bladder. She'd held back out of correct telephone etiquette, but everyone had a breaking point. A sigh of relief escaped her.

"Are you peeing?" Lynn asked.

How could she tell? Swan plucked the air freshener from the back of the commode and spritzed the air, as if that could disguise her failure of nerve. How many overachievers out there had to trot to the john just when things were getting challenging? This had to be a club with a membership of one.

"I'll take care of the check," she assured Lynne. "Have fun, but if you're not back in time for the L.A. show, I'm coming to get you."

"So I guess the audition went badly?" Lynne persisted. "If you're in the bathroom, it must have been bad."

"Sometimes people just have to go. I was in here when you called."

Lynne sighed. "How bad was it, Swan? You might as well tell me."

"Terrible." Swan shuddered at the thought. "I molested a repairman, thinking he was one of the models."

"Way to go!" Lynn chortled with delight. "Was he cute?"

Swan found herself smirking into the mouthpiece. "Cute doesn't begin to describe this guy. He's sex on the cloven hoof, sent from the hottest region of hell to torment me."

"Wow, *that* good?"

"Dark hair, blue eyes, the longest legs I've ever seen." Including the third one. "Just my type."

"I didn't know you had a type."

"I didn't, either." Swan sighed, perfectly aware that she would never see the man again. Lynne would have gotten his business card and his bank balance before she let him go. Probably a saliva sample, as well.

"Well, it sounds like *you're* having fun, you vixen. How's the model search going otherwise?"

"I still haven't found anyone who can dance and unbutton his fly at the same time. I never realized what an art form that was. We should have called the modeling agency instead of letting Gerard recruit his friends."

"Well, then call the modeling agency."

"And how do you suggest we pay them?"

"With the check you're picking up tomorrow!"

That prompted Swan's second sigh of relief. Of course, they had money now. Maybe they could even afford to pay Gerard's back wages. Oh, happy day. Now all she needed was for Lynne to come back safely and the show could go on.

"Gotta go," Lynne said. "Something's moving and it isn't me."

"Be careful!" Swan pleaded, but her partner had already hung up. And with the sound of Lynne's voice went Swan's elation. Somehow Swan was going to have to get through the launch party tomorrow night and probably the L.A. show on her own. The odds of Lynne getting back for either seemed slim. But Swan wasn't alone. She had her indispensable Gerard—and some emergency funding to ease the pain.

Thanks to Art Long, she thought. Lynne had been dating him for a couple of months now, and Art was the one who'd suggested they use the villa as collateral for a business loan. Lynne's mom and stepdad had retired and moved to the Florida Keys, leaving her the charming, three-story mansion. Unfortunately, Lynne could barely afford the taxes, and her mother's one condition was that she cover all costs in maintaining the house.

Swan had moved in last year to help defray expenses and they'd converted the villa's first floor into their design center and offices. But they were still running short every month. Then La Bomba, a trendy west-coast clothing chain, offered to show Brief Encounters's wares exclusively and to promote them with a fashion show tour. It looked as if the struggle was over. But only in the long term. In the short term, their manufacturing costs had soared and they had yet to recoup any of the money. If the shows didn't generate strong sales...

Well, Swan wasn't going to think about that.

Art had pushed the paperwork through in record time, and now it seemed he was willing to participate in a bit of forgery, as well. Lynne had her ways, but Swan wasn't sure she wanted to know how Lynne had managed to wrap a banker around her little finger.

Swan's crisis seemed to be over, so she quickly finished. Washing her hands, she glanced at herself in the oval mirror above the marble sink, but did not like what she saw. She looked exactly like what she was: a thirty-year-old woman who'd had to sacrifice most of her "me" time to keep a business afloat. Her aquamarine eyes were her best feature, but even their rather exotic almond shape couldn't stop them from looking stressed and weary.

Tired of fighting with her long auburn hair, she'd gone after it with a claw clip and it was now back where it belonged, sitting on top of her head. She was grateful for its rich luster, but she probably could have used a stylist—a few highlights wouldn't have hurt, either. Still, all the sacrifices had been worth it, especially now. She'd come a long way since she and Lynne had joined forces. They both had.

They'd grown up together, though under very different circumstances. Swan's mother, Pat, had worked for Lynne's mother as a housekeeper, but they were both single moms and had many things in common, which was probably why their working relationship had developed into a lasting friendship. Eventually Lynne's mother, Felice, had remarried, but she and Pat had remained close. Pat still worked as a housekeeper for another very wealthy family. Her duties now mostly involved supervising the household staff. Whenever she could, she traveled to Florida to visit Felice.

Swan owed much to her mother. It was Pat who had taught her to sew and to piece whole outfits together from whatever material was available. Swan took to it quickly, once fashioning slacks and a blazer from a corduroy bedspread. But her mother was also a cautious and fearful soul who believed that dreams were dangerous and pursuing them even more so. She'd never wanted Swan to do anything but follow safely in her footsteps. "It's steady work," she liked to say. "You'll never go hungry or lack for a roof over your head."

Maybe that was another reason Swan felt the need to prove herself. Her doting mom was waiting for her to fail.

Swan felt as if she were carrying Brief Encounters squarely on her shoulders right now, and everything she and Lynne had was at stake. It wasn't just their business, it was this house, too....

But if she didn't stop thinking like that, she would never get out of the loo.

She peeked up and down the hallway before letting herself out of the bathroom. Somewhere loose in this building was a dangerously attractive telephone repairman with a twitch, and she did not want to run into him again.

SWAN HAD ALWAYS FOUND banks a bit stifling, but this morning was different. She was absolutely thrilled to be at the Manhattan Beach branch of First National Heritage. Her pulse was alive with excitement as she walked into the heart of the brick-and-marble building and looked around for the man she needed. Now, where was Arthur Long?

She searched for a tall, lanky man with a heavily jelled crew cut and round Harry-Potter-like glasses. Swan didn't know a whole lot about Art, except that he was a loan officer at First National and Lynne was quite taken with him. Art was cute in a bankish way, and he had a habit of looking you straight in the eyes and clasping your hand the way a minister would. Unfortunately, he reminded her more of a salesman than a minister. He talked fast and breathy, and he liked to slip your name into the conversation as often as possible, as if to cement the fact that you were friends, darnit.

There he was, coming out of one of the bank's offices. She waved and managed to catch his eye. He headed her way, all horn-rimmed spectacles and big wide smile. Probably a perfectly nice guy, she thought, wondering why she wasn't lucky enough to be attracted to one of the nice guys of the world. Her first—and last—romantic disaster had been a limo driver, a bad boy down to his muscle-man T-shirts and unfiltered cigarettes. And now she was losing her mind over a telephone repairman who was too sexy for his tool kit?

She could feel the heat rising all over again as she thought about what she'd done to him. What she didn't understand was why she couldn't get him out of her head. She'd even dreamed about him last night, and of course what had she done in the dream but give in to her crazy impulse and touch him. *The entire vibrating length of him.* What happened after that was the stuff of X-rated videos. It could probably have gotten them arrested in some states.

"Right this way," Art said, seemingly unaware of his client's rocketing blood pressure as he guided her into his office. "Have a seat and we'll have this taken care of in a couple of minutes."

Swan managed to sit in an overstuffed leather chair and return Art's smile without giving away her breathy, over-heated condition. She forced herself to take in her surroundings. The size of the room and the quality of the decor were impressive. The desk looked as though it might be mahogany, and there was a matching credenza against the wall. Apparently Art was doing well. She was glad someone was. Was that gleam of gold on his wrist a Rolex watch?

"I can't tell you how much Lynne and I appreciate this," she assured Art. "I just wish she could be here."

His nod said he did, too. "She told me about Gvon. If all goes well, and I know it will, Swan, you two could be doing your fall show in New York next year."

He seemed very understanding about Lynne's sea voyage with another man, but it was widely believed that Gvon's interest in women was solely limited to the clothes he designed for them, so perhaps Art's masculinity wasn't threatened.

Art dragged a large folder of papers from the side of

his desk to the center. Even though there was no one else in his office, he lowered his voice. "We just need you to sign Lynne's name on a couple of these documents. As long as we have her permission, there's no problem. Basically, this stuff gets filed away and no one ever looks at it again."

Swan shifted uneasily. She wished she could be as casual about this little bit of forgery as Art and Lynne. Still, there weren't any other options. They needed the money now. The fate of their tour was on the line—and if the tour was on the line, so was their business.

"Okay," she said. "It isn't as if I haven't done this plenty of times—Lynne and I are always signing each other's names to forms, but never loan documents."

Art pulled a Cross pen from his pocket and handed it to her. "It'll be fine, Swan. There and there." He pointed to the appropriate places.

Unlike Swan's carefully controlled signature, Lynne's was a flamboyant scrawl that was completely illegible. It fit her carefree personality perfectly. Art slid the document that named the house as collateral over to her. Swan made a practiced twirl with her right hand and then laid pen to paper and signed her partner's name.

"I hope there aren't any problems with this," she said. "Lynne would be devastated if she lost that house. It's been in her family for ages, you know."

Art just grinned and swept the papers into a neat pile. "You two are unstoppable, trust me. You have a great future ahead of you."

"If only you were an underwear buyer." Swan watched as Art bundled the documents into a fan folder. From his top desk drawer he took out a check and a leather-bound book. "How's a hundred grand sound?" he said, handing her the check.

Swan's hand trembled as she took the money from him.

Her breath faded as she looked at it. *One hundred thousand dollars.*

"I had this organizer made up especially for your whirlwind tour," Art said, holding up the leather book. "It has your company name embossed on the pages and there's a digital order book in the back to keep track of your skyrocketing orders."

Swan had a mental image of the old organizer in her bag, which was falling apart from wear. The book he handed her was beautifully crafted. The organizer section was made of high-quality paper with their company name inscribed in beautiful lettering. The other section contained several useful compartments, including the one that held a tiny computerized order book. Swan was sure the package must have cost several hundred dollars.

"Thank you!" she exclaimed softy. "It's beautiful. Lynne will be as thrilled as I am."

"Listen, when she gets back, we'll all get together and have dinner. My treat."

Swan shook her head in protest. "*Our* treat, and we'll wrestle you for the check. You've been much too good to us."

Despite the banker specs, Art had a dashing smile and he flashed it now. "What red-blooded guy would turn down a chance to wrestle two beautiful women?"

Once Swan had gathered up her belongings, Art escorted her as far as the door of his office when a ringing phone stopped him. Swan quickly thanked him again and left. As she walked through the lobby, heading toward double glass doors leading to the bright sunshine outside, she had a thought that almost frightened her.

No turning back now.

MOMENTS BEFORE THE PARTY was about to start that evening, Swan stepped out onto the patio and allowed herself a moment to take in the magical world that lay before her in the estate's gardens. She clutched her new leather organizer, where she'd jotted her commentary for the show, and took a breath. Gerard had outdone himself. She couldn't imagine how he'd managed to put together such an elegant display on a party budget that bordered on embarrassing. Buffet tables sat on the left and right of a rented champagne fountain. Japanese lanterns hung in colorful patterns, augmenting the starlight from a crystal-clear sky above. At the far end of the garden Gerard had set up a runway, accented by delicate white lights. The entire space had become a place of wonder and delight.

"Are you pleased?" Gerard asked as he hurried up the flagstone steps and joined her. He took a moment to check out Swan's outfit and gave her a surprised blink of approval. It was a daring black silk halter top with a bias-cut skirt that she'd put together a couple of summers back, wondering if there would ever be an occasion to wear it. To gear yourself up for a bold move, this was the dress to wear, she thought. And tonight was the night.

"If you're not thrilled with all of this," he said, "I'm going to hang myself. Just like that nanny did in *The Omen*."

The way he stood with his hands on his hips and his face all expectant made Swan laugh. Gerard was no taller than five feet six and on the plump side these days but his heart was large, and that was what mattered. Plus, whatever he lacked in stature, he definitely made up for in Sturm and Drang.

"Gerard, I *love* it! How on earth did you ever manage this?"

He flipped his hand casually. "Oh, it was nothing. A little of this, a little of that, and a lot of discount shopping."

"I'll never be able to repay you. Not just for this, for

everything you've done these past few days. I couldn't have made it without your help."

"My pleasure, Duckling." He loved to call her Duckling instead of Swan, but at least he didn't put the U-word in front of it. "Lest you forget," he said, "I'm your biggest cheerleader. It isn't every day that a couple of feisty independents decide to strike out on their own, especially in this business—and you know how I love an underdog."

He headed off, beckoning her to come with him. "The guests will be arriving any minute, and you're the receiving line. Once you greet everybody and get them eating, drinking and mingling, I'll do the honors and introduce you."

Swan had been on the run for days, but suddenly her nervousness caught up with her. And it wasn't just the stress of the tour, as if that wasn't enough. She'd been having vivid dreams at night and flashbacks during the day, all of them erotic and all of them starring long-legged men with bulging tool kits. She never knew when the lurid images would pop into her head, and it was playing hell with her composure.

"I wish you were coming with me on the road trip," she said, trailing after Gerard. "If you were there, I wouldn't feel so…so…"

"Helpless? Vulnerable? Terrified?" Gerard offered.

Swan nodded. "Any one of those would fill the blank."

Gerard grabbed her hand and led her back into the house and down to the foyer. Her black-beaded heels clicked on the marble steps and her skirt swished against her legs. The knowledge that at least she'd dressed for the part boosted her confidence. She left her organizer on an occasional table as he went to open the door and usher in the first of the guests. *Here we go,* she thought, taking a deep breath.

The guest list had been a calculated move with calculated risks. The *L.A. Times* and the *Long Beach Press Telegram* were both sending their assistant fashion editors tonight. Photographers from *In Style* magazine and *Details* were scheduled to show up, as well. The risk was that they would pan the line. Veteran designers could weather bad reviews, but hopefuls could be wiped out by just one, especially if it was the premier show.

Besides the press, the small staff of people who had actually worked with Lynne and Swan to get the new line from idea to reality had been invited, along with the managers of the Los Angeles La Bomba boutique. Swan's mother had been invited, too, of course, but Pat McKenna was too concerned about the risks her daughter was taking to show up and witness them in person.

May she be wrong about that, Swan thought. *With all due respect, may she be dead wrong.*

Once she'd greeted everyone, Swan began mingling, making her way through the house and out into the gardens. It was quite a heady experience seeing so many enthusiastic faces and hearing the buzz of excitement about her new creations. Jan Hudson, the manager of La Bomba, rushed up to her.

"Wonderful party!" she said, clasping Swan's hand. "We can't wait for you to bring the show to the store. Everything is ready to go." She glanced around. "Where's your partner in crime?"

Jan clearly meant Lynne, but there was no time for Swan to explain. She was being summoned.

"It's show time!" Gerard called, waving at her from across the wide expanse of neatly trimmed grass. He was climbing the steps to the stage and runway that he and his buddies had built.

"Good luck," Jan said as Swan excused herself.

Swan silently rehearsed her opening lines as she headed for the stage. She wasn't accustomed to public speaking, but the show had to go on, and she was the one who had to deliver it. Fortunately she had the organizer notes to back her up if she went blank. And this bold black dress as her shield.

Just don't let me have to whiz, she prayed.

Gerard tapped the microphone with his hand. Three loud thumps assaulted the quiet night air. "Ladies and gentlemen," he said, "she is not only the designer of the hottest new line of male undies in recent memory—which will be sold exclusively through the La Bomba boutiques, I might add—she is also our master of ceremonies tonight. I give you Swan McKenna!"

Waving to the clapping crowd, Swan hurried up two creaky wooden steps to join Gerard at the podium.

"Swan McKenna!" he bellowed again. Gerard gave her a thumbs-up before disappearing behind the curtain of the makeshift stage. He'd also volunteered himself and his motley crew to run the slide show, lights and sound system.

"Thank you all for coming," Swan said, still a little breathless. Her voice sounded loud and hollow as it came through the speakers. "Some of you may have noticed that my partner, Lynne Carmichael, isn't with us tonight. She was called away on a business matter, but she sends her love and her gratitude for your support."

Swan sucked in a breath and smiled. "And now, I would like to present a sneak preview of Brief Encounters's first-ever line of male undergarments. This is our fall collection, and we have for your viewing pleasure our Romeo Underwear, our Hero Bodywear and our Machismo Activewear!"

On that cue, Gerard flipped on the sound system and the night erupted with Jerry Lee Lewis wailing out "Great Balls of Fire." The audience applauded as three male models burst onto the stage and began their routine. Behind them, projected on a black silk screen, were huge color slides of other pieces from the fall line. The photos had been Swan's idea, and it had cut down significantly on their need for models.

"Starting the show is our Romeo for tonight, Brad!" The applause was instantaneous as Brad took center stage. He wore an Armani tuxedo jacket and very little else. In one hand, he clutched a dozen roses, and in the other, a heart-shaped box of candy. His lower parts were encased in a snug-fitting thong that was glow-in-the-dark pink. But even Swan wasn't prepared when the lights went out. For a few moments, all you could see was a disembodied hot-pink thong bobbing around.

Not unlike my dreams, Swan thought ironically.

The crowd howled and flashbulbs popped as photographers jostled one another for a better angle.

"The Romeo imprint is for the romantic at heart," Swan said. "The man who knows how to sweet-talk and candy-walk his way right into his lover's heart. Romeo gets his Juliet every time when he's wearing a Brief Encounters design!"

As Brad left the stage, the second model came forward. He wore a traditional red fireman's helmet and had a length of fire hose draped over his bare shoulder as he strode confidently down the runway. "For the damsel in distress, for the adventuress, and for all who love a man in uniform, bring on the heroes!"

This round of applause was even louder than the first. Swan noticed that a few of the women in the audience were actually getting to their feet to get a better look at Sam the Fireman. Sam's formfitting briefs were fire-engine red with black suspender-like straps attached. When he got to the end of the lighted runway, he stopped and yanked the hose from his shoulder, pointing the nozzle at the audience.

"What do you think, ladies?" Swan asked cheerfully. "Is he hot enough for you? Should we hose him down?"

Sam dazzled them with a raffish grin before bowing his head. As he turned, the audience got their first good look at his tightly knotted buttocks, and the normally tranquil garden gave up a roar of approval.

"Whew," Swan said, wiping her brow in exaggerated fashion. "We better cool things off." There were loud groans of protest and Swan laughed. "You don't want to cool off? Not even with a swim? How about a swim with the man who's bold enough to wear Machismo?"

Model number three sprinted onto the runway in a black bikini swimsuit that left little to the imagination. Atop his head was a black swimming cap and goggles. Tall, tanned and sleek as a panther, he made his way down the runway.

Swan gave her spiel on the Machismo line and allowed the raucous response to build as she waved all three models back onto center stage. "This is only the preview," she shouted, trying to be heard over the noise. "The entire line can be seen tomorrow night at the La Bomba boutique on Melrose. Again, thank you all for coming!"

With that, she grabbed her organizer from the podium and descended into a throng of well-wishers. Her sense of relief outweighed everything else, but the success of the event began to dawn on her as she was swept into one embrace after another. Her guests, professional and otherwise, seemed thrilled by the program—and happy for her. Maybe it was safe to say that the fashion show was a hit. She only hoped the line was, too.

The press rushed over with questions about the show, and there was a line of people waiting to extend their congratulations. Swan held out through most of it, savoring the sweetness of Brief Encounters's first victory, and wishing Lynne had been here to share it. She had to find

Gerard to thank him, too. But finally, she had no choice. The need to excuse herself was becoming more urgent every second.

"Brava!" someone called out as Swan hurried into the house. Some of the guests had moved inside from the garden, and she smiled, waving as she sailed by them. The closest bathroom was in the hall, under the foyer staircase. She turned the knob, grateful that she had made it. Locked! From inside someone said, "Out in a sec."

But Swan didn't have much more than a second. She trotted down the hall and ducked into one of the guest rooms. The bathroom door was open and the light was off. Empty.

In record time she had her ruffled skirt hiked up and her panties and panty hose down to her ankles. She'd worn panties because her new Tanga Totally Nude panty hose were quite risqué without them—and also because of the problem that had brought her to the bathroom. A psychologist friend had told her that her sense of urgency was nothing more than a reaction to stress. Swan didn't disagree, but tell that to her bladder on a night such as this.

It hit her suddenly how exhausted she was. The past few days had been a whirlwind of activity, but she had made it through, and she had made it through on her own. It had not only gone well, it had gone better than she'd dreamed it might—the perfect day, really.

Lord, she was tired. She could go to sleep right here.

Letting her eyes drift shut, she reached for the toilet tissue. A few seconds later she heard a creaking noise and she slowly opened her eyes again. A few seconds? Swan blinked several times. It must have been long enough for her to have fallen into a deep sleep—because she was now dreaming that there was a man in her bathroom—a very tall, angry-looking man holding a big gold badge.

"Swan McKenna?" he said. "You're under arrest."

3

IT WAS A GOOD THING Swan had already finished her personal business. Otherwise she would have left a puddle on the bathroom floor. Under arrest? He had to be kidding. "Gerard!" she called. Her assistant must have put this guy up to it. "Get out of my bathroom," she croaked at the intruder when there was no immediate response from Gerard. Leaning toward the partially open door, she shouted again, "Gerard! Are you out there? This isn't funny. Get this policeman person out of my bathroom! The auditions are over!"

"FBI, ma'am," the intruder said. His voice was quiet and calm in the face of her distress. "And I'm not going anywhere. *You* are. To jail."

Swan couldn't even stand to demand that he leave. She was sitting on the throne with her panties down and her skirt up. This had to be some crazy prank Gerard thought up with the help of his male model friends, although this guy didn't seem to be one of them. He hadn't been part of the crew. But now that she thought about it, she had seen him somewhere before.

"If you don't leave instantly, I'm calling the law," she warned. She grabbed a plastic plunger from its holder on the floor, as if to swing it at him.

"Ma'am, I *am* the law." He flashed the badge again. "Rob Gaines, Special Agent, FBI. Now put that thing down and get up. Slowly."

Swan peered at him for so long that it suddenly hit her

where she'd seen him before. "I know you," she gasped. "You're not FBI, you're that telephone repairman! Did you think you could fool me by changing costumes?"

"Trust me, Ms. McKenna, this is no costume. Now set the plunger down and put up your hands. Keep them where I can see them at all times."

He wasn't the sexy-as-sin telephone repairman who'd been invading her dreams for the past two days? He was a government agent? Boy, could she pick 'em. Swan wanted desperately to think that this was a dream, too, a very bad one, but as she scrutinized his dark hair and hot blue eyes, she realized something. *It was him—and he wasn't looking at her hands.*

She followed his gaze to the length of thigh exposed by her hiked-up skirt. Apparently, FBI agents weren't bashful about getting an eyeful. She dropped the plunger and tugged her skirt to her knees.

"Do you *mind?*" she said. "I'd like to finish up without an audience."

"Sorry, ma'am, we can't do that," another voice said.

Swan looked around Gaines and saw a second man at the bathroom door. He was as tall as Gaines but possibly twenty pounds heavier, with short-cropped, sandy-blond hair that looked as if it might be prematurely graying.

"Joe Harris, FBI," he said.

"Are you selling tickets out there or what?" she snapped. "I'd like some privacy, please."

"Swan? Is everything all right?" Gerard was suddenly peering over the shoulder of Joe Harris. "Who are these men, Ducks?"

"Oh, no," she moaned. "You don't know them, either?"

Gaines had never taken his gaze from her person, and if that wasn't disconcerting enough, he didn't blink. Not once. The man had no reflexes—and his burning gaze had her heart thumping in that strange and unfamiliar way again. His jeans and work shirt were gone, replaced by a navy single-breasted suit that looked *way* too good on him. He could have been an old-fashioned G-man with his dark, sardonic eyebrows and his seen-it-all-and-then-some scowl.

He shot her a warning look that basically said, *Don't do anything to make me pull my gun and shoot you,* and then he turned to his partner. "I can handle this, Joe."

Joe didn't seem to agree. "You may need a witness in case she claims you molested her or something."

"I can handle it," Gaines insisted. "Shut the door and take her friend with you."

Harris backed Gerard out and once the two of them were gone, Gaines kicked the door shut with his foot. "Take care of business," he ordered Swan, apparently referring to her nature call, "and make it snappy."

"I'll take care of business," she said, yanking some tissue from the dispenser, "as soon as you look the other way."

He turned sideways, clearly intending to watch her without staring right at her. It was all she was going to get, Swan realized, secretly furious at him for betraying her this way. How could he have let her think that he was some poor, defenseless, oversexed telephone repairman when all the time he was setting her up? A moment later she was bending down, wondering if she could get her panties and panty hose up all at once. She'd never been able to do it before, but she'd never been under surveillance in her own bathroom, either.

She arranged the slippery silk panties and the gossamer hose in her fingers and began easing both up her calves. Once she had them high enough, she would quickly stand and tug everything over her hips. At the same time her skirt would fall down, covering all the vital places. It could work, but it was a delicate operation.

Her calves were covered and she was inching the panty hose over her knees when he let out a sharp sigh of impatience. She began to hurry and the panties slipped from her fingers and balled up in the nylons. She kept going out of fear, but every tug made it worse. The nylons had curled into an airtight roll, sucking the panties in with them. They looked like link sausages. Damn! Now she would have to start all over.

"Time's up," he announced.

"Wait a minute!" Springing to her feet, Swan brushed her skirt down and gingerly coaxed the lingerie up at the same time. For a second she thought it was going to unfurl, but that glimmer of hope was her downfall. It made her hurry even more. She couldn't see what she was doing because of the skirt's ruffly hem, so she yanked the silly thing back up and stuffed a wad of it in her mouth, clenching her teeth to hold it while she worked. She felt like a Flamenco dancer with an entire bouquet of roses in her teeth.

Now the black silk material was rolling up, too! It had slipped in between her tummy and her underwear. She would soon be nothing but one big airtight wad, encased in nylon.

"Cuuduuupleeeeleeee!" she mumbled, asking him nicely to leave.

Her skirt was disappearing and her halter top would be next. Everything she owned had decided to tie itself into knots, including her tongue.

"Neeeeesummpriiisee." She needed *privacy*. Couldn't he see that?

Her struggles just twisted things tighter. And now her fingers were caught. Desperate, she released the skirt from her teeth and began to fumble inside her panty hose in

earnest. She had to find her bikinis and separate the warring pieces of lingerie. Her hand was still buried inside
her undies when he glanced her way, but there was nothing she could do about it. She'd been taken hostage by
her underwear.

"What are you doing?" Gaines asked.

"Concealing a weapon," she said sarcastically.

Big mistake. Big.

Evidently, federal law enforcement officers didn't appreciate a little harmless gun humor. Without warning,
Gaines spun around to face her. His eyes narrowed in
disbelief as he saw her Houdini-like predicament. If someone had tossed her off a bridge, she would have drowned
before she could get her hands free.

Swan tried to extricate herself, but she couldn't. It was
like being restrained with Saran Wrap. Somehow she had
created a slipknot, perhaps out of an elastic leg hole, and
it wasn't about to let go of her fingers.

Gaines closed the distance between them in two easy
strides. "What have you got in there?"

"Nothing! It's just my underwear!"

"The hell you say. You're trying to shove something
into your panties."

Swan gave him a look of utter exasperation. "I am not
trying to shove anything *into* my panties. I'm trying to
get something *out of* them. And it's not working."

Before she could explain, she felt herself being spun
around like a toy top. The way he gripped her wrist and
pulled, he didn't seem to care whether or not he left her
fingers behind. Fortunately it only took one firm tug to
free her and then he yanked both of her hands behind her
back.

"Hey, is that necessary?" she said as handcuffs locked
down on her wrists.

"We're going to clear this up and we're going to clear it up now."

Gaines turned her around and scrutinized her from head to toe. It was obvious from his perplexed expression that he had no idea how a woman could have been strait-jacketed by her own clothing in mere moments. And with no help from anyone else.

"You did this to yourself?" he asked.

Swan glanced down and let out a little moan of despair. A skirt that would normally have covered her legs to mid-calf now exposed her from her belly button downward. The link-sausage undies were an awful sight, but at least she wasn't dealing with full-frontal nudity. She was too mortified to even consider what her backside must look like. From the way it felt, she was going to have to keep her rear to the wall at all times.

Swan wasn't sure it was possible to be more humiliated.

Rob Gaines proved her wrong.

"I have to search you," he said.

Swan shook her head so hard she nearly lost her balance. "I want a female officer to search me!"

His shrug said, *Sure, whatever you want, lady.* "Let's go then."

He pointed to the door, but she didn't move. "Go where? I can't even walk."

"Headquarters. If you want a female, that's where we're going."

If angry glares could burn, he would have been charcoal briquettes. "All right," she sighed. "Get it over with then."

"I should call in my partner," he said.

"No! Search me, dammit. Frisk me, pat me down, probe my body cavities, whatever the hell you have to do, just do it and get it over with."

"Thanks for all the options," he said dryly. He placed

his palms on her waist and began to frisk her in a way that was totally professional but not at all reassuring. He was thorough and patient as he slid his hands along the curves and swells of her body. He never touched her inappropriately. He never even spoke, but there was something about the feathery pressure of his fingers, or maybe it was his smoky aftershave or the heat of his breathing, that elicited what Swan could only call unwelcome sensations. *Whew*. He was everywhere with his velvet-soft hands, even inside her thighs.

Swan's stomach took an express ride down, and her heart went the opposite direction. A weird tremble crept into her breathing, and she very nearly emitted an audible sigh of relief when he stopped. If her panties weren't damp before, they certainly were now.

"Thanks," she said, willing strength back into her legs.

Apparently satisfied that she was unarmed, he stepped back and studied her hopelessly snarled clothing. "Want me to fix that?"

It was either him or the bomb squad. "Sure."

"Okay, but it may take surgical intervention."

"Meaning you're going to cut off my underwear?"

"Meaning I'll try to untangle it, but if I can't, this is Plan B." He pulled a penknife from an inner pocket of his jacket and set it on the vanity table. "Either way, I'll have to go in."

"Go in where? Hey!" Swan gasped as he stretched her panty hose out like a slingshot and delved into her drawers. "Hey, stop that!"

His hand was much too large not to touch things it shouldn't. So much for professionalism. Something brushed her pubic hair and she let out a squeal.

"What is this?" she cried, "some kind of macho payback for pulling your pants down?"

To his credit, he didn't respond. He went about his

business, feeling around some more, working the knots like a safecracker. He plucked and toggled and tugged, but nothing seemed to give way. When he went to pull his hand out, it didn't give, either. He was stuck.

Swan let out a horrified gasp. This could not be happening.

"We seem to have a problem," he said.

"No, we don't," she informed him in barely audible tones. "Just amputate your hand at the wrist and we'll be fine."

His expression told her he didn't think much of her suggestion. In fact, if she'd been a zoo animal, and he'd had a tranquilizer gun, she would have been headed for a very long nap.

"I was thinking of something a little less drastic," he intoned.

"Like what?" She didn't trust any part of this. He wasn't moving his hand, but she couldn't help thinking that his eyes were unnaturally bright, and his breathing had deepened. It mortified her to think that he might have discovered the damp spot. Fiend. He was enjoying this.

"Like this wad of nylon must be ballistic," he told her. "It could stop a bullet. I recommend Plan B."

"These are my best black panties! And my last pair of Tanga panty hose!"

"Would you like us to be buried in them?" he inquired politely. "Because that's how long it will take to get the damn things unsnarled."

"Oh, use the scissors in the drawer," she said crossly, gesturing to the vanity where he'd set the penknife.

Just moments later Swan's panty hose were in shreds and so were her nerves. She told herself that going commando was preferable to having an FBI agent in her pants, but as Gaines snipped away at her underwear, she wondered how this entry would look in her journal. "Tonight

I was handcuffed in my bathroom while an FBI agent surgically removed his hand from my panty hose, after which he hauled me to jail and threw me in a holding cell with hookers and drug addicts.''

A shudder started at the base of her heels and slithered up her spine.

"Hold still," he said. "I'm almost there."

She didn't ask where. She just closed her eyes and held her breath until she felt the wad begin to give way. A moment later his fingers were no longer nestled against her private parts and the garrote that was strangling her stomach was gone! With a few more snips of the scissors, he had the lingerie free and he was gingerly peeling it off her. He even made sure her lower extremities were covered with her skirt. What a prince.

What was that he was humming? "Natural Woman?"

She opened her eyes and was surprised to find him standing there, studying her intently, his hands planted on his hips. She could hardly believe this was the same man who'd nearly achieved lift-off in her design center. He could have had the decency to look a little flustered, couldn't he? Especially when she was breathing like a distance runner. All she could think about at that moment was the satisfaction of breaking through his reserve and making him squirm, too.

"I'm going to take the cuffs off," he said, leveling a firm gaze at her. "But I don't want any problems. Understand?"

He even waited for her to nod.

The moment her hands were free, Swan adjusted her blouse and skirt, as if that could restore her respectability. "This is outrageous," she said in a trembling voice. "How dare you come in here and accuse me of— What am I accused of anyway?"

"You're under arrest for several counts of bank fraud, embezzlement, conspiracy and forgery. Serious stuff."

Swan gaped at him as he took a card from his coat pocket and began to Mirandize her. He was as nonchalant as if he'd never been messing around in her pants, as if he hadn't made her tremble and gasp.

She heard the words about her rights, heard what he said about lawyers and about how anything she said *could* and *would* be used against her in a court of law. She heard every bit of it, but none of it truly registered. It felt as if she were not in her own skin anymore. Was she going into shock?

"Do you understand your rights as I've explained them to you?"

"Uh—"

"I need a yes or no."

She gave him a defiant look, her spirit flooding back. "Yes, I understand my rights, and I also understand that I haven't done anything wrong. You and your buddy out there have made a terrible mistake."

"Have we?" he said. "It's all on videotape."

"Videotape of what?"

"Of you, forging a name on loan documents and walking out of the bank with an unauthorized bank draft for—"

"*Unauthorized?*" Until this very moment Swan had clung to the notion that this was a practical joke or some kind of mistake. Now, with a clarity that made her heart tumble, she understood what was happening. She didn't know what he meant by "unauthorized check," but she had signed Lynne's name to the loan papers and somehow the Feds had found out. Those *were* serious charges.

But she could explain them!

She forced herself to breathe, even to smile. "It is a

mistake. All you have to do is call Art Long at First National Heritage. He'll explain everything.''

Art would probably lose his job over this, she realized, if he hadn't already. She didn't want that to happen, but she didn't want to go to jail, either.

''Art Long has been taken into custody. He's cooling his heels down at the federal building right now. And by the way, he cracked under pressure and told us everything.''

She stared at him in amazement. ''You arrested Arthur? What did he do?''

''Conspired with you to rob First National Heritage.''

''No! That's ridiculous. Lynne Carmichael and I got a loan from the bank. I did sign her name, yes, but I had her permission, and she's my business partner.''

Gaines nodded, not particularly interested, apparently. ''Long gave you some papers today and a book,'' he said. ''A gift, I believe. Where is that book now?''

Swan shook her head, confused. ''The organizer?''

''Yes.''

''It's right there.'' She pointed to the floor between the commode and the vanity. In her haste to get her panties down, she had set it there.

Gaines took some rubber gloves from his coat pocket and tugged them onto his hands. He picked up the organizer, gave it a cursory once-over, and then opened the bathroom door a crack. ''Hey, Joe, you want to witness this?''

From her vantage point, Swan could see Gerard as he sat on a chair in the far corner of the bedroom. He looked forlorn and frightened. Joe Harris stood over him, scribbling notes on a small pocket-size pad. Gerard glanced up and shrugged, obviously as much in the dark as she was herself. Harris said something to Gerard that she couldn't hear. Gerard nodded weakly and stood up. He offered Swan a tiny smile and then left the room.

Special Agent Harris pulled on his own pair of gloves as he entered the bathroom. "Find it?" he asked.

Gaines casually waved the engraved book to prove he had it.

Swan's stomach was in knots as both men focused on her. She felt like a lab specimen. "What does this have to do with the loan papers?" she asked.

Neither man replied. The silent treatment in full swing. Gaines plucked out the cashier's check she'd picked up from Art Long yesterday. He handed it to Harris, who studied it for a moment and then slipped it into a clear plastic bag he'd taken from his pocket. As Harris was doing this, Gaines picked up the penknife that he'd planned to operate with and carefully cut a razor-fine slit down the inside of the book's back cover. Swan was aghast. He'd ruined it! Wasn't her underwear enough?

"What are you doing with my check?" she asked Harris. And then to Gaines, "Look what you've done to my organizer!"

"Evidence," Harris said.

"Evidence," Gaines said.

"Evidence of what? I've done nothing wrong. It's all a mistake. Lynn will tell you that!"

Gaines arched his brows. "*This* is a mistake?"

Swan watched in silence as he carefully removed a piece of paper that had obviously been hidden between the book cover and its back piece. He held it up for her to see. It was another cashier's check of some sort. It was made out to Lynne Carmichael and the amount brought a gasp of disbelief.

Four million, nine-hundred-thousand dollars and no cents.

"What's that?" she whispered.

Harris waved the plastic bag that contained her check. "Altogether, that's five million in embezzled bank funds."

Too much was happening too quickly. Too many questions were ricocheting inside her mind for her to grasp even one and examine it closely. Swan staggered back, lowered the lid on the commode and sat down. "Is there more?" she asked.

Harris frowned. "What? Money?"

Swan shook her head. She should be going crazy, but instead she was going numb. "No. Surprises. Are there any more surprises?"

Gaines gave both the book and the check to Harris, who was apparently in charge of submitting them as evidence. "I'll tag and bag these," Harris said as he stepped out of the bathroom. "It'll take a few minutes. You got her?"

After Harris had left, Swan glanced pleadingly at Rob Gaines. "I really need you to explain what's going on. This is all a mistake. I didn't know anything about that check, the big one."

For a long moment he simply stood there studying her as he slowly peeled the rubber gloves from his hands. She wondered if he was going to speak to her at all, when, finally, he leaned against the edge of the vanity.

"There's no mistake, Ms. McKenna," he said. "You and Lynne are up to your necks in this, however—"

He seemed to be deliberating again, but she sensed there was more on the man's mind than bank robberies. Possibly a lot more. Possibly her.

"However what?" she asked.

"Well, there might be a way that we could work something out."

"Okay," she said slowly. She had a bad feeling about where he was going with this, but, at the same time, her vital signs were whipping themselves into a frenzy again.

Her skin was feverish and her hairline was damp. He seemed to be able to do that to her under just about any damn circumstances.

"Just tell me what you want," she implored.

That triggered a glance from him that nearly made her vital signs stop. It had all the smoldering intensity of an illicit touch and Swan was rocked back by it. But she'd barely had time to register the impact when she was wondering if the whole thing had been her imagination.

All at once he was the government agent again—standing tall, arms crossed with the authority of a hanging judge, and when he spoke, it was cool and professional.

"The FBI can count on your cooperation then?" he said. "We have a tough case on our hands, and you could be useful to us."

She nodded. "Of course, I'll cooperate. Tell me what's going on."

Gaines relaxed his stance and began. If he'd been harboring any prurient urges, they were well concealed. "Your friend, Art Long, is one of the best con men in the business," he explained. "It's taken us years, but we finally have him where we want him. Only there's a problem. Long didn't work this scam alone. Someone inside the bank helped him, someone highly placed. We want that person, too."

"But how can I help? Lynne and I don't work at the bank. Surely you must know that."

"We do. But we also know that Ms. Carmichael and Art Long have been seeing each other socially. We know Long has visited this house and spent time with both you and Carmichael."

"You've had us under surveillance?"

He ignored her and went on. "What we don't know is whether you and your partner were duped by Long or whether you're part of his scheme."

"We were duped," she assured him. "Lynn and I thought Art wanted to help us. And, I swear to you, Lynne doesn't know any more about this than I do."

"Speaking of Ms. Carmichael, where is she?"

"She's with a designer. A *big* designer, who might be interested in sponsoring our line under his label. This could be the break of a lifetime."

"That explains *what* she's doing. Now, *where* is she doing it?"

Swan shifted and felt cool air swirling around inside her skirt. It was quite a draft. "I don't know," she said. It wasn't exactly a lie. "They're on a yacht somewhere on the high seas."

"Ever hear of obstruction of justice?"

"I don't know where she is!" Was her skirt still hiked up? Swan twisted around to look and nearly swooned as the blood rushed out of her head. God, wasn't bladder urgency enough? Gaines caught her elbow to steady her. His grasp on her bare arm was firm, though not overly so. But his fingers were hot and strong, and she almost wished he would do something more with them. She didn't want to think what exactly, but *something*.

"Take it easy," he said.

Swan released a breath that helped clear her head a bit. "I'm fine," she said, but it sounded as hollow as she felt. "Just tell me there're no more surprises. I don't think I can take any more tonight."

She looked up at him, saw his expression and groaned inwardly.

"I've got one more," he said, "and you aren't going to like it."

4

"MS. MCKENNA! Come back here!"

Rob Gaines belted out the command as Swan brushed past him and walked into the adjoining bedroom. She needed some space to clear her head and she needed it now. In less than twenty minutes he'd accused her of horrendous crimes and strip-searched her in a way that gave new meaning to the term.

What was next? *Stop or I'll shoot?*

"That was not a request," Gaines barked. "Stop or I'll—"

Swan stopped. Oh, yes, she did. She stopped so suddenly she tilted forward like a ski jumper about to go off the ramp.

"I think we need to establish some ground rules," he said. "First, turn around, and second, look deeply into my eyes and listen carefully to every word I say—as carefully as you've ever listened to anything in your life, because compared to this, none of that other BS matters."

Swan wanted to tell him that his superior tone was not necessary but, of course, she didn't. She turned, looked straight into his glacial-blue eyes, and felt as if her breath had been flash-frozen in her chest. If time travel were possible, this guy had been sent from the Ice Age. Even his impossibly long eyelashes did nothing to warm the chill.

"Rule number one," he said, "since I'm the one with the badge and the gun, I'm in charge here. Rule number two, since you're the one about to be wearing the hand-cuffs again, you're not in charge. You're the suspect. And rule number three, don't ever walk away from the guy with the gun because he might think you're trying to es-cape, and if he did think that, he would have to do ev-erything in his power to stop you—and that would not be good.''

Not good for whom, she thought, mustering up some defiance. He'd probably love to pull out that big old six-shooter of his and blast away.

''Is that all?'' she asked.

''Rule number *four,* you're in a shitload of trouble, Ms. McKenna. It wouldn't be an exaggeration to say that your very life is in my hands, so if I were you, I'd be *very* nice to my hands.''

Swan was drawn like a magnet to the body parts he mentioned, and they were exactly the kind of hands she loved on a man. Hard from use, brown from the sun, with strong, tapered fingers and a palm plenty wide enough to handle a football. Veins could be seen running down from his forearm, and the feathering of hair above his knuckles matched the sooty black of his lashes.

She was obsessing over the hands of a man who was a threat to her very existence. How normal was that? For that matter, how normal was anything that had happened in the past twenty-four hours? Maybe the threat he posed had something to do with it. He'd just told her that he held her life in his hands and the idea of being that vul-nerable to a man, especially this man—

''Are we clear on the rules?'' he asked.

''You're the guy with the gun.'' She gave him a tight nod. What else could she do? ''And, by the way, what is this gun fixation of yours? You know what guns are, don't you? Compensation for an inadequate penis.''

He shot a look at her that questioned her will to live.

"Maybe we should talk about *your* penis fixation," he said. "And while we're at it, I don't feel the slightest bit inadequate."

That was no big surprise, but it brought a sting of awareness to her cheeks anyway. She also felt a thrust of something deeper, quicker and significantly hotter in her belly. She *had* to get a grip.

"Back to business," he said. "I'm giving you a choice, which is more than most felony suspects get. Either you agree to help us catch Long's accomplice or you and Art can have adjoining cells. Which is it going to be?"

Swan went icy cold. "That's a choice? Everything Lynne and I have worked for is about to be destroyed, and you want me to pitch in and help so you and that other bully with a badge can use our show as a sting operation to catch someone you can't catch yourself!"

"Yeah, that about sums it up."

He actually seemed pleased with her assessment, and that was the last straw for Swan. She slumped down on the edge of the bed and covered her face with her hands. *"This is not happening,"* she whispered. If she kept her eyes closed long enough and said the words passionately enough, maybe this nightmare would go away. And it would take Rob Gaines with it.

Gaines sat down next to her. His voice took on an explanatory tone, along with a hint of compassion.

"Listen," he said, "you're going to be dragged into this mess whether you agree to help us or not. Now I know that stinks, but that's just the way it is."

Swan glanced up at him. "What do you mean?"

"Art Long is smart. He's been conning people for years but he's not *this* smart. He didn't put this plan into action by himself. Large amounts of money have been electronically transferred, and according to the bank examiners who tipped us, he doesn't have the authority to do that on his own. Long hasn't confessed to having an accomplice, but he had help from someone inside."

"Inside the bank? How am I supposed to help you with that? Lynne and I don't know anyone at the bank besides Art."

"That's what you claim, but *someone* opened an account under Lynne's name and has been electronically transferring funds into that account. This same someone then issued a cashier's check for those funds in the name of Lynne Carmichael—a check that you picked up after forging Lynne's name. And now Lynne has conveniently disappeared."

"Well, when you put it like that, of course we look guilty." She pressed two fingers to her temple and hit exactly the spot where it was beginning to throb. "But Lynne *hasn't* conveniently disappeared. She's away on legitimate business, and I know nothing about any electronic transfers." Frowning, she said, "What did you mean that I would be dragged into this whether I help you or not?"

Gaines rose and slipped his hands into the pockets of his charcoal slacks. She was reminded of the man in the gray flannel suit, except for one or two discrepancies— the rakish dark hair and disreputable blue eyes. There were con men in every profession, she reminded herself.

"You're a marked woman, Ms. McKenna. You say you're not in on this with Art Long, and if that's true, then one thing is certain. Art did not intend for you to keep the five million. Someone was going to 'relieve' you of all that money—likely Art himself—and then split it with his accomplice."

Swan didn't like where this was going. "Are you suggesting that his accomplice might come after the money? Or after me because he believes I have the money?"

"You're starting to get the picture," he said. "If you

work with us, we'll provide you protection. When the accomplice makes his move, we can be there to make ours. You won't be hurt, and we'll have our coconspirator."

Swan rose and walked to the double doors that led to a balcony above the gardens. White, lacy sheers covered the glass panes. She moved one aside and peered into darkness that was as opaque as an inkwell. The doors were closed, but she could hear the low roar of the ocean, and closer, the purr of traffic on a side street. The beach was always busy in the summer.

"When do you think this person might make a move?" she asked him. "Am I in danger now?" She needed the truth, no matter how bad it was.

Rob Gaines considered the value of lying to her and decided against it. There was nothing to be gained by giving her a false sense of security. Right now she was vulnerable enough to listen to what he had to say and frightened enough to accept it.

"You could be," he told her, "which is why Joe and I are staying here tonight. I doubt anyone's going to hit this place, though. They'll wait for the confusion of the fashion shows. You're being promoted as the designer of the line, which means you'll be easy to find, and you'll be distracted. Thieves love chaos."

"Swell," she said. "I'm being used as bait. I could be thumped on the head at any time, robbed and left for dead. And what happens when this accomplice discovers that I don't have the five million dollars? I'm history, right?"

She shoved a handful of auburn hair away from her face and stared him down with an accusatory expression.

Not if I can help it, he thought. Her rising agitation gave off a scent that was part frightened woman and part French perfume. Both were totally alluring, and both were Swan McKenna. She could be hell in high heels one min-

ute and visibly apprehensive the next, just as she was now.
Rob preferred her vulnerable. She was much easier to handle. He was also aware that if she weren't a suspect, he
would have had a hard time keeping his distance. And the
hell of it was, he wasn't sure she would have stopped
him.

"Relax," he said, his voice softening. "Joe and I
haven't lost anyone yet. We'll set up a security plan. If
you do exactly as you're told, you'll be safe. We can
protect you, but only if you cooperate."

She hugged herself and he could see gooseflesh creeping up her arms.

"And what do I get out of this," she asked, "besides
a nervous breakdown?"

"Immunity from prosecution. You'll probably have to
testify against Art and his accomplice in court, but, otherwise, you're off the hook."

"What about Lynne?"

"That depends on Lynne. Partial immunity, possibly
full, if she's willing to testify."

"Immunity from prosecution for something we didn't
do? You'll excuse me if I don't sound grateful."

She swung her head and cast him a hard glance, her
red hair dancing. Rob suspected she was about to slip on
her high heels again and give him a hard time. But he
didn't have any more time to play.

"I need an answer," he said. "Say yes, Ms. McKenna.
It's the only smart thing to do."

Smart or not, Swan wasn't sure she had a choice. There
was no guarantee that Rob Gaines wouldn't haul her off
to jail if she refused to help. That would be disastrous for
Brief Encounters, and the bad press could be enough to
ruin them, even if her name was cleared. But bait for a
sting operation?

On the other hand, it was also possible that whoever

was helping Art Long had been frightened off and wouldn't come after the money. That would make this whole exercise pointless. But there was no way to be sure of that, and five million dollars was a lot to walk away from.

"Did you say yes, Ms. McKenna?" Gaines intoned. "I didn't hear you."

"*Yes,* Ms. McKenna." She was giving up, but not happily. "You know," she said, "if you and Joe are planning to go undercover, you could always be underwear models."

She took some pleasure in watching his face go pale at the thought.

"I saw what you put those guys through tonight," he muttered, "and I wouldn't be caught dead wearing one of those nut buckets."

"Nut buckets?" Swan chuckled. First time she'd ever heard her thongs called that. It was also nice to know that she could still laugh.

"You'll have people setting up the stage, doing the lights and the sound, that sort of thing?" he asked. Swan nodded. "Good, because Joe and I will blend in as a couple of workmen. We'll do everything possible to stay out of your way. But you need to keep in mind that we're conducting an investigation, and you're still one of the suspects."

"How could I forget? I'm getting tired of protesting my innocence, and you're probably tired of hearing it, but someday you're going to be damn embarrassed about the way you're treating a woman who gives pennies back to store clerks when they make the wrong change."

She expected some kind of wisecrack and when it didn't come she stared at him hard. Maybe she was daring him. "Go ahead and say it," she invited. "Tell me what an idiot I am for getting myself mixed up in this loan fiasco. But don't tell me I'm a thief, because I'm not.''

He was suddenly very serious. The dark lashes lowered, masking his expression. ''If you think I don't want you cleared of these charges, you're wrong. Nothing would make me happier. I mean it.''

The way he said *I mean it* made her stomach go weirdly light. This wasn't butterflies or anything like it. It was as if the force of gravity had suddenly been lessened and everything might lift right off the ground.

''*Nothing* would make you happier? Why would you care what happens to me? You don't even know me.''

He lifted his head. ''I have my reasons.''

''Your quest to catch Art Long, right? And I'm your means to that end? Is that why you care?'' She told herself to let it go, but she couldn't. She wanted to grill him. She wanted to put him under bright lights in a darkened room and interrogate him until he surrendered them, one by one. Call it payback.

Maybe it was her imagination, or just wishful thinking, but she had the feeling he wouldn't mind spending some time with her in a darkened room, either. He hadn't smiled, hadn't even looked as if he might, but there was an energy brewing in the cool blue irises hidden under those lashes, and it was sexual.

Her soul-searching came to an abrupt end as Joe Harris walked into the room.

''Everything is booked,'' he said to Gaines, who simply nodded.

It took Swan a moment or two to figure out what he was talking about, and then it hit her that Rob had given Joe her loan check along with the other one. ''I'm getting my money back, right?''

Harris looked at her as if she'd lost her mind. ''That's

evidence, Ms. McKenna. No way you're getting that check.''

"You can't mean that.'' Swan's voice went faint. "I need that money! Lynne and I have costs to cover for this tour. If I can't come up with the money, it will ruin our relationship with the boutique chain. They may even cancel the tour, and I still have to pay for the launch party. I put that on a credit card!''

Harris and Gaines looked at one another. Apparently even tough FBI agents could be surprised.

"I'm serious,'' she said. "Lynne and I went broke getting the line manufactured. Part of the loan from First National was to cover modeling fees, travel expenses and lodging. I won't even go into the stack of delinquent bills I have on my desk. Without that money, there won't *be* any shows.''

Gaines raised his hand for silence. After a moment's reflection he spoke to his partner. "We could put in for an emergency requisition.''

"Worth a try,'' Harris said. "All they can do is say no.''

Voices filtered up from below and Swan suddenly remembered her party, her guests. The fashion press was down there, along with the brass from La Bomba. She had no idea where Gerard was or what was going on downstairs. The last time she'd seen him, he was being ushered out of the room. He may have been taken in for questioning for all she knew. That would mean her guests were down there, fending for themselves. She had to go. Someone had to do damage control, and there was no one but her!

Without even thinking to ask permission, she breezed past the two agents and headed for the veranda. As she reached the doorway, she realized she'd just broken every one of Rob Gaines's four rules and there was nothing she could do about it. Hell with it. Let him shoot her in the back. He might be doing her a favor.

IT WASN'T QUITE AS BAD as Swan had thought. Gerard hadn't been hauled off in a squad car. He'd been holding down the fort until she got back, and her guests didn't seem to have any idea what was going on. That much she could be grateful for. They didn't even notice that her outfit was a wrinkled mess.

She tried to think of some way to bring the evening to a close, but no one seemed in any particular hurry to leave, which, ironically, was the sign of a successful party. Something to celebrate, except in this case there were two government agents in her guest bedroom, and she did not want them mingling.

Too late. She caught sight of Joe Harris by the buffet table. He was helping himself to a healthy slice of Gouda cheese, but he was also watching her. Swan looked around for Gaines, but didn't see him. She hoped it was because he was working on getting them some funds for the shows. That should keep him busy, and meanwhile his absence gave her another idea. There was something else she had to do tonight, and it would be far easier if she didn't have to deal with Rob Gaines.

Gerard was heading her way with a small cluster of guests, hopefully to say good-night. She caught his eye and pretended to be adjusting her earrings. She was actually pointing toward Joe Harris. By now she and her assistant could read each other's minds. She was asking Gerard to cover for her and he gave her a knowing nod. He excused himself and picked up a tray of canopies, hurrying over to where Harris was standing. In typical Gerard fashion, he had the agent engrossed in herb-stuffed mushrooms and conversation within seconds.

Swan strolled out with the departing guests. She wasn't

making a break for it. She just needed to make a phone call, and privacy was essential. At the front door, she thanked everyone for coming. As her guests descended the steps, she slipped into the conservatory—a plant-filled porch with a slanted-glass ceiling—and closed the door behind her.

She dialed her own voice mail and found a message waiting from Lynne. The girls had decided beforehand that if Lynne had news she'd leave a message rather than disturb Swan during the launch party. It had seemed like a wonderful idea at the time.

Lynne was short and to the point. "So far, so good. Gvon is playing it cool, but there's an excellent vibe here, Swan. He's interested. Very interested. More later!" *Click.* Lynne was gone.

There was no justice in a universe that allowed her partner to be on a pleasure cruise while she was dealing with this nightmare. But there was a hidden blessing in Lynne's being incommunicado, and even Swan had to admit it. Gaines would certainly have taken Lynne into custody if he could have found her, and that would have been the end of Brief Encounters's blossoming relationship with Gvon.

Swan also hoped—and prayed—that her friend had had nothing to do with Art Long's scheme. Not that Lynne would ever resort to stealing five million dollars, but she might have unknowingly been involved, and Swan felt the need to protect her, especially now.

She dialed Lynne's cell number. As the phone rang, she turned and faced the darkness, gazing through the panes of the glassed-in porch. *Was* someone out there? Someone waiting for his chance to catch her off guard? Could Rob Gaines protect her?

After three rings and Lynne's cheery intro, Swan left her hushed message.

"It's Swan. Listen carefully, Lynne, this is *not* a joke. The FBI is here and they think you and I are involved in an embezzlement scheme with Art Long. We're in big trouble, and I mean *big*. I can't talk right now, but I'll call you later and fill you in. Meanwhile, whatever you do, don't come back here."

Swan hung up, relieved to have gotten that out of the way. She exhaled deeply, aware that the stress was beginning to affect her. She was reeling inside, like a pedestrian who'd been sideswiped by a car and left spinning. She didn't know which way to fall. Amazingly, though, she didn't have to go to the bathroom. Maybe she was beyond that now. Maybe this debacle would cure her.

"I just hate it when people lie to me," Rob Gaines said.

Swan whirled around, her heart hammering, and found him leaning casually against the casement in the doorway. He came forward and took the phone from her hand. He pushed the Redial button and listened for a few seconds before hanging up. "Voice mail, huh?"

"I don't know where she is," Swan said. "I swear I don't."

Gaines nodded, his lips tightly pursed. "But you know how to contact her? You know how to warn her that we're looking for her?"

"It's not what it looks like," Swan said. "Really, it's not."

He didn't have to say it. She knew he wasn't going to believe a word she said now. Not one single word.

IT WAS A LITTLE AFTER TWO in the morning when Rob swung his legs off the leather couch in the study and slipped his shoes back on. He couldn't sleep anyway, so he might as well spell Joe on watch. The second and third floors of the Carmichael villa were used as living quarters.

Rob was on the second floor just down the hall from Swan McKenna's bedroom.

The whole place was quiet as a tomb as he stepped out into the hallway.

Rob wasn't normally impressed with material things—in his line of work the wealthy were too often the very crooks he was investigating—but he was impressed with this place. The floors were travertine marble with black diamonds of granite that called the eye forward. The art on the walls looked as if it might be of museum quality; everything about the house was old and elegant. Graceful Kentia palms in porcelain pots lined the hallways and the ornate wrought-iron balustrade on the stairway looked original.

Going down that stairway felt a little like stepping back in time.

As Rob rounded the corner on the lower floor, he saw his partner flaked out on one of the settees in the foyer. A copy of the *Wall Street Journal* blanketed Joe Harris's chest as he snored the night away. Rob shook his head, wondering why he was surprised. Something was going on with Joe lately. He was coming up on his fiftieth birthday, and he seemed depressed about it. Maybe it was a midlife crisis. The only thing on his mind lately was retiring and heading for some tropical island. Rob had had to remind him more than once that he wasn't retired yet.

Rob quickly found something that concerned him much more than Joe's midlife crisis. The French doors that led to the terrace were standing wide open, as if someone had flung them apart and walked out.

"Damn," he said under his breath. He was about to wake Joe and start a search when he saw a lone figure moving slowly along the center path of the garden that led to the gazebo.

Rob left Joe sleeping in the foyer. No sense getting his

partner involved now. He could handle this alone. The late summer night was unusually clear and the moonlight provided plenty of illumination as he descended the marble steps that led to the gardens. The lone figure was Swan, and she'd made her way to the end of the path that had earlier been aglow with Japanese lanterns. A black row of manicured hedges lay before her and the Pacific Ocean beyond. It didn't appear that she was trying to escape, but she could be planning to meet someone. Her partner? On the other hand, she might just be out for some air.

He slipped into the shadows to watch her for a moment.

As his eyes became accustomed to the dark he noticed she wore only a cotton shift of some kind that swirled around her legs like a breeze as she walked. It was light, simple, plain. Not what he would have expected from someone who designed wickedly sexy underwear for a living. She was barefoot, and Gaines noticed how gently her feet moved along the path.

The woman is light against the dark, he thought. And then wondered where that had come from. He wasn't a poet, wasn't even a sentimentalist, but the words fit her perfectly.

It must be that little bit of moonlight she was wearing. The material wasn't exactly sheer, but the way it caught light as she walked made it appear almost translucent. And unless it was his imagination, the curvy darkness underneath was her nude body. He was suddenly very alert. His pulse quickened as if he'd seen a concealed weapon. Maybe that's exactly what she was, he thought. He couldn't make out detail, but the darkness of her form was uninterrupted, which suggested she had not replaced the underwear he'd had to cut off her.

He felt a twitch beneath the fabric of his suit pants. Something down deep was stirring to life, straining against its own weight. *Christ*. The last thing he needed now was another hard-on. The same thing had happened when she'd been playing with his zipper. That was no big surprise, considering everything else she'd been doing. But apparently things had progressed. Now just looking at her could get a reaction, which wasn't good news for an FBI agent who was trying to keep a suspect under surveillance and to pull off a tricky sting operation at the same time. Funny how he kept reminding her she was a suspect, but he couldn't seem to keep that fact in his own head.

She's a suspect, Rob.

She's quick, smart, devious.

And lovely in the moonlight. Adrift, lonely, lovely. All those things that made a man want to come to a woman's aid. Only he couldn't come to Swan McKenna's aid, not in the way she needed him to. If he wanted to stop Art Long, he had no choice but to use her in this operation, and he did want to stop Art Long.

Five years ago Rob had been assigned witness protection duty over one Paula Warren. The twenty-six-year-old socialite had a history of emotional problems, but there was something about the woman that had captured Rob's imagination. He hadn't been sexually attracted to her— although she'd made it perfectly clear that she had designs on him. It was more of a protective thing with Paula. She'd seemed lost, and her track record with abusive men hadn't made things any easier for her. When she'd agreed to testify against Art Long and the financial scam he'd put together, she'd become Rob's personal charge.

The woman's erratic behavior had made Rob's life a living hell and nearly cost him his badge. And then she'd killed herself—or so the coroner said. Rob had some doubts about that. He'd never been able to prove it, but he believed Art Long was directly or indirectly tied to

Paula's death. Worse, she'd been Rob's responsibility, and he'd let her down. He should have been there to stop her.

Rob had been waiting all this time for another chance at Art Long, and the last thing he needed now was his conscience bothering him. What he did need was absolute control—of his mind, of his body, and of Swan McKenna, his suspect. There was a code of conduct to be followed, lines that couldn't be crossed. It wasn't confusing. It was utterly simple, and he knew better than most the cost of straying.

He'd crossed the line only once, years ago, and he'd promised himself it would never happen again. That's why it didn't make sense that she could be getting to him when no other woman had in years. He hadn't allowed it. Maybe what bothered him most at the moment was exactly that. He didn't know what made her different. Why her? Why now?

As he was pondering that question, an ocean breeze blew across the garden, lifting the tail end of her nightshirt. *Damn.* He was right. She wasn't wearing panties. Even Mother Nature was conspiring against him.

Suspects who were up to something were more furtive about it than this. That's what he told himself as he headed into the garden to check on her. His approach was soundless, but he cleared his throat when he was a few feet away. No point in scaring the hell out of her again.

When she turned, the breeze caught her auburn hair and blew it across her face. Rob's instinct was to clear it away from her eyes. She looked pensive, not startled and, for some reason, that was like a knife going through him.

This was worse than he thought. Now he was feeling gentle *and* horny.

"You shouldn't be out here," he said.

"I know. And in case you're wondering, I'm not breaking rule number three. This isn't an escape attempt. I was just taking a last look at the garden—and thinking about the launch party.''

"It seemed to go off pretty well," he offered. She was clearly upset and at least he could be civil.

"It did go well. It's just…"

Swan turned, her gaze sweeping over the remains of the party. "It's funny how you work for so long on a dream, and when it finally comes you realize everything will be different from that moment on. But it wasn't supposed to be different in this way. Not like *this*. It seems so unfair, and yet it's my fault. I shouldn't have signed those forms. I shouldn't even have gone to the bank."

"Hey, you've had a lot dumped in your lap these past twenty-four hours," he reminded her. "Don't be too hard on yourself."

"Why not?" Her lashes fluttered in his direction. "Oh, I forgot, that's *your* job."

Rob shrugged off the insult. Luckily she couldn't wound him that way.

Swan sighed and brushed the hair from her face. She held it in her hand, her head tilted just slightly. Rob had never seen anything more graceful in his life.

"I'm sorry," she said. "One of the reasons I came out here was to try to make some sense of what's happening. I guess I'm lucky not to be in jail, right?"

He didn't answer and she went right on. "I decided a little while ago," she said, "that the best course of action is to cooperate as fully as I can. I won't give you any trouble, and hopefully you and Agent Harris can get this resolved as quickly as possible."

He nodded, more relieved than he cared to admit.

"I'm not after you," he told her. "I'm after the truth and, right now, I don't know what that is. Until I do, you're a suspect, but you're also a potential witness. Either way, I have no other choice than to dog your every step. I have to be your shadow, Swan. It's for your protection. It's not personal.''

Yeah, right. If she'd had any idea how personal it was, she would have slapped him into next week. When he wasn't contemplating her character, he was fantasizing about this incredibly hot redhead dropping to her knees in front of his aroused body. At this very moment he was thinking about the fact that she was naked under her gown made of moonlight, and it hid nothing from his view. If he took her in his arms, he would feel the yielding softness of her breasts and her thighs and her curly red mound.

That wasn't personal, was it?

5

"SOMEONE SHOULD TELL the models that Elvis has left the building." Rob shook his head and muttered, "If I see one more pelvic thrust, I'm going to be sick."

Joe Harris let out a snick of laughter. "Relax, man, it's not that bad. With the possible exception of you, it looks like everyone here is having a great time."

Harris was right about that. La Bomba's L.A. boutique was packed with customers, mostly females, and there didn't seem to be a disappointed face in this Saturday afternoon crowd. On the drive up from Manhattan Beach this morning, Rob had envisioned the boutique as being some tiny, chic shop about the size of a walk-in closet. What he found was a store with at least two thousand square feet of assorted lingerie items for both sexes. The back corner by the fitting rooms had been cleared by the staff and a small stage and sound system set up for the runway portion of Swan's presentation. Merchandise had been moved out of the way to make room for over a hundred folding chairs, but it wasn't enough. Customers were standing as far back as the front door.

Swan was at the podium now, emceeing the show—with more damn enthusiasm than Rob would have liked, if he was being honest. She wasn't the only enthusiastic one, either. Each new model brought a boisterous round of applause from the almost entirely female audience. This crowd covered all ages—everything from teenagers to grandmothers.

Rob had not been prepared for that, not for white-haired grandmothers. He kept waiting for one of them to holler, "Where's the beef?" If that happened, he was leaving. Let Joe keep track of the designing genius who was responsible for this pandemonium. At least one thing was going according to plan. The leather organizer—Swan's gift from Art Long—was sitting in plain sight on the podium. She'd been using it for her show notes.

The organizer was the key to Rob's entire operation, and the plan was simple. Swan was to keep the book with her at all times, and she was never to be out of sight of either Joe or Rob. Other than that, she was to act as if she had no idea there was anything in the organizer other than her appointments, her "to do" lists and her notes. In other words, as normal as possible.

Nobody should have a problem with those instructions, right?

Rob grimaced. *Wrong.* She'd already slipped away twice to make nature calls without telling anyone. Rob could understand her reluctance to ask permission to go to the bathroom, but what the hell was she doing in there? He'd heard female bladders were smaller, but no one had to go that often. He would discuss that with her after the show.

He and Joe had dressed as lighting technicians—work shirts, jeans and tool belts—which gave them free access to the backstage area, as well as the ability to keep Swan in sight at all times without attracting too much attention to themselves.

Now, twenty-two minutes into the show, they hadn't seen anything out of the ordinary—except a parade of male models dancing and prancing their nearly naked butts down the runway, at times wearing nothing much bigger than a candy bar wrapper.

Thongs? How could men wear those things?

"May they get diaper rash and die," Rob said under his breath.

Joe nudged him in the ribs. "You know what they say about guys like you. Latent tendencies, that's what they say."

"Would you like to die now or later?" Rob asked.

Harris laughed. "Easy, boy, easy. Maybe it's just me, but I think Ms. McKenna's got herself a winner here. Look at this place. The women are jammed in here and they seem to love everything they're seeing. What do you bet they buy her out afterward?"

Joe pointed toward the runway where a beefed-up model was turning in slow degrees to give the audience a good look at his faux fur thong. "Take that thong, right there—"

"No, thank you," Rob replied dryly.

"There can't be more than two dollars of material in that thing and it's selling for what? Twenty bucks or so? Man, you can't beat that."

"Yeah, well, the Bureau is going to beat *us* if we don't scope out this place. You take the right side and I'll take the left."

"Work, work, work," Joe grumbled as he turned and headed for the far side of the runway.

"Hey, try not to fall asleep, okay?" Rob called after him.

Interesting that Rob had picked the side of the runway where Swan was situated. He'd given some thought to letting his partner have "Swan detail" for a change. Joe was a seasoned agent and, in theory, he was every bit as well trained and prepared as Rob was. But even as Rob had debated the possibility, he'd known it was never going to happen. Nobody was guarding Swan McKenna's body but him.

There were plenty of reasons why that made sense, and

one of them was location. They were in L.A., close to the crime scene, and Rob had reasoned that the accomplice was more likely to strike here than to follow them up the coast. In a situation such as this, he felt the need to be everywhere—not just watching Swan, but watching everything, everyone—to be omnipresent. Joe was more laid back in nature, not as vigilant. Or at least that's how Rob sized it up. And to be fair, Joe didn't have the same motivation Rob did, either. He had no scores to settle with Art Long. This wasn't a grudge match for Joe Harris.

That's why Rob cared so much. Because of Art Long. This *wasn't* about Swan McKenna, except as a means to an end.

That's what Rob told himself as he watched her auburn hair shimmer with every move of her head. Her smile was radiant. Her presentation was charged with energy, and she seemed animated to the point of trembling. She was either excited or nervous, he didn't know which, but he'd never seen her as vibrant.

He had to give her credit. She was good up there. She was selling her underwear, and she was good. He got a kick out of the way she giggled when someone called out from the audience—and he hated the way his chest tightened as he watched her. In another couple of minutes he was going to be fighting for breath. He was vigilant, all right, vigilant in noticing every detail of the way she looked, the way she talked, the way she engaged the crowd.

He'd called her only a *means to an end?* Who was he kidding?

He turned his attention to the crowd and immediately noticed a spectator who seemed out of place. First of all, he was male. Second, he had shoulders like a linebacker and, third, his head was shaved clean but his face hadn't seen a razor in days. His sleeveless denim jacket had biker graffiti stitched on the back, but Rob couldn't make out the writing at this distance.

More suspiciously, he was staring at Swan as though he couldn't take his eyes off her. Rob understood the impulse, but he didn't like seeing another male in that state, especially under these circumstances.

Maybe it was nothing. Maybe the guy enjoyed wearing the occasional thong, but Rob intended to get closer to him all the same. It was then that he felt it—nothing he could put his finger on, just a tickle at the base of his neck. But he'd had the sensation before and it had never failed to alert him that trouble was present.

As one of the few men there, Rob stood out, too. He compensated for that by pretending to gauge the light with a meter as he worked his way around the fringes of the crowd. The biker hadn't noticed him and Rob was within fifteen feet of the man when a loud burst of cheering distracted him.

Rob glanced up to see a model dressed in a black tuxedo on the runway. The women were going crazy. Apparently this hunk of beefcake had just dramatically ripped off his jacket, shirt and tie—they were on the floor behind him—but he was now having a problem with his pants. He fumbled with the buttons, glanced up at the audience with a helpless shrug, and fumbled some more.

Right, Rob thought, that guy is about as helpless as a rattlesnake.

"Let me!" several women called. One started toward the stage and was actually stopped by the store's security.

"What's this?" Swan pretended to be surprised. "A gentleman in distress? We can't have that, can we, ladies?"

"Nooooo!" The reaction to Swan's question was loud enough to hurt Rob's ears.

"Think I should help him?" Swan asked them.

Hell, no! Rob thought.

"Yesssssssss!"

"Well, if you insist!" Swan came around the podium and joined the model center stage. She circled him slowly, boldly looking him over, as if she were sizing him up in all ways possible.

The back of Rob's neck had begun to warm considerably. *What was she up to?* He glanced around and saw that the biker had been stopped in his tracks, too. Interesting that she was still having the same effect on both of them.

Rob hadn't realized how short her black-and-white linen sundress was until he saw it from this angle. It was four inches above her knee, and for a petite woman, her legs seemed remarkably long. The sheath wasn't just short but formfitting, too. It hugged her behind in ways he didn't even want to try to describe. If she had to squat down for any reason, she'd have two more cheeks to powder.

"Are you having problems?" Swan asked the model.

The stud muffin's shrug was even more exaggerated this time. He was obviously trying to give the crowd a good show, but Rob didn't care. He didn't like this man.

Swan put her hands on her hips and looked out at the expectant audience. "Well, we're not going to let this stop our show, are we?"

The audience erupted in a wild chorus of agreement. Swan grabbed the model's tuxedo pants, right above his hips, and gave a mighty pull. The pants came apart at the seams—obviously stage clothes—leaving the model naked except for a bright red thong that cupped his equipment. Like some rodeo cowgirl, Swan swung the pants over her head as she headed victoriously back to the podium. Mission accomplished. The hapless model was now free to continue his runway walk.

Rob was speechless.

The audience wasn't. There seemed to be no end to their glee. Rob had begun to wonder if he'd stepped into some alternate universe. Women weren't supposed to act like this, were they? Hooting and whistling? He'd been in strip clubs that were less lively.

He scanned the audience, but saw nothing that reassured him. These weren't just grandmothers, they were housewives, secretaries and soccer moms, for heaven's sake. Shouldn't they be home baking cookies or changing diapers? He knew how ridiculously chauvinistic that sounded, but he couldn't seem to help himself. Sexist thoughts flooded his brain. All he needed now was a snout and some pig ears.

Men had been ogling women for years, he reminded himself. Why shouldn't women turn the tables? Logical as that was, he was still steamed at Swan's display on the stage. Worse, he was steamed at himself for being steamed. What right did he have to be jealous or angry? She wasn't his woman. She was his responsibility, but she wasn't his woman. If she wanted to make a spectacle out of herself, that was her business.

"And there you have it, ladies and gentlemen," Swan announced. "The fall line from Brief Encounters. We hope you enjoyed the show, and please remember every item you've seen today can be purchased only at La Bomba boutiques. Thank you for coming!"

As the crowd rose from their seats and began to disperse, Rob realized he'd lost the biker. *Brilliant, Gaines. You're zero for two. The suspect has vanished—and so has your alleged mind.*

Swan received a rousing round of applause as she stepped away from the podium and made her way down to the sales floor. Rob noticed that she had the organizer tucked securely under her arm. At least she'd done that much right. The temptation to hold her responsible was powerful, but he had no one to blame but himself. The fashion shows were her gig. Catching criminals and protecting civilians was his—and if he didn't get his act together, they were about to have another problem. If someone was planning to go for that organizer, it would be now, while she was in the midst of the adoring throng.

Rob glanced over at Harris and they exchanged nods. Joe started making his way toward the front entrance as Rob eased his way back to where Swan stood speaking with a cluster of well-wishers. The store's events director, a twenty-something woman with energy to spare, joined the gathering, and soon everyone was talking at the same time.

Rob couldn't make out a single word, but that wasn't what concerned him. He had Swan in his sights, but he needed to watch the crowd, too, and he had no idea what he was looking for. The biker was a little obvious. He might even be a decoy, meant to draw fire while the accomplice made his—or her—move. Rob hadn't ruled out either sex. Art Long was known to victimize women, but he'd also partnered up with them in the past, and a woman bank executive could easily blend in with this decidedly feminine crowd.

Rob began disassembling the light stand closest to where Swan was standing. He had already exchanged a glance with her to let her know that he was near and she was safe. She'd acknowledged him with an imperceptible nod. She was aware of him, alert. That was good.

Most of the audience had swarmed back into the store proper, and the racks were crowded with customers looking over Brief Encounters merchandise. Women were already lined up at the checkout counters, ready to buy, but Rob could see that it was going to take a while for the store to clear out. Calling them a swarm was pretty accurate, he realized ironically. All the activity did remind him a little of bees, with their steady and determined yet somehow frantic buzzing.

Or maybe it only sounded frantic to a man.

Was that sexist, too? He was never really sure.

It was a full half hour before the customers began to dissipate. Fifteen minutes later, only a handful of patrons and staff remained.

"I don't think it's going to happen," Joe Harris said as he walked over to Swan and Rob. "I'm going to check the stockroom and the fitting rooms one more time."

As Joe walked away, Swan casually asked Rob how he liked the show.

Rob's answer was a noncommittal shrug.

"You didn't like it?" She seemed surprised.

"I didn't get to see much of it. I was working, remember?"

The brightness of her smile faded, as if she'd hoped for some other response. Did she actually expect him to like the show?

"I'm not into beefcake," he said. "The music was great, but as far as the guys and those torture traps you had them wearing...I think that's a girl thing."

"Yesterday it was nut buckets and today it's torture traps? I guess it's safe to say you don't like thongs."

"I don't like underwear, period."

Her smile made another quick appearance, but it was different this time, a little shy maybe. Was that color rising in her cheeks? She wasn't easy to track. It was almost as if she had two contradictory personalities warring for control. The woman who blushed and looked away, eyelashes fluttering when she was flustered, and the one who could bring down the house with her daring, as she'd just done on stage. Apparently he was going to have the pleasure of figuring out who the real Swan McKenna was—

the sex kitten who yanked off men's pants or the bewildered, barefoot maiden he'd followed into the villa gardens. Of course, the maiden hadn't been wearing underwear, either, now that he thought about it.

"So what did you think of the skit?" she asked.

"You mean, the guy who couldn't get his zipper down? That was a skit?"

"Right, wasn't that a hoot? The ladies loved it."

"A real hoot," he said, giving her a skeptical look. "Whose bright idea was it to rip the guy's pants off?"

"Mine," she said proudly, "and you're the one who inspired that idea."

"Excuse me?" Rob was getting more annoyed by the minute, although he couldn't fathom why. "What is this thing you have about getting men out of their pants?"

She cocked her head with a hint of amazement. "Are you angry?" she said. "You are! You're angry. I think that's sweet."

"What are you talking about?" He *was* angry, and there was nothing sweet about it—or this conversation. It was none of his business how much or how little she enjoyed herself while on stage with half-naked men. It was his job to keep her safe, not virtuous.

"You're jealous," she said. Her laughter tinkled softly and her hair shimmered with rich lights as it moved around her face. It was falling into her eyes again, and he'd begun to think of that as a conspiracy to bring down the government. It was effective enough.

"Listen—" he started.

"Oh, I know, I know," she said, waving him off. "You're too big and tough to be sweet. FBI guys probably aren't allowed to get jealous. It's not on the list of acceptable emotions."

Her voice went soft and feathery. "But I still think it's very sweet."

She was looking at him as if she needed him to believe that, and Rob knew he was at a crossroads here. Whatever he said now would determine what path the two of them would take. He could own up, admit to the jealousy and perhaps ease the tension between them. But that would bring them closer. And it could open them up to talking about things that weren't on the list of acceptable emotions, as she had so succinctly put it. Or he could take the other path and admit to nothing, which was exactly what he should be feeling. *Nothing.* That just might drag him out of this emotional miasma and put his head back into this case.

Rob knew the geography of these crossroads well. Five years ago he had chosen the first path and it had ended with a woman dead, a broken engagement, and an FBI agent looking at hard time in federal prison. That agent was him. History had a way of repeating itself, but it wasn't going to repeat itself now.

"Look, I don't want to hurt your feelings," he said, "but this is going nowhere, okay? Whether or not you think I'm sweet is the last thing on my mind at the moment. It wouldn't even make my top ten list. You're in trouble and there's a crook running free. That's what's on my mind, and it should be what's on your mind, too—the *only* thing on your mind."

"What *is* your problem?" she said.

"When I'm not careful, people die," he shot back savagely. "That's my problem."

The color in her cheeks deepened, but there was no pleasure in its brightness now. She was shocked, and hurt, too. He could see that clearly, and as much as he didn't like it, some things had to be done.

"I know how important your job is," she said, "but we're not on opposite sides. We don't have to be enemies. I could help, if you'd let me."

"You want to help? Stick to business. Lay off that 'sweet' garbage."

For a second she looked as if she might want to slap him. Instead she met his gaze straight-on, met it hard. "Fine, but there's just one more thing. I haven't lied to you, despite what you might think. I haven't lied once, not even about Lynne. But I'm not convinced that you're not lying to me—and to yourself."

She turned and walked away, wounded pride evident in the tilt of her chin. He would have preferred the slap.

THE MAN WAS BURNING with jealousy. Swan knew it even if he didn't. And if he *was* jealous, that meant he had feelings. Either he wanted her for himself, or he couldn't deal with the thought of her wanting anyone else, which was pretty much the same thing. Both possibilities seemed logical to her, and since she and Rob Gaines were going to be trapped together in a car for the next several hours, this was the perfect time to clear things up.

"Permission to speak?" she asked him curtly.

"Denied," Rob said just as curtly.

Swan closed the organizer on her lap with a sigh of exasperation. If anyone in this car had the right to be angry, it was her. Why was he pouting? They were three-and-a-half hours into a seven-hour car trip to San Francisco, where the next show was scheduled, and he'd barely taken his eyes off the road the entire time. The only time he'd spoken was to inform her of their travel plans.

Once he and Joe had decided that the accomplice was not going to put in an appearance at the L.A. show, they'd packed up Swan's SUV with as much stage equipment, wardrobe, props and makeup as it could hold. The rented trailer they were pulling contained the rest. Joe Harris and

Gerard Nichols were following in the unmarked sedan that had been assigned to the agents.

At the last minute Swan had begged Gerard to come along, and he'd all but jumped at the offer. She'd done it with Rob's okay, of course—she obviously wasn't supposed to think a thought without Rob's okay—but she was glad Gerard had agreed. She needed at least one friend on this trip.

Swan picked lint from the knee of her khaki jeans. She was tempted to ask herself what Lynne would do. No doubt her partner would have driven Rob Gaines up a wall by now, but Swan doubted even Lynne could have cracked his defenses. He was Fort Gaines. She'd never met a man more determined not to get involved, which in all probability meant that he actually *wanted* to get involved.

Even if he didn't know it.

As the moments slipped by, Swan found herself nodding. That last thought had triggered an idea. Fortunately the freeway traffic was light. They were virtually the only ones on the road, so if something should *accidentally* spill in the special agent's lap, it would be inconvenient rather than dangerous. She loosened the seat belt to give herself some maneuvering room and reached through the space between the two front seats. Her purse was on the back seat and she'd tucked a bottle of aspirin inside.

"What are you doing?" Rob asked.

"I can't reach my purse. I'm going to have to get up on my knees."

She really did make an effort to get herself turned around without invading his space, but it couldn't be done. She bumped him with her shoulder as she leaned through the opening between the seats, and her arm brushed against him repeatedly as she riffled through her overstuffed purse in search of the aspirin. And, okay, maybe she overdid her struggle with the aspirin bottle when she finally found it, but it had one of those safety caps and she'd never been able to release them.

"Are you any good with these?" she asked him, grimacing as she pressed down with the heel of her hand and twisted the cap.

"It's all one motion," he said. "Push and turn at the same time."

Swan did what he said, pushing and turning until the cap popped off as if it were on springs. Startled, she began to wobble in her kneeling position, and Rob switched lanes, perhaps to slow the car down. But all was lost. The cap dropped into his lap, followed by the aspirin bottle and then Swan, herself, who was still on her knees.

It wasn't exactly the disaster she'd envisioned. It was better. She caught herself with her hands, which landed on each of his thighs, and his physical reaction was swift and thrilling. She could feel muscles locking as if someone was turning dead bolts. He took a hand off the wheel to brace her, but that pushed her farther off balance and, for several seconds, she was facedown in the kindling heat of Rob Gaines's loins.

Neither one of them could get her up, although Swan honestly wasn't trying very hard. The car jerked as he changed lanes again, which sent her rocking back and forth. He was actually making it worse, she realized. If he'd stayed in the original lane, she would have been peeling herself off him by now.

"Hang on," he said. "I'm pulling over."

Swan nodded obediently, her fingers sinking into the rippling muscles of his thighs. *Well, he told her to hang on.* It might have felt as if she were massaging him, but she was just trying to get a better grip. She could feel the heat rising off his body in waves, but there was very little she could do about it. She pushed herself up, only to fall back again as he came to a stop.

He cut the engine and grasped her by her shoulders. "I've got you," he said. "You can let go now."

Reluctantly, Swan let herself be lifted off him, but not for long. "Oh, look what I've done," she cried. "The pills, they're all over you!"

"It's just aspirin," he said. "Forget it."

"Not a problem," she insisted, rearranging herself to clean him up. "It'll just take a minute." He muttered an expletive, which she ignored. Of course, she had to brush the pills off him in a manner that required her to delve into the folds of his jeans, where the little buggers were hiding. Busying herself, she stroked and brushed and plucked, intent on finding every pill from his fly on down.

"That's good enough," he told her as her fingers crept into the juncture of his thighs. But she kept right on going, venturing into the forbidden zone. *My, my,* she thought, *lookee what's happening to the unflappable lawman.*

He grabbed her wrist and jerked her hand out of there. "I *said* that's enough."

"I'm not done!" Breathless, she met his angry gaze and held it until he'd pulled her within inches of his mouth.

"What are you doing?" he said under his breath. "What the hell are you doing?"

"Nothing," she whispered. Swan had no idea where they were or who might be outside the steamy enclosure that her SUV had become. She couldn't see anything but the man who was devouring her with his eyes. She couldn't hear anything but the heat jetting through his nostrils and the wild thunder of her own anticipation.

She could already taste his fiery anger. She wanted to taste it, but as she moved to kiss him, he held her back.

"You're lying," he said. "This isn't nothing, and you know it."

"*I'm* lying?" She flinched under his fiery gaze. "What about you? Look at you." She was visibly trembling, but she took some satisfaction in the fact that he was shaken, too. His face was mottled with heat and she could hear it in his voice.

He stared at her blankly. "What about me? I'm fine."

"Oh, please! Don't tell me you didn't want to kiss me, Rob Gaines. Don't even try. You were crazy to do it."

"Crazy is right. I'd have to be crazy." He released her and started up the engine, pulling the SUV out with such speed that she slid backward in the seat. If there were any pills left in his seat, they were dust by now.

"That didn't happen," he said when they were back on the freeway.

"What didn't happen? You didn't almost kiss me, or I didn't spill my only bottle of aspirin?"

"You know exactly what I mean." He let out an explosive breath. "Now, let's change the subject."

Swan released the breath she'd been holding, too. Maybe that was a little too close for comfort. She hadn't actually meant it to go that far, but she would never understand how he could sit there and deny the electricity in this car. They could have solved California's energy crisis.

Swan brushed aspirin dust from her jeans and, after an uncomfortable stretch of silence, she finally did change the subject. "I doubt if this is on your list of acceptable topics," she admitted, "but I'm curious about something you said earlier."

"What was that?"

"About people dying when you're not careful." He'd said it with such passion that she couldn't believe it had anything to do with her dying. She, who wasn't even in his top ten. It had sounded like something deeply personal, something from his past.

"You're right," he said. "It's not on the list. Pick another topic. In fact, why don't I pick one? There's something I'm curious about."

"What's that?"

"Your bladder."

"That's not on *my* list," she said.

He cut her a look. "Sorry, you don't get a list. You've been hitting the rest rooms about a dozen times a day by my best count, and you're not supposed to be out of my sight, remember? If I can't see you, I can't protect you."

"So come in there with me. Give the ladies a real thrill."

He heaved a sigh. "You're not going to make it easy, are you?"

Now I'm the difficult one?

"It's a nervous disorder," she said, shrugging it off, "like your twitch. When I get anxious I feel…pressure." It was more information than she wanted him to have, given that he was responsible for most of the nervousness. She glanced over to make sure he wasn't smirking, but he wasn't even looking her way.

"No more bathroom excursions unless you tell me or Joe first," he said. "That would be the perfect place for someone to ambush you."

All business, this man. "Fine," she agreed with a roll of her eyes.

"And speaking of excursions, where the hell *is* your partner, Lynne?"

Swan had actually been expecting that question. "Somewhere on the high seas," she told him, "and that's the God's truth. She's with the designer I told you about."

"Why hasn't she called you?" His eyes were narrowing by degrees as he looked over at her. "Or has she and you haven't told me about it?"

"Her cell phone probably doesn't work from the middle of the Pacific."

"Ever hear of ship-to-shore?"

"If there's an emergency, I'm sure she'll contact me."

"You don't consider this an emergency?" He snorted. "If she doesn't call soon, she and Geee-von will be talking to the Coast Guard."

Swan had a few questions of her own hanging, but the tension in the car was too thick right now. Rob had told her the four of them would have two adjoining rooms in San Francisco, and the agency would pay for their hotel, but he hadn't said who would be in which room with whom. She was burning to know how he planned to arrange things. She was also more than a little curious whether the agency had approved funds for the next show.

Determined to calm down, she looked out the passenger side window. She'd always loved the last few dying moments of daylight, when the sky turned every shade of blue and purple imaginable. It took her back to the summers of her childhood. As soon as the dinner chores were done, she and her mother would go out and sit on the porch or the lawn of whatever house they were living in, and watch the sun set. It was still Swan's favorite time of day, but it wasn't having the effect she'd hoped.

Pat McKenna was a great believer in simple truths, and she'd tried hard to instill them in her daughter. What a cruel twist of fate it was that on some level she might well have felt vindicated by the situation Swan was now in. Not because she actually wanted Swan to fail, but because she, herself, had given up so much out of fear. This would have convinced her that she'd done the right thing and that the daughter she loved to distraction was destined to learn the hard way, despite everything Pat had done.

Swan was beginning to fear that her mother had been right all along.

She let the seat back a few notches and made herself as comfortable as she could under the circumstances. Rest would be good. Sleep would be better. She was exhausted. There had been little sleep last night and this entire day had been nonstop activity. As she closed her eyes she wondered if Rob Gaines was as acutely aware of her as she was of him at this moment. And she wondered what it would take to get him to admit it. Medieval torture devices sounded good, but it was probably something far more subtle.

She had every intention of figuring it out.

SWAN WAS JUST COMING OUT of the bathroom as Rob hung up the phone. She'd slipped into one of the hotel's thick cotton robes and she tied it securely as she walked into the spacious room's combination living and bedroom area. The hot shower had been heavenly, exactly what she needed after the long drive. Her bare feet were still damp against the soft nap of the carpeting.

Joe and Gerard were in the adjoining room, unpacking. Rob had insisted that the common door between the rooms be kept open at all times, but he'd made it very clear that he was bunking with Swan. She still didn't know quite what to make of that.

"The funds weren't approved," Rob said without preamble.

"What?" Swan nearly tripped over the rug in her haste to know if she'd heard him correctly. His expression alone was grave enough to frighten her. "What did you say?"

"The Bureau doesn't finance peep shows, as they put it. They turned down the requisition."

She hadn't expected this, not for a moment. The stress of the past thirty-two hours suddenly overwhelmed her. It felt as if everything she'd worked for was disintegrating before her very eyes.

"How can they not approve it?" she asked him. "Without that money, there aren't going to be any fashion shows. And if there aren't any fashion shows, there isn't going to be any sting operation. They realize that, don't they? *You realize that, don't you?*"

She was close to yelling when Joe and Gerard suddenly appeared in the doorway.

"What happened?" Joe asked. "They turned us down?"

Rob nodded, and Gerard gave out a gasp. He marched straight across the room and pulled Swan into his arms, giving her a consoling hug. "Those bastards," he muttered.

Swan extricated herself and confronted Rob as if he were the one who had said no. "Tell them this isn't acceptable. It's not just their sting operation, it's my company. We won't survive without this tour. Brief Encounters won't survive."

"Look, I'm sorry," Rob said.

"Sorry?" She nearly sputtered. "Sorry? You can't let this happen. You have to do something! Why are they willing to sacrifice their precious sting operation now?"

"They believe Long's accomplice is more likely to make a move if you stay in the vicinity of the crime scene. That was my theory, too, but I've changed my mind."

"Changed how?" she asked.

He tried to explain. "I think the accomplice hasn't made a move because it's too close to home. He or she lives and works in this area, so the farther away, the safer and more anonymous it is. Unfortunately, I can't convince the powers that be. Even if they were comfortable with the idea of your shows, they don't see the need to finance them if they believe they can get their guy without them."

"I won't do it," she said, her voice dropping to a mere vibration. "I won't go back there and let them use me as bait for their trap. Not after this. They can throw me in jail, dammit. I won't do it."

Rob walked over to her, as if to calm her down, but she turned away from him. She wasn't going to let him touch her.

"Let's think about this," he said. "There must be some way to salvage the shows. What is it you need for this one in San Francisco?"

"Models. Living, breathing men to wear the underwear. I can't do the show without them."

Gerard pitched in. "Maybe I can make some phone calls? I have lots of friends in Frisco."

Swan nixed that instantly. "We tried that, Gerard. You're a doll for offering, but I can't go through auditions again. Remember the snakes, the fire swallower, the Marquis?"

"The phone repairman," Gerard said, winking at Swan. Everyone laughed, but Gerard protested. "Don't be so quick to scoff. Our Rob would have brought down the house in that outfit."

Swan was not going there. "Even if your friends were willing," she told Gerard, "we wouldn't have time to assemble everyone and rehearse them."

"How many models do you need?" Joe asked.

"I'd like ten, but I could probably get by with eight, even six," she said. "I'd need a bare minimum of six, but wait!" She began to pace, an idea forming. "If I came up with more skits, like the breakaway tuxedo, I might get by with half that many. There would be plenty of time for the other two to change while I was on stage with the third."

"Sounds like you might be able to do it with three." It was Joe again, making the observation.

"Maybe," she said, concentrating fiercely, "maybe…if I could come up with enough material to fill say three to five minutes per outfit."

"We have three men right here in this room."

Swan wondered about her hearing. Joe Harris couldn't possibly have said… She turned to him in confusion and saw the guyish smirk on his face. Okay, he was probably kidding. "Were you actually suggesting—?"

"He's not suggesting anything," Rob said firmly.

"That's a fabulous idea!" Gerard let out one of his little squeals. "I've wanted to model all my life. If only I weren't so…chubby."

"You're not too chubby." Joe yanked his shirt out of his pants and revealed his ample spare tire. He began unbuttoning the shirt. "Look at me."

"Joe!" Rob stared at his partner in abject horror. "Put your shirt back on. You're not doing this. *We're* not doing this!"

Gerard turned to Rob in mild exasperation. "What is your problem, Mr. Antsy Pants? You're the one with the great body."

Joe was actually grinning. "How tough could it be?" he said. "I know how to wear underwear. I do it every day."

"It's a cinch," Gerard chimed in.

Of course, Rob Gaines didn't wear underwear, but Swan felt no need to point that out. By now they were all looking at poor Rob, who'd backed up a few steps, as if the distance could save him. "Oh, no," he said, "no way."

He'd begun to sweat. The beads were visible on his forehead.

For a long pregnant moment no one did anything but stare at Rob. Swan began to feel sorry for him. But not that sorry. She walked to the king-size bed and sat down heavily.

"We can't very well make him do something he doesn't want to do," she said. "Besides he'd never work out anyway. He hasn't got what it takes, I'm afraid. He's missing the big three."

"What big three?" Rob asked suspiciously.

"The three things a model has to convey to the audience in order to win them over—openness, sincerity and charisma."

"I thought all you needed was the big *two* for one of those nut buckets?" Rob's grin was hopeful, but no one was laughing.

Gerard sniffed. "If the two he had were bigger, maybe he wouldn't be afraid to wear one of those nut buckets."

Oh, they're plenty *big,* Swan thought.

"Maybe you should be worrying about your two," Rob warned Gerard, who pretended to be horrified and went to hide behind Swan.

"We're not afraid of you G-men," Gerard said, peeking over Swan's shoulder. "Be nice, or you'll be sorry. Swan'll come over there and bitch-slap you. Right, Swan?"

"Gerard," Swan said, shaking her head in despair. It was time to put an end to the silliness. None of it was having any effect on Rob anyway, who'd entrenched himself across the room, his arms folded and his legs braced.

Swan threw up her hands and walked to the locked and bolted door of the hotel. She wanted to throw it open and let some air into the hot, stuffy room, but that wasn't possible, she realized. She was a hunted woman. It wasn't enough that her life was a train wreck, she was being stalked, and she had no idea what to do. Her partner was long gone, and Swan couldn't even call her mother, who would be terrified for her, and rightfully so.

"I'll model for you."

Swan heard the uncertain male voice behind her. She swung around in surprise. It was Joe Harris standing there, looking like a sacrificial lamb. He didn't seem at all certain of himself, and Swan could sympathize. He'd just deserted his very stubborn partner for her.

"You'll have to show me how," he said, "but I'll do it if you want me to."

"Now there's a guy with the big two." Gerard stepped forward proudly. "Count me in."

Swan was touched, really touched, but she couldn't accept their offers. "We have three labels," she explained. "Romeos, Heroes and Machismos. It can't be done without three models." She cast one last meaningful glance Rob's way. "It's too bad," she sighed. "Rob would have made the perfect hero."

Joe and Gerard pivoted as one to glare at Gaines, who by now was all the way up against the wall and almost as pale as the off-white paint.

"No way," he vowed. "Over my cold, dead body," he vowed.

Swan's eyelashes fluttered as she tried not to smile. Sounded like the last words of a condemned man to her.

6

"How am I supposed to size you when you're going up and down like a weather balloon?"

Rob had no acceptable answer for Swan's question. What man wouldn't be going up and down if a woman were doing to him what she was doing to him? She had her hands all over him, and there was nothing he could do to stop her this time. He was now officially an underwear model. He'd finally cracked under the pressure, and it was a sad story. In the middle of the night in a seedy motel room, he'd hung his head in defeat and agreed to demean himself. Now he had to endure this fitting ritual.

Of course, she hadn't told him about that.

Swan was on her knees in front of him, a tape measure in her hands and a red pincushion hooked to her wrist with a cute little matching elastic band—the picture of a busy seamstress, innocently going about her work. But you couldn't tell him she didn't know what she was really doing. Thank God she'd let him wear a pair of shorts for the sizing. Boxer briefs she'd called them, apparently because they clung to the body like briefs, but had legs about as long as boxers. He still felt naked.

She'd measured his hips in several places, and she'd been messing around in his crotch area, too. She might as well have been sizing him for a condom. That's how familiar she was getting with his tormented male anatomy.

"Which way do you prefer your weather balloons?" he asked dryly. "Up? Or down?"

She had nothing to say about that, but he got a reaction from her—a nice tight little swallow—and for that much he was grateful. Sexual torment should be equal, and she was way behind.

Finally she stopped fiddling with him, tilted back and looked up at him. The color was high on her cheeks.

"Seems we have a problem here," she said. "Do you think it could be nerves? I have some tea that might calm you down."

"I'm not nervous. This is what happens to men when women fondle them."

She blinked at him as if to say, *Excuse me?* "First of all, I'm not fondling you. I'm sizing you. And second, Gerard didn't go up and down like a weather balloon when I measured him, and neither did Joe."

"Well, hell, Gerard's gay, and I'm beginning to wonder about Joe. Any red-blooded guy would react."

"Oh, I see." Now she was measuring the outside of his leg from his hip to the top of his thigh. "So erections are on the FBI list of acceptable responses?"

"Yeah, sure."

"Well, then, congratulations. I'm sure the Bureau would be proud of you, but they're not on the list of acceptable responses for male underwear models."

He shrugged off her concerns. "This isn't going to happen during the show. You won't be on your knees in front of me, blowing…hot air on me."

"Don't be so sure. You and I will be doing a skit together. I haven't worked out all the details, but we can't have this problem. Think what the ladies would do."

Rob didn't want to think about that. "I'll count to ten backward, or you could pack me with ice." Not that it was necessary at this point. He was currently in the "down" mode, thanks to all this chitchat. If she kept it up, his weather balloon would probably wither away to nothing.

"Don't tempt me," she said. "Fortunately we have ways of dealing with difficult peni. Gerard?" she called, looking over her shoulder at the open doorway to the adjoining rooms.

Gerard and Joe were in there assembling props for the new skits. They'd been working on runway moves earlier, and Gerard had reported that Joe was making good progress with his Sam the Fireman routine. It wasn't news Rob wanted to hear. He had no idea what was going on with his partner, but Joe had sided with Swan and Gerard in their effort to shame him into this situation. The three of them had made him feel as though the show couldn't go on without him. Maybe that was true. He didn't want Swan to lose her deal with the boutiques, and he didn't agree with the Bureau's Assistant Special Agent in Charge that Long's accomplice was more likely to make a move on home territory. But mostly he didn't want his sting operation canceled.

"Gerard," Swan called again. "Could you find the accessories trunk and bring me a Number Two, please?"

"Sure thing, Duckling," Gerard replied from the other room.

"A Number Two what?" Rob asked.

"You'll see in a minute," she said, intent on her measurements.

Rob heard Gerard digging through one of the cases Swan had brought along. A moment later, Gerard joined them.

"Here you go." He handed Swan a long, tubular cotton object and returned to the other room. It reminded Rob of a rolled-up sock.

"This ought to do it," Swan said as she held it up.

"What the hell is that?"

"It's a crotch stuffer, size two." She studied his lower regions, making little measuring motions with her hands. She shut one eye and looked him up and down, then side to side. "You may need a three."

"No way in hell do I need a three!"

"Yes, I think you're right. Gerard," she called, "bring me a four, would you?"

"Oh, my," Gerard said from the other room. "We haven't had to use a four since Viagra came out. I'm not sure we even have one anymore, but I'll look."

Rob felt like a slab of meat on the scale. Give them a tenderizer mallet and they could finish him off.

Swan was still studying him, and perhaps unconsciously—though he wasn't so sure—she began tapping the crotch stuffer against her lips. After a moment, her eyes seemed to unfocus and her lashes quivered as if she were in deep thought. She began to run the stuffer along her lips, lingering here and there, and it was one of the most erotic things Rob had ever seen, even if she didn't know what she was doing.

Damn. Rob felt it coming, and there was nothing he could do to stop it. This was going to be the mother of all weather balloons. His testicles began to tingle and he felt that first tightening of deep scrotal muscle. As his penis began to lengthen, the friction of tender flesh against the cotton material only enhanced the sensation.

Swan's eyes widened as she watched the change occur. The crotch stuffer was now pressed firmly against her lips, her mouth slightly open.

Rob's mind was filling with erotic images of Swan and those damnably sweet lips of hers. But in his imagination it wasn't a cotton sock she had pressed to her lips, it was his hot, aching shaft. He tried to think of something else, but the image was too powerful.

God, he was hard. Talk about a difficult penis. Let's

see what she could do with this stick of dynamite, he thought. He had to clear his throat to keep from laughing.

Swan glanced up at him, her cheeks a little pinker now than they were a moment ago. She cleared her throat. "Never mind, Gerard," she croaked.

"Well, I wish you'd make up your mind," Gerard huffed. "We have work to do in here."

"I guess you're not nervous anymore?" she said, glancing up.

Rob wondered if he was blushing. He was sure as hell warm enough. "Look, it doesn't mean anything," he said. "It's just a physical reflex."

"Oh, really? I'm surprised it isn't your nose that's growing, like Pinocchio."

"What's that supposed to mean?"

"You know exactly what it means." She was echoing his comment in the SUV yesterday and her tone was superior enough to have come from a Sunday school teacher.

Rob met her skeptical gaze and wished he could tell her exactly what was going on in his head at that moment. That seemed to be what she wanted, access to his inner world, his inner self, his inner something. And lawman or not, he was still human. The only thing he was in touch with right now was his inner demon, and that horned creature wanted to take her beautiful face in his hands and hold it perfectly still while he slid his number four right into the heaven that was her open mouth. Was that on the list of her acceptable responses?

He wanted to do a few other things, too, such as remove the clothes from her busy little seamstress's body with his teeth, and whisper up and down the entire length of her with his hot demon's breath. He wanted to make her so crazy excited she didn't know a pincushion from a tape measure. But more than anything else, he wanted to penetrate her shiny wet lips with his ragingly hard cock.

Swan tapped the cotton tubing against her lips, blissfully unaware of Rob's demonic listmaking. It had begun to occur to her that she rather liked sparring with this tough FBI agent. Their give-and-take was honestly quite exhilarating—and so was knowing that his body had a mind of its own, so to speak. She was beginning to wonder if it might respond to any little old thing she did, whether he wanted it to or not. Now *that* was exhilarating.

"I guess federal agents lead a pretty austere life, don't they?" she mused out loud. "I mean, with all the rules and regulations and such?"

"I wouldn't call it austere, but we're trained to be in control."

"Really? All the time? Isn't there any situation where you could—you know—let go and enjoy yourself?"

"Not with you," he said, an odd little groan in his voice.

Swan's heart wavered and nearly stumbled over itself. She should have let it go. This was the time to stop playing. She could hear it in his voice, but something in the very tension he exuded was beginning to get to her. Her bra felt oddly tight and her skin was tingling against the warm silk cups. Something was happening in the pit of her stomach, too, a gentle tugging sensation.

"I guess what you're saying is that you're not allowed to get involved with someone like me, a suspect or a victim or whatever I am. Is that right?"

"That's exactly right."

"You're not even allowed to have feelings?"

"Agents can have feelings, Swan. We're only human. But we aren't allowed to act on them."

A few insights came to her at that moment. She understood perfectly the need for law enforcement personnel to maintain a certain distance from the people they worked with, but she wondered if the pressures of his job weren't so extreme that he had learned to keep everyone in his life at arm's length. No wonder he was so emotionally isolated. And, really, what harm would it do if he found a little pleasure with someone?

The other thought—the second one—was one of the more wicked ideas she'd ever had in her life. If he really wasn't allowed to act on his feelings, that explained why he hadn't followed through on the kiss they almost had in the car yesterday. It also meant she could flirt with impunity. She could be bold and daring, flirtatious, outrageous—everything she'd always secretly wanted to be. And there was nothing he could do about it.

Girl, you should be ashamed of yourself for even having the thought.

Swan couldn't tell whether that was Lynne's voice in her head or her mother's. This was getting scary.

"Okay," she said, moving on, "we're ready to see how much altering you need."

"You're altering *me?*"

"A figure of speech," she assured him. "Don't go anywhere. I'll be right back. You're going to love this part."

Before he could protest, Swan escaped into the other room where Joe and Gerard were rehearsing, and sorted through the rack of clothing designated for the San Francisco show. When she returned to Rob, her hands were discreetly behind her back, and she had assumed the demeanor of the mature, thirty-year-old businesswoman that she was.

"Now, we're going to be professional about this. Agreed?"

Rob's nod was hesitant. "Agreed."

Swan nearly lost her battle with the giggles as she brought her hands forward and held up a thong made of vibrant royal blue Lycra with black elastic hip straps. She actually heard Rob gulp, then let out some sort of woeful moan.

He took the thong and without saying a word went into the bathroom and shut the door behind him. She didn't hear the lock click, so apparently he planned to come back out some day.

While Rob was changing, Swan went back to Joe and Gerard's room. The two of them actually seemed to be having fun. For a man close to fifty, Joe was in very good physical shape, despite the spare tire he'd complained about. He wasn't as sculpted as Rob, but he was far above average. What won her over, though, was his personality as he proudly demonstrated his runway walk and turns for her. He wore red, white and blue boxer briefs and Swan decided he was going to be a perfect Sam the Fireman.

Gerard's red-and-blue cape lifted like wings as he came over to join Swan. He was wearing his superhero outfit, complete with bright yellow briefs, and he was smiling like a new dad. "That boy can strut," he said of Joe, who was concentrating on a couple of poses. "How's our brooding brute in the other room?"

"Not very happy about any of this."

"He looked pretty happy to me," Gerard countered. "Or should I say, his shorts looked happy? What were you doing to that poor man anyway?"

"Nothing! I'm sizing him for the line. What else would I be doing?"

As Gerard scrutinized her flushed face, his expression became more concerned. "Listen, be careful, Swan. These bodyguard situations are fraught with emotional peril. Don't you watch the movies?"

"Gerard, I'm fine. Worry about the show, not me."

"Hey, I'm worried sick about the show. I just don't want to see you get hurt, and he's the kind of man who can hurt a woman. Trust me. I know about these things. I've had my heart broken a time or two by the strong, silent type."

She patted his arm. "You're such a good friend."

"Yes, I am. Now away with you. I want to teach this FBI man how to handle a hose."

His eyebrows wiggled with evil glee, and Swan laughed. "Behave yourself," she said as she left.

There seemed a million details to remember for this evening's performance. She and Gerard had brainstormed new ideas until the small hours of the morning. Even with the skits to stretch things out, they would only be able to show half the line at most, which would cut the live portion of the show significantly. Luckily, Lynne had seen to it that every item in their fall line was photographed, and Gerard had the slides with him. What couldn't be modeled in person would be shown on a silk screen projection at the back of the stage.

"No giggling," Gaines said as he opened the bathroom door to come out.

Swan went nearly breathless as he stepped out and approached her.

The dark blue thong clung to him like a shimmering hand. That particular shade of royal blue against his tawny skin made her think of sultans and languid harem girls, for some reason. And the thickly banded muscles of his thighs made her think of the things sultans and harem girls did. Impossibly erotic things. He was beautiful.

"It's a little loose on the sides," she said, her breath snagging in her throat.

He was beautiful. She picked up her sewing basket and carried it over to where he stood. There was no way she could make the needed adjustments while standing. She sank down on one knee and gently slipped her fingers between his warm flesh and the soft black bands. She gazed upward and saw him looking down at her. There was no question that he worked out. His abs had the kind of definition you'd find in an ad for bodybuilders. They rose and fell with his breathing in a slow, rhythmic fashion. And his blue eyes had darkened to the point that they nearly matched the dense hue of the thong he wore.

"I just need to tighten this strap up a little," she said. Her voice felt small and distant, as if someone else were talking.

"Sure," he said.

It wasn't intentional—or perhaps it was—that her fingertips slid down his hip. Her breath hitched as she noticed the soft cup that held him move ever so slightly.

What if she were to place her hand on that? Hold him the way the cup of the thong did? What would that feel like?

Hot and heavy, she imagined. Maleness, in its purest form.

"Let's get this over with," he said.

His voice sounded ragged, and Swan was torn between desires. She didn't want to cause him any further embarrassment, but she was also fascinated by what might happen if she lingered—what might happen to her as well as to him. The tingling sensation in her breasts had turned into prickly heat, and the warmth in her belly was radiating deeper.

The blue sack began to swell as if air were being forced into it.

She pulled her hands away from his flesh.

"Seriously," she said, "what if this happens on stage?"

Rob shook his head. "Don't write any skits with you down on your knees in front of me, and I'll be fine. I'm not wearing one of those socks."

"No," she agreed. "That would only make it worse."

She made the adjustments with safety pins and stood up. She felt a bit light-headed, but that could have been because of how quickly she rose. It might also have been because the blood was flowing to another part of her anatomy, but she wasn't going to let herself dwell on that.

"If you're up to it," she said, "Gerard has a few things he wants to show you. Runway moves."

"I'm up to it, trust me. I think I'll be safer in there than in here."

Swan didn't allow herself to watch as he strode across the room and disappeared through the door. She was tempted, though, and she hadn't been doing a very good job of keeping any of her impulses in check. It was probably a fortunate thing that one of them was honor-bound not to do anything crazy. Otherwise, Sam the Fireman might have had to come in here and hose them both down.

"ARE YOU AWAKE?" Swan asked. She lay in the king-size bed, her eyes wide open, staring into the dark void of the hotel room. It had been nearly 2:00 a.m. by the time the four of them had finished up and lain down. That was an hour ago, and she hadn't been to sleep yet. She needed some of that calming herbal tea she'd offered Rob, but she was afraid she would wake him if she got out of bed.

"Not anymore," came a groggy response.

"Oh, sorry." She could barely make him out, resting on the couch with his feet propped up on the table.

"That's okay," he said, sitting up to stretch. "I'm not supposed to be sleeping anyway. God, what an exhausting day."

Luckily he couldn't see her smiling. They hadn't done anything but size him, fit him for the underwear, and practice for the show. That was exhausting? He probably would have been happier in a pedal-to-the-metal, tire-shredding car chase. She saw him so clearly as a man who was in his element when he was dealing with danger. She suspected the only thing he wouldn't risk was his emotions.

"Why doesn't Joe ever stand guard?" Swan asked.

"Is that what—" Rob seemed to be looking her way, staring at her in the dark. "He'll get his chance," he said.

Swan wished she could see the expression on his face. Maybe then she could figure out what he'd been going to say. *Is that what you want, Swan? Is that what you need? Joe, instead of me?* She wanted to see if there'd been a flicker of disappointment in his expression, anything to tell her that she might have had some emotional impact on him. He couldn't be that impervious.

Abruptly she asked, "Have you ever been in love, Gaines?"

"I was engaged once, but it didn't work out," he said.

If he'd been talking to a man, that answer might have ended the conversation, but he was talking to Swan, and all he'd done with his little nugget of information was seriously whet her appetite.

"How long ago?" she asked.

"A very long time," he said. "Forever."

"Forever's a long time," she agreed. "And you've had no relationships since. That must be tough."

"No tougher than having one. Relationships are hell. Case in point, this situation."

"You call this a relationship?"

"That's my point. It isn't, and it's already hell. Think what it would be like if it was."

Swan had no rejoinder and the room went quiet again. She was about to give up and just lie there some more, staring at the ceiling, but he surprised her by picking up the thread.

"And what about you?" he asked. "Boyfriend? Fiancé? Secret lover stashed away someplace?"

Swan had to smile. "You said yourself that I was under surveillance, and I'm sure you did a background check. That means you already know there isn't anyone in my life." *And hasn't been for quite some time.*

Swan stretched her arms out to her sides. Her fingertips didn't come close to reaching the edges of the huge king-size bed. "If you want to know," she said, "my last date was over two years ago. I've been completely involved with the line since then."

She heard the sofa groan as he turned, or was it him who'd made that mournful noise? She wondered if his back was bothering him after all the driving he'd done. "I've yet to see you make a personal call," she said. "Don't you have any family? Brothers? Sisters?"

"I have a little sister. She's all that's left now."

"Oh, I'm sorry. You lost the rest of your family?" Swan rolled over to look at him. She was surprised and filled with sympathy, but she didn't sit up. He'd already volunteered more than she'd expected, and she sensed that to overreact might cause him to back off. Besides, there was very little sadness in his voice. It was mostly resignation.

"It's not what you're thinking," he said. "No one died tragically, but things were bad at home, so bad that Dad took off. I guess I was about eleven when he left, and my sister was seven. He never came back, and my mom got progressively worse after that."

"She was ill?"

"You could call it that. I'd call it other things, like slow suicide."

"That sounds tragic to me," she said. She guessed that he was talking about drugs or alcohol, but she didn't ask. Again, she sensed they were heading into dangerous emotional territory, but she also knew that if he let himself open up and talk about it, it might help.

Apparently he didn't think so. He'd gone quiet over there on the couch and the silence felt like a barrier she was reluctant to breach, even to tell him again how sorry she was. "That must have been very hard," was all she said.

"A lot of other kids have it far worse."

She took one more step, one more risk. "Your sister, is she all right?"

Swan thought she saw him nod, although it was hard to tell in the darkness.

"My sister joined the military," he said. "She's stationed in Germany right now. I don't talk to her as often as I should."

There, for the first time, she detected regret, maybe even sadness, but with a hint of pride mixed in. He loved his sister, or at least Swan wanted to think so, and perhaps he'd had a hand in raising her. She was certain he would discount it if she asked, but it sounded as if he'd had to take on responsibilities that no eleven-year-old should ever be faced with.

"I lost my father, too," she volunteered, "but it wasn't like what happened to you."

"I know," Gaines said. "He was a rock musician with dreams of stardom, and your mom made the mistake of thinking she could change him. They weren't even married a year when she divorced him, but by that time she was already pregnant with you."

"How do you know all that?"

"It's in your file."

Swan rolled back onto the pillow with a sigh. "That is so unfair, Gaines. I just want you to know that."

"What?" he asked.

"Is there anything you *don't* know about me?" Swan

had never actually met her father. He was gone before she was born and apparently he'd never looked back. The last they'd heard was that he'd joined a hippie commune somewhere in the Pacific Northwest. That was ten years ago and Swan had never felt a need to contact him. But Gaines probably knew that, too.

"I know some facts," he was saying, "but that's all. Other than your vital statistics and a bit of background information, you're still very much a mystery to me, McKenna."

Swan was slightly mollified by that—and since he'd actually bothered to ask about her romantic relationships, there was a little something she could share. "Maybe you'd like to know a secret then?"

"I'd almost pay money for that, McKenna."

She was glad he couldn't see her smile. "I once had a huge crush on this driver who worked for Lynne's mother. I was just a kid—sixteen—and he was in his twenties, but very buff, if you know what I mean. He used to walk around shirtless. Lynne and I used to sneak up to her bedroom and talk about him for hours. She knew I was infatuated and she kept egging me on, daring me to go outside and talk to him while he washed the cars. I think she may have nudged him in my direction, too. I couldn't get her to admit it, but I wouldn't have put it past her."

"Sixteen?" Gaines said, disbelieving. "You were jailbait. That guy should have known better."

Her voice softened. "I wish one of us had known better."

"Did you actually hook up with him?"

Swan hesitated, wondering if she should be telling him any of this. He could so easily judge her for something done at an age when the hormones are flowing and young girls don't make very good decisions for themselves. Besides, it was probably the only wild thing she'd ever done, really. But he wouldn't know that.

"Swan? What happened with this guy?"

So…he *was* interested. She rather liked that thought, and she did want to tell him the rest of it. "I took him some lemonade one hot afternoon, and my mother saw us talking while he worked on the cars. She lectured me for hours afterward about the dangers of mingling with the male sex. She told me that men like him couldn't be trusted, and if I were to risk my heart, it should be with someone kind and decent, but as far as she was concerned there weren't any decent men out there, so the smartest thing I could do was learn to take care of myself."

"And that was the end of it?"

"God, no, that was the beginning. I had Lynne tell him that I wasn't allowed to talk to him anymore, and she came back, bubbling about his plan that he and I meet in the five-car garage where he did mechanical things. He also lived there, in an attached apartment. Naturally, I had to go, and it wasn't long before we were meeting each other there on a regular basis—in secret, of course."

She sat up and pulled up her legs, covering them with the comforter. "You know the rest of the story. I fell in love with him, and he broke my heart, just the way my mother said he would. It only lasted a couple of months before he dumped me for a waitress who worked at one of the coffee shops on the beach. When I asked him why, he said she had interesting things to talk about—she didn't bore him. God, that hurt. I thought I'd die it hurt so badly."

She could feel the pain of it now and wished she'd never started this conversation. She'd been pushing for a peek into Rob Gaines's secret heart and instead she'd exposed all the hurt in her own. Maybe she hadn't learned anything.

"It sounds like you really loved this guy."

"I did—in that passionate, all-or-nothing way that teen-age girls do. But I think what I really needed was for him to love and accept me. I was so confused about who I was, and where I was going, and I came out of that feeling worse about myself."

"And you probably believed everything your mother told you about men, right?"

"I did, yes." That was very perceptive of him, she realized. "She'd had me pretty well convinced that men couldn't be trusted, and then he came along and proved her right. I think I gave up on relationships before I'd even had one. I certainly didn't hold out much hope of finding the kind, decent guy my mother talked about."

"I feel as if I should apologize for my gender," he said quietly. "That should never have happened to you." As if to offer reparation, he added, "Speaking of personal calls, you're free to make them. Obviously you shouldn't mention the sting operation, but there must be someone you want to contact, maybe your mother?"

Swan shook her head. "Thanks, but I'd have to lie through my teeth, and I don't think I can do that right now."

Through the shadows, she saw Rob stand up and stretch. He gave out a soft groan as he did some side-to-side stretching. She was watching him so intently that when he turned her way, she thought he was coming over to the bed.

"You better get some sleep," was all he said.

Swan pulled the comforter to her chin and curled up into a ball. "What about you? When do you sleep?"

"I'll get Joe up at seven, then I'll shower and get a few hours." He moved back to the sofa and sat down. She watched as his shadow began to melt into the darkness of the far side of the room.

"Thanks," she said softly.

"For what?"

"For talking. For just talking with me."

"Anytime."

Her lips formed a smile. "Same here."

ROB HAD NEVER WANTED to chicken out of anything more in his entire life. There were too many women in this place, too much noise and commotion, and not nearly enough clothing. The only thing covering his nearly naked body was the terry robe that Swan had borrowed from the hotel and, to make matters worse, this La Bomba boutique had decided to serve champagne to the audience.

Too many *women?* He was in bad shape. He never thought he'd hear himself admitting to that. Fear was not on the list of acceptable emotions for an FBI agent. It could disable you faster than a bullet, and Rob had always had automaton-like control over his emotions until now. He was barely on a nodding acquaintance with fear, and he hadn't known how lucky he was.

His gut was busier than a popcorn machine. His forehead was damp and his hands were numb. Luckily he wouldn't be needing them for much of anything anyway. If his feet went numb, he was going to be in trouble.

The thought of strutting around, bare-assed, in front of a couple hundred women had turned him into a basket case. Soon *he* would be needing to pee. Good luck in this thing, he thought, looking down at the forest-green thong that could just be seen through the opening of his terry robe. He'd already been made up, fitted and stuffed. Yes, stuffed. Swan had insisted he wear at least a number four, which she'd sworn was nothing more than a panty liner. She'd said it would keep the "details" from showing.

She'd also put some bronze body gel all over him that smelled like coconuts.

He'd have a swarm of flies following him onstage. And a panty liner? What more could you do to humiliate a man? He swiftly opted not to think about it. She would find a way.

At least he'd found the courage to untie the robe and let it hang open. Now he was trying to get used to the idea of walking out there without it. Out there, being the runway. He and the other two models, Joe and Gerard, were waiting in the backstage area of the San Francisco La Bomba boutique, and the place was abuzz with last-minute preparations for the show. There were people running around Rob had never seen before, which made him nervous from a security standpoint, but Gerard had sworn they were all okay. His friends. And since Rob and Joe were both in the show, Rob had arranged for some backup. He'd spoken with the store's security force, alerting them to be on the lookout for any suspicious behavior.

It wasn't the ideal backup plan, but it was better than having to explain why he and Joe were wearing nut buckets to his fellow agents. And the show had to go on. Rob was impressed with how much organization an underwear gig took. Costumes had to be hung on rolling racks, sorted by model name and the sequence they would be worn in the show. Music and lights had to be cued, almost down to the microsecond, it seemed. The sound system that would carry Swan's voice had to be tested and retested, adjusted and readjusted, until it was perfect. And all of this work was done by what amounted to a skeleton crew of volunteers. Fortunately, some of the boutique's staff had pitched in, too.

Gerard, who would be modeling three changes himself, was acting as backstage director, and Rob had to give the man credit. He knew what he was doing. He'd insisted on a dress rehearsal this afternoon and now, with less than ten minutes to show time, Rob was glad they had. If nothing else, he knew where he was supposed to walk and where his stop marks were.

Just make your marks, don't trip over your own feet on the way, and everything will be fine. That's what Swan had been telling him all morning.

His partner seemed immune to this insanity. Like Rob and Gerard, Joe was wearing a robe that Swan had borrowed from the hotel. But unlike Rob—who had not been able to sit still for more than two minutes at a stretch—Joe had parked himself on a folding metal chair at a folding metal table and was intently reading Friday's edition of the *Wall Street Journal.* The idiot was more engrossed in the paper than he was in this three-ring circus. Didn't he know danger when it stared him in the face? A threat you could understand and combat was one thing. Rob thrived on that. This was high noon, and they were unarmed.

Swan was standing by one of the sound system consoles, speaking with a technician friend of Gerard's. Today she was wearing a silvery top that actually laced up the back, revealing snippets of her flesh, and matching slacks that tapered at the ankle. *The woman was hot.*

She wasn't more than thirty feet from him, but Rob couldn't make out what she was saying over the noise. She glanced over at him and smiled. His answering smile felt alien on his face, the way a man would look if something were squeezing his nuts and he was trying to pretend it felt good. Actually, something was squeezing Rob's nuts. And it did not feel good. Maybe that's why his hands and feet were going numb.

He watched as Swan nodded to the tech and then headed his way. She had the organizer tucked firmly under her arm.

"How are you doing?" she asked.

"Just dandy, thanks. I think I have to pee."

"No way. There isn't time."

"How would you like me to tell you that when *you* get the urge?"

She patted his arm as if he were a child. "You'll be fine," she said. "They're going to love you."

"I don't want them to love me. I want them to go away."

Fat chance of that, he thought. The noise level in the audience was growing louder by the second. Evidently they were ready for a show and ready for it now.

"Let's go!" Swan called to Gerard and Joe. She gathered the three men together, apparently for a pep rally. "All right, fellas, it's show time. If there are any last-minute questions, ask them now. Rob, you're up first. But don't come out until you hear your cue."

From the other side of the curtain, somewhere out in the assembled audience, a woman shrilled, "Where's the beef?" A chorus of laughter followed.

Rob took it as a sign of his deliverance. "It sounds like they want hamburgers," he said. "Maybe Joe could take my place, and I could make a fast-food run? It'd only take me a minute."

Gerard pushed Rob toward the curtain. "Give 'em hell," he said.

Rob was sure his feet were going numb, but he had the presence of mind to drag Joe close. "Remember our contingency plan," he said. "While I'm out there, you watch Swan's back. Watch her every damn second, and keep your eye on the book, too, because she's going to have to leave it at the podium while she's involved in the skits."

"Roger Wilco." Joe grinned broadly. "Listen to them out there." He shook his head in pure male wonder.

"Have you ever heard women make noises like that? I've been waiting for this my whole life."

Rob felt actual despair. "You're sick, you know that?"

"Well, here goes," Swan said, taking a deep breath and heading for the stage. "Break a leg, guys."

Not the best thing to say to a man with numb feet!

Rob watched as she vanished around the black curtain and took the podium. He heard a round of applause and exhaled deeply. Given a choice, he'd rather be enduring a colonoscopy without anesthesia right now. Anything would be better than this, and it felt as though he had a tube up his butt anyway. Thongs were more uncomfortable than he could ever have imagined.

"All right, boys," Gerard announced as he slipped off his robe. "Get naked, get your props and take your places." He clapped his hands briskly as if that would make them move faster.

Rob wanted to kill him. He wanted to strangle him with a pair of Brief Encounters underwear, preferably one of the faux fur thongs.

"Have some fun with it," Joe whispered to Rob.

"Yeah, right," Rob mumbled as he took off his robe. *Suck it in, man. I mean, literally, suck it in.*

Swan's amplified voice rang throughout the store as she made her introductory statements. The tumultuous response she received made Rob wonder if the women were coming right up onto the stage. That thought worried him. He could tell from Swan's voice that even she was a bit overwhelmed.

SWAN FELT LIKE A LION tamer at the circus, wondering if her big cat was going to bolt. This raring-to-go crowd was enough to freak out a seasoned model, much less her three newbies. Joe and Gerard would be fine. Even if they didn't look like pros, their personalities would carry them through. Rob was the wild card. She knew he wouldn't deliberately sabotage the show, but he was showing signs of stage fright and if he let it take over, it could freeze him in his tracks. A few days ago she might have relished the thought of him being the object of laughter and ridicule, but not now.

It surprised her how much she did not want that to happen, but she felt helpless to prevent it. There was one thing she could do, although there wouldn't be time to warn the guys in advance. If she brought either Joe or Gerard out first, it might break the ice and relieve some of the tension. Of course, it could do just the opposite, but she was going to try it anyway. Her intro would cue the right lights and music, and the guys were lined up and ready back there. She knew Gerard had seen to that.

Swan reached under the podium and pulled out a referee's shirt, a hat and a whistle. The shirt had black-and-white stripes and the cap matched it. She slipped on the shirt, leaving it unbuttoned, and popped the cap on her head backward. Here goes, she thought, adjusting her wireless microphone headpiece.

"Ladies and gentlemen, Joe and his bouncing balls!"

Joe charged out from behind the curtain as if he'd read Swan's mind. He was dribbling a basketball and wearing briefs in a black mesh design with a jock strap lining. His skill during rehearsal had surprised everyone, including Rob, and luckily it hadn't been a fluke. Joe made it to his mark at center stage where he did some fancy footwork, weaving the ball through his legs and then spinning it on one finger, which almost worked. When the ball hit his head, he gave it a soccer bop and caught it behind him, which brought whistles and cheers.

Mistakes weren't fatal. You could recover. Swan hoped Rob got that message. "Joe is wearing briefs that breathe from our sportswear line," she told the crowd. "We call the line Machismo Activewear, and it doesn't matter what sport your man is into, he'll appreciate the comfort and support this design provides.''

She blew her referee's whistle loudly and grabbed a second basketball from inside the podium stand and then jogged down the runway toward Joe. She was a little nervous herself, but his goofy grin relaxed her. Swan tossed him the second ball, and Joe began his routine all over again, actually dribbling both balls at once.

"Joe and his bouncing balls!" she said, throwing out her arm.

He did some footwork and that was supposed to be the end of the routine, but Joe didn't show any signs of stopping. He turned to the excited crowd and dribbled both balls down the runway, right to the very end, then whipped around, bounced first one ball, then the other, high off his knee and caught them. A round of applause broke out as he looked over his shoulder and wiggled his backside. The entire room went up, cheering in unison.

Swan was just as surprised and tickled as the audience. "That's our Joe. Pretty ballsy, I must say! Want to give your man some bounce, ladies? Take home something from our Machismo line."

Joe was taking his bows and soaking up all the attention he could get as he backed up the runway. Swan had begun to think she would need to go down and get him. She blew several blasts on her whistle, and reluctantly he turned and headed for the curtain, blowing kisses all the way.

No stage fright for that one.

Swan decided to stall a little longer and call Gerard out next. Knowing Joe was a hard act to follow, she pumped the crowd up even higher, ending her intro with, "Are you ready for our next Machismo man? Meet Gerard and his heart-throbbing thighs!"

Gerard made his entrance doing a wheelie on a bicycle he'd borrowed from one of his San Francisco buddies. He wore a pair of thigh-length silver biker briefs with a black racing stripe, a black leather jacket and gloves as he pedaled down the runway, hit the brakes at the end and dismounted.

"Haven't we all secretly fantasized about a biker guy?" Swan asked.

While she gave her spiel about the garment's functionality and its "no-slip grip on the thighs," Gerard began to slowly strip, taking off his gloves and flinging them into the crowd. The women were on their feet as he peeled off the jacket, one sleeve at a time. Moments later he had the jacket stretched out behind him like a bath towel, turning in a circle, rotating his hips, Carmen Miranda-style.

It was more funny than sexy, and the audience howled. Swan hiccuped a giggling sound. Before it was over, she had to restrain herself from pounding on the podium at the hilarity of it. "Want his thighs to make your heart throb, ladies?" she said. "Give your guy a pair of our Machismo biker briefs."

Gerard flung the jacket into the crowd, remounted the bike from the rear, as if he were leaping onto a horse, and pedaled offstage, doing one last wheelie before he disappeared.

It was Rob's turn. Each of the first two skits had taken about four and a half minutes, so he'd had almost ten minutes to get his nerves in line. She hoped he'd been able to do that.

"And now, for a total change of pace," Swan said as the music dropped low and then ended with the sound of beating drums. "Recall the hunters and gatherers of old, if you would, the trackers who stole noiselessly through the forest, the Indians who rode the plains. Recall those early adventurers as we give you our boldest, sexiest, and most daring sportswear, the Huntsman.''

Rob stepped out from behind the curtain. He carried a wooden crossbow in his right hand. A quiver of arrows was strapped across his chest and hung on his back. His face was impassive, but there was no hesitation in his stride. It was long-limbed, muscular and purposeful as he started down the runway into lights that made him look as though he was gleaming.

His stony countenance had the desired effect. The entire audience seemed to take in a breath at the same time, and Swan joined them. The drum music grew more powerful, filling the room as the lights went down. A blinding spotlight hit him, but he didn't waver. He was a hunter, primed for the kill. There was no smiling or joking this time. There wasn't even a sound. For this vignette, his focus was perfect.

He pulled an arrow from the quiver and armed the crossbow. His shoulders rippled with strength as he braced his legs and aimed toward the ceiling. It looked as if he intended to shoot a star from the night sky. For a moment Swan thought he might. They had not rehearsed this, and she didn't know what to say, so she wisely stayed silent.

There was a smattering of applause that quickly stopped. The audience didn't seem to know what to do, either. Swan could hear sighs and other subdued vocal effects from the women. His performance had had the effect of rendering them nearly speechless, and Swan knew something they didn't. It wasn't a performance, wasn't an act. This was Rob, stripped down to the raw male that he really was. She wasn't sure how she felt about that as he lowered the bow, turned and walked past her up the runway.

"The Huntsman," was all she said.

Fortunately the music began to blast and the slide show

began. As emcee, she would be describing some of the qualities of all three lines as her models changed for the next round of skits. One down, two to go, she thought. Maybe they would make it through this. The Machismo Activewear segment had gone better than she had dared hope.

Swan's luck held out through the Romeo line. Joe modeled Fly Boy, the line's shocking pink boxers with an innovative Velcro fly, which he was happy to demonstrate, much to the crowd's delight. Gerard came out in Sweet Talker, a tiny thong with lush red lips imprinted in a strategic place. Rob wore slinky silk pajama bottoms in zebra stripes and a faint smile.

Swan didn't dare to think he might be enjoying himself, but she knew the audience was. They were up on their feet with every one of her introductions, and she was thrilled. But again, she knew something they didn't.

They hadn't seen anything yet.

Joe launched the Hero line with his Sam the Fireman— and drew two-fingered whistles with his cocky red helmet, canvas hose and red, white and blue boxers. Gerard bounded onstage next, a superhero in hot yellow briefs and a red and blue cape. During rehearsal, Swan had pressed a sticky-back triangle on his chest with a large crimson G.

"Who says your man has to be in top physical condition to be your hero?" Swan announced as Gerard posed and preened, flexing nonexistent muscles. Her research had shown that most men were not in top physical shape, and Gerard brought home the fact that it didn't matter what you looked like, you could be sexy and daring if you wanted to.

Gerard's exit was a dead run backstage, his arms outstretched as if he actually expected to take off and fly before he disappeared through the curtain.

"Do you have a soldier of fortune at home?" Swan asked the crowd. "Would you like one? Maybe an aviator, a sailor or a Green Beret?"

That was Rob's cue. And his entrance brought more hushed sounds of appreciation from the house. He was doing it again, Swan realized. He was knocking their socks off, and her feelings were oddly mixed about that. It was great for her line, but what would it do to a man's ego knowing all these women were hot for him? Rendered speechless by the very sight of him? Rob hadn't struck her as a guy who was aware of his appeal. She'd just as soon it stayed that way, although why she should have cared about the size of his ego, she didn't know.

He looked good in camouflage, she had to admit. *Damn* good.

He was wearing the line's cammy thong, and she may have sized it a little too small because it appeared to be packed. No wonder the women couldn't speak. His only other clothing was a pair of military boots, open-laced. It was a look that exuded power and physical threat, whether it was meant to or not. Slashed in vertical lines on his chest were ribbons of black and green cammy paint. The same had been applied to his high cheekbones, and the word that lodged itself in Swan's brain was *dangerous*.

She felt something tumble in her belly as she registered the full effect. It had to be the lights. She didn't recall him looking this way before—so formidable—but then maybe she hadn't let herself. They'd been at such odds.

The music suddenly changed and it hit her that she had a show to emcee. Rob had reached his mark and he was waiting center stage, his back to her. His shoulders were squared, his backside flexed. It was not a sight for the faint of heart, and Swan was beginning to have second thoughts about their skit.

Her props, a round-brimmed drill sergeant's hat and a

riding crop, were stashed in the podium stand. She popped the hat on her head and rested the riding crop against her shoulder.

"Paraaaaaade rest!" she said as she walked over to Rob.

Rob snapped into position with his hands clasped behind his back and his feet spread apart at shoulder width. Swan had deliberately given him routines that didn't require him to "dance or prance," and he'd seemed appreciative. But he might not be when he found out what was coming. She'd added the riding crop as a last-minute prop.

"I think it's time to inspect our big bad soldier man," she said. "See what he's made of. What do you think?"

The audience was all for it.

Swan circled him, her chin high as she tapped the crop into her palm. "A man who wears the Hero line is always ready for close-order drills, isn't that right, soldier?" Swan gave his bare butt a little snap with the crop. Just hard enough to get his attention.

The crowd loved it and encouraged her to give him another.

"Where the hell did that come from?" Gaines said through his teeth.

"Did I hear a '*Yes*, ma'am'?" She snapped him again, a little more smartly this time. It actually left a pinkish mark on one cheek, and she glanced up to see his reaction. His jaw was clenched, but that was probably due to surprise. She hadn't told him about the prop because she hadn't intended to use it. Gerard had given it to her as a joke "to keep that Neanderthal in line."

What had possessed her to change her mind was still a mystery to her. Maybe she wanted to shake up his composure a little, despite the risk of doing so in the middle of the show. Maybe she just wanted to get a bit better acquainted with that beautiful backside of his.

Swan began circling him. Slowly. Her gaze took in every part of his toned physique. Was he always this taut and twitchy? The man was a curled fist. He was quite magnificent, really, although she mostly associated that word with landscapes. She found herself particularly drawn to the brawny muscles of his back and shoulders. What would it be like to run her hands over those massive cords? she wondered. She'd measured him for underwear, but what would it be like to actually touch him intimately?

It was such a temptation. Everything about this situation spelled temptation for her because he couldn't do anything. He wasn't even allowed to speak to her. The urge to get a rise out of him was irresistible. It was all so *not* Swan McKenna. She hadn't had an irresistible urge since high school, and the one she'd had back then had gotten her into enough trouble to last her a lifetime.

She came around, passing in front of him but not without first examining him as closely in front as she had in back. "Well, he certainly passes my inspection," she said. The crowd agreed.

She ran the tip of the crop over the swells of his pecs and then, just because she was enjoying herself, she tickled his collarbones and gave his Adam's apple a tantalizingly slow circle. Would it move? she wondered.

It did. And he made a little growling sound that sent a thrill through her.

"I wonder if he's any good with *fox holes?*" Her voice was deeper and more sultry than she'd ever imagined it could be. Suddenly it didn't feel as if she was acting anymore. "Or hand-to-hand?" She omitted the word combat, leaving the audience to fill in their own blanks.

When she checked out his expression, she saw that she had nothing less than a beast on a short chain. His blue eyes were icy-hot, and he was beautifully clenched from head to toe. Even the breath jetting through his nostrils was taut. The audience thought it was all part of the act, but Swan knew this man would probably take the riding crop to her if given half a chance, and it wouldn't be a tap or a snap.

She ran the tip of the crop down his war-painted chest and over his vise-grip abs. When it got to the top of the thong, she whisked it lightly from side to side, hip to hip. Some of the women in the crowd issued a collective sigh. They would probably have loved it if she dipped inside with the crop, pulled open the band of the thong and took a little peek. Did she dare?

"Hiding any grenades in there?" she asked him.

It seemed like such a good idea, and this was show biz, after all. The common goal was to sell underwear, wasn't it? But when she glanced up, she wasn't so sure. There was no mistaking the torch that smoldered within this soldier. His gaze could have singed the hair from her body, and his jaw worked against its own tightness. Apparently he wasn't having as good a time as everyone else.

She briefly pulled the microphone away from her mouth, pretending to adjust it. "We're selling underwear," she said under her breath. "It's not a big deal. Relax and have fun with it, okay?"

"Oh, I intend to have fun," he said ominously.

It sounded like a threat and she reacted by turning to the audience. "Did you hear me order him not to talk?" They shouted yes en masse and she nodded in agreement. They were all with her on this. They wanted this bad boy to get his comeuppance and what could she do but try to oblige them?

"Apparently he's a slow learner," she said.

She strolled around behind him and pursed her lips in thought. After a moment's contemplation, she hooked a finger in the T-strap of his thong, stretched it like a slingshot and let it fly.

The growl that came out of his mouth was downright primitive. A shockwave rippled up and down his spine, and Swan's smile froze on her face. Sometimes you didn't realize you'd crossed the line until you were so far over it, there was no getting back. Her heart spasmed with fear and her mind followed, leaping to the only logical conclusion it could. She was a dead woman. She had better catch the next plane to Bora Bora and hide in the jungle with the blood-sucking leeches and the pythons, because she was a dead woman.

THE PLAN had been for Swan to mingle with the crowd when the show was over and let it be seen that she was carrying the organizer. At some point, on a signal from Rob, she would go to a designated point in the store and wait there alone. She would pretend to be making a cell phone call. That would give the accomplice an opportunity to approach. Of course, Swan would be under surveillance the entire time, with both Rob and Joe ready to intercede.

Instead, Swan rushed backstage as soon as the show was over. She'd thought Rob might be waiting for her when she got done, but she saw only Gerard and his motley crew, celebrating their success with some grocery store champagne. Joe was with them, too. Swan gave the group a V for victory sign, but she didn't join them. She went straight back to the small dressing room the store had allowed them to use. Maybe Rob was still changing.

The place looked empty as she entered, and she was actually relieved. She wanted to apologize, but it might be better if they both had some time to cool off. Unless she'd misread him completely, he was ready to chew up the scenery, and she needed to calm down, too. Luckily the dressing room was large and had a makeup table and a sink. She let the water run until it was refreshingly cool, and as she blotted her face, she listened to her breathing deepen and relax. This was just what she needed.

She was still bent over the basin, eyes closed, when she felt a tap on her shoulder. She didn't have to turn around. She saw him in the mirror the instant she opened her eyes. He'd changed into street clothes—blue jeans and a chambray work shirt, which should have tamed the beast a bit. It hadn't.

He had definitely misplaced his smile.

"You," he said in a low voice.

His dark gaze ricocheted off the mirror.

Before Swan could say "You, what?" he'd spun her around on her heels and backed her against the basin. If the sink hadn't been there, she would have been on her butt. "I was looking for you," she hastened to tell him.

"Is that right?"

Was that a riding crop in his hand? Swan glanced at the chair where she'd left hers and her heart sank. She'd been disarmed. "I wanted to apologize."

"Oh? To apologize for what?" He began tapping the end of the crop into his palm, just as she'd done. Sharp little snapping sounds filled the space between them. "It wouldn't be for this, would it?"

Uh-oh, she thought.

Swan slid to her right, but Rob sidestepped her, cutting off her escape route. She forced an unsteady smile. "You know, you were a big hit out there. Everyone loved you. They'll be talking about it for days." Maybe if she fed his male ego the beast inside would mellow out and take a nap.

"I could have done better," he said in a dangerously low voice, "if I'd had a little more experience with a riding crop. Why don't I get some now?"

His index finger snagged her waistband at the clasp and he pulled her toward him. Swan's heels skidded across

the floor when she tried to resist. At the moment he had
the upper hand in every way—or at least that's what her
shivering skin was telling her.

Rob began circling her the way she had circled him
earlier. She watched as his eyes traveled slowly over her
body. When he got behind her, she felt the ties to her
silver lame top suddenly release. Her hands flew up to
keep it from falling and exposing her breasts. She wore
no bra—which he knew, of course.

"What are you doing?" Her head snapped around, but
he'd already completed his circle.

"Oops," he said casually, "or should I say, relax and
have fun with it?"

Again his eyes roamed freely over her body, especially
the hands that were covering her breasts. He lowered the
crop and began sliding its tip up her thigh. The pressure
left a tingling sharpness in its wake and Swan began to
wonder where he was going next. She sucked in her belly
as he tapped her there, lingering to draw a lazy circle
around her belly button, which was exposed by the material she'd clutched.

Swan didn't know whether her heart was crazy from
excitement or fear. One thing was for sure. The beast was
off his leash.

"Maybe I should inspect *you* now?" he suggested.
"See what you're made of. Isn't that what you said earlier?" He answered his own question with a nod. "Yes,
it was. I remember it clearly."

"It was a skit, Rob. I didn't mean anything by it."

If he'd been smiling at all, it vanished without a trace.
"Did I give you permission to speak?" he said.

Swan felt the cheeks of her behind tighten in anticipation. She was going to get a smack. She just knew it.
And she was right. Rob gave her a smart little tap with
the crop. "Ouch!" she said. "I didn't swat you like that."

It hadn't actually hurt, but she wanted him to think it did. Unfortunately she couldn't see his expression without turning around or craning her neck, and neither of those moves seemed like a good idea.

"That's true," he said. "It was more like this." He gave her other cheek a pop, and this time it did smart. "Now that's a swat."

Swan winced, but she didn't move a muscle as he came to stand in front of her. He placed the tip of the crop between her collarbones and traced it down to her breastbone, and then he applied just enough pressure to back her all the way to the wall. She stopped only when her shoulders came up against something solid. She couldn't retreat any farther, but he stepped in another few inches until he was all but face-to-face with her.

He was looking at her the way a man looks at a woman that he's planning to kiss. Or take over his knee and spank.

"You can't do this," she got out, but just barely.

"I'm the one with the crop," he replied. "I can do what I want. Isn't that how you played it on stage?"

"You're a Federal agent, and I'm a suspect. It's against the rules, right? You aren't allowed to lay a hand on me, unless I…resist you, or something."

That didn't come off quite right. She *was* resisting him, and she wasn't even sure she wanted to. But still, he wasn't allowed to do this stuff, swat her with riding crops and take liberties with her belly button. Suspects had rights, too, didn't they? She should have watched more crime shows growing up.

"Perhaps I should demonstrate my 'fox hole' skills," he said. "Some 'hand-to-hand'?" His breath was so hot and close it was making her light-headed. "Or maybe I should just press you to the wall and kiss you, McKenna."

"You can't," she whispered.

"I don't see anyone stopping me," he said.

Swan felt the tip of the leather crop against the tender flesh under her chin. He was tilting her head up. Bringing her lips up to his. Bending to kiss her.

She closed her eyes, offering herself and imagining the sweet, illicit thrill of being pressed to the wall and held there with his body, every virile inch of it. Her skin burned with anticipation, her senses burned.

His lips rubbed hers lightly and she moaned with pleasure.

Just as she angled her head to kiss him back, the fitting room door banged open. Joe Harris stopped in his tracks as he saw the two of them. "Hey, what's going on here?"

Rob stepped back and looked at his partner. "Nothing, just…practicing a skit."

Joe scrutinized both of them, taking in Swan's disheveled state and the blouse that barely covered her. He closed the door behind him and spoke to Rob in worried tones. "Man, whatever it is you're doing with her, you can't be doing it. You know that."

Actually, Rob did know that. Or he should have. Joe's shocked question brought him swiftly back to reality—and so did Swan's dazed expression. If her blouse had dropped to the floor, she would have been topless, he realized. And when he looked down and saw the riding crop in his hand, he stepped back, disgusted at himself.

What the hell had he been thinking? And how far would he have gone?

Rob knew how far he *wanted* to go.

He handed his partner the crop, yanked his windbreaker off the back of the chair and walked out of the room, leaving the two of them to stare after him. No one had ever been able to push him into losing control the way this woman could. It was uncanny.

But it wasn't her fault. He was the guy in charge. Joe would have to baby-sit their suspect for a while. Rob had to get his head together, and he had to do it now.

8

SWAN HAD NEVER BEFORE thought of making an ice pack out of her knee-high nylons, but she had succeeded. Joe Harris had brought her back to the hotel from the fashion show, and on the way he'd picked up some fast food from the grocery store deli and a twelve-pack of soda. He'd also filled the ice bucket when they got to the hotel. That was about the time Swan realized the annoying din in her head was a headache. She was grateful that Gerard had volunteered to stay behind at La Bomba to supervise the loading of their equipment into Swan's SUV and the rented trailer. She didn't know where Gaines was, and she didn't care. He'd stormed out of the dressing room without saying where he was going, and that was an hour ago.

Swan hadn't bothered to change her clothes or eat. She'd gone straight for the ice. The leaky pack was wrapped in a hand towel from the bathroom, and she was lying on the bed, pressing it gingerly against the cymbals clashing in her temple.

Joe was stretched out on the couch across the room, his feet resting on the coffee table as he tapped out numbers on a handheld device. On the way over here, he'd told her that he was trying to salvage his dwindling retirement account, and she'd sympathized. She knew what it was like to be desperate for money. She hardly knew what it was like not to be.

She moved the ice and hit a tender spot. Apparently

she groaned louder than she'd realized because Joe glanced over at her. "Are you all right?" he asked.

She couldn't shake her head. It hurt too much.

"Rob didn't hurt you, did he?" That possibility actually got him off the couch. He came over to the bed and peered down at her.

"He didn't hit me, if that's what you're thinking," she said, talking as softly as she could. "But my head feels like a five-alarm fire, and I never had headaches until I met *him.*"

Her logic seemed to amuse him. "Guilt by proximity? That's a tough rap to beat."

"Guilt by cornering me in a dressing room." Guilt by almost kissing her, and then getting furious at her instead. Guilt by making her *want* him to kiss her!

Swan didn't have the strength to continue her mental indictment, but it was true that she hadn't been prone to headaches before meeting Rob Gaines. Maybe it was hormonal. She probably had enough estrogen running in her veins to set up her own donor bank. She did hope the pain wasn't a migraine. She'd heard those could be caused by hormones.

"That dressing room thing was a fluke, Swan. Rob doesn't allow himself to be in close proximity like that. I don't know if I should be saying this, but he had a bad experience a few years back."

"Really?" She struggled to sit up. "Is that why he's so intense?"

Joe's shrug was its own kind of confirmation.

"Do you know what happened?" Swan didn't care how much pain it gave her to ask the questions. This was new and untilled soil.

"Actually, it was a lot like this mess." He walked back, sprawled on the couch and wasted no time getting back to his numbers.

"Like this mess? What do you mean, Joe? *Joe?*"

He didn't look up. "It wasn't a bank scam," he said, "but it did involve Art Long and a woman he duped. Her name was Paula Warren and she was a witness for the prosecution. Rob was supposed to be protecting her."

"And what happened? They got involved?" She wasn't sure where that question had come from, but she certainly wanted to know the answer. She was sitting up now and rivulets of melted ice were running down her face. She didn't care.

He tore himself away from the handheld and gave her a doleful look. "I've already said too much. Rob would kill me."

"Who's going to tell Rob? I'm just trying to understand him, Joe. It would make everything so much easier. He's incredibly guarded, and I keep thinking it's me. There are times I could swear that he hates me."

"He doesn't hate you. If he hates anyone, it's himself."

"Did he fall in love with this woman, this witness?" She had to know if he was prone to that sort of thing, like actors who fell in love with their costars.

"If anything, it was the other way around. Paula was a spoiled socialite, used to getting her way, and when Rob rejected her, she ratted on him, said he came on to her, that he used his authority to coerce her into having sex with him. That got him fired—and it only got worse from there. Before it was over, he came close to doing hard time."

"Rob was fired from the Bureau? But he's an agent now."

"He was reinstated after a board of inquiry found out that Paula was a very sick girl. She'd falsely accused other men of molesting her, including her own brother. Her history of emotional problems was so bad it ruined her credibility on the stand. The prosecution destroyed her."

"But why would Rob hate himself for that? It wasn't his fault."

Harris put his work down with a sigh. He was obviously sorry he'd started up with the inquisitive Ms. Swan McKenna, and he just wanted to get it over with.

"Paula came from money," he explained, "and she had the kind of social contacts Art Long needed. He'd put together an investment scam and he convinced her it was legit in order to get her to refer her rich friends. We busted them both, offered her a deal, and she took it. Rob was assigned the unenviable job of protecting her until she could testify."

"And that's when they got involved?"

"That's when *she* got involved. I'm not sure how it all happened, but she developed this romantic attachment for him. In her mind, he was more than her protector. He was her knight in shining armor. She fell hard, but I know Rob well enough to know those feelings were never reciprocated. He did his job. He protected her, but it wasn't romantic like that."

Swan still didn't understand why Rob might have hated himself, but she'd heard enough to know why he had such a rigid code of ethics. It was personal as well as professional. "You said he did hard time?"

"I said he *almost* did hard time, and we're not going there."

Joe's sudden scowl dared her to ask another question, but something that Rob had said recently came back to her. He'd told her that people got killed when he wasn't careful. "Just this one more thing, Joe, *please,* and then I promise to leave you alone. Did Paula Warren die while under Rob's protection?"

He nodded wearily. "And Rob took it hard. It wasn't his fault, but he still can't see it that way."

"How did it happen?" she asked.

"It was a bad rap, and that's all I'm going to say. Rob paid a high price for it. The scandal shadowed him for years. It cost him promotions, his reputation, and eventually even his fiancée. But he's back now. The acting head of the L.A. office is currently under fire, and there are rumors Rob might be the one to replace him. But that mess changed him."

Joe took a swig from his soda can and helped himself to one of the spring rolls he'd picked up at the store. "I never told you this," he said, waving the roll at her, "and you didn't hear it."

She smiled, but with some care. "Hear what?"

He went back to his calculations and she tried to get comfortable, but there was too much on her mind to sleep. She turned gingerly from one side to the other, until finally Joe spoke up.

"Listen, if the headache's that bad, I can go out and get you something."

The phone rang before she could answer him and Swan winced at the sound. He mumbled, "Hello?" listened a minute, then dropped the receiver back in the cradle. "Wrong number," he said, getting up. "Look, I'm not getting anything done anyway, and there's got to be a drugstore nearby."

"Thanks," Swan said. "Maybe you should go. Tomorrow's another big day and I need to be ready for it." They were heading out early for Seattle, and it was a long drive. Gerard would fly up ahead of them to start setting up for the show, but Swan had a million things to do in the meantime.

Joe tapped the door on his way out. "Lock it up behind me."

The ice pack had turned the nightstand into a puddle. Swan got herself up and took what was left of it to the bathroom. She left it in the sink and stole a peek at herself in the mirror. She actually felt a little better than she looked, which was depressing. The ice must have helped. With one eye shut, she straightened her hair, wondering why she cared about her appearance at a moment like this.

That made her smile ruefully, which made her wince in pain.

Rob might walk in at any moment, that was why. He might walk in, find her utterly irresistible in her suffering and press her up against the bathroom sink, his breath hot on her throat, his hands hot on her body.

Another utterly pointless fantasy, but she couldn't stop it. She shuddered with the pleasure that flooded into her memory banks. It washed over her like an ocean swell and it was hard to believe that she could react so strongly. The undertow was amazing. One steamy encounter with an FBI agent and she was as much a puddle as the ice.

The phone rang as she was blotting a little stray mascara from beneath her right eye. Her heart kicked up to about twice its normal pace and she made a blind rush for the phone on the nightstand, headache forgotten.

Please don't let it be Joe or Gerard or the hotel management.

"Hello?" she said, trying to sound sultry rather than sick. Her disappointment was sharp when she heard a woman's voice on the other end.

"Ms. McKenna? We haven't met, but I'm a big fan of yours. I was at your show this afternoon, and I tried to get your attention, but you left the stage so suddenly I wasn't able to intercept you. I hope you don't mind, but I got the name of your hotel from the manager at La Bomba."

"Of course, I don't mind," Swan said, "but who am I talking to?"

"Oh, Stella Diamont from Sebastiani! And I can't tell you how much I loved your premier line. It was all very sexy and ingenious, especially your use of less-than-perfect models.''

"Really?" Swan couldn't quite catch her breath. Stella Diamont was the head buyer for all the North American Sebastiani retail outlets. "I'm terribly flattered, but—"

"Yes, I know. You have an exclusive contract with La Bomba. That's exactly what I want to talk to you about. To be perfectly honest, we'd like to steal you away, as soon as your contract is fulfilled.''

"Really?" Swan was repeating herself, but it was better than shrieking, which was what she wanted to do.

"Yes, Ms. McKenna, really. I'm wondering if we might talk about that. I know this is all very last minute, but I'm right across the street from you in a cute little coffee shop, and I have a few minutes before I have to leave for the airport. Any chance you could pop over for a chat?''

Swan didn't hesitate. "Yes, of course. Just give me five to make myself presentable.''

"Looking forward to it," the other woman said. "I'll be wearing a white linen blazer, navy slacks, and a big smile.''

Swan had trouble hanging up the phone she was so stunned. If Lynne had been there, she and Swan would have been dancing for joy. To have interest from a retail chain such as Sebastiani was inconceivable. This was better than Gvon!

As Swan whisked a brush through her hair, she could feel her temple give out a couple of weak throbs. The headache was not gone, but it was manageable enough to ignore. What concerned her more was leaving without telling anyone, but Joe wasn't there and she couldn't wait until he got back.

She had Rob's pager number, and she probably ought to have used it, but she had no idea where he was, and he most certainly wouldn't have allowed her to go on her own. If he'd allowed her to go at all, he would have wanted her to wait until he got there, and she didn't have that kind of time. Even if he was five minutes away, that was too long.

She spent the next thirty seconds putting on her lipstick, looking for her shoes and convincing herself that it was okay to dash across the street for a few minutes to meet a hugely important buyer who wanted to throw piles of money at the company. After all, it was a warm August evening and the sun would be out for several more hours. Who would try to harm her in broad daylight?

SWAN GLANCED over her shoulder to see if there were any FBI men chasing her with handcuffs. It looked clear, so she pushed through the glass doors of the hotel lobby. The coffee shop could be seen from her side of the street. It was the anchor restaurant at the end of an upscale strip mall. She could walk over there in no time.

She had her shoulder bag looped over her head the way the safety experts advised, and she'd zipped the organizer inside. She'd been instructed to keep it with her at all times. She knew Rob hadn't meant a situation such as this, but it seemed safer to take it with her than to leave it in the hotel room. Honestly, the more she thought about this sting operation, the more ridiculous the whole thing seemed. Art Long's accomplice—if he even had one— surely must know by now that Art had been arrested. Only a fool would attempt to steal the organizer without knowing for certain that the check was still inside it. Swan had the distinct feeling that Rob Gaines was fishing in an empty lake.

Warm sunshine fell on her face and arms and it felt wonderful. Just the simple act of being alone felt wonderful. Other than her bathroom time, she hadn't been out of eyeshot of either Joe or Rob. Someone was always watching her, always telling her what to do and what not to do. You could only take so much of that.

Besides, once this operation was over, Rob Gaines would be moving on to his next assignment. He'd walk away as if nothing had happened, leaving Swan and Lynne to put the pieces of their company back together again. Meeting with this buyer might be breaking his rules, but she had an obligation to her company, and she had to put that above any obligation she might have to him.

Swan stood at the corner, impatiently waiting for the light to change and the jammed lanes of traffic to clear. It was rush hour and Stella Diamont had picked the busiest time of day to meet. The light changed and Swan made a dash for the other side of the street. She was beginning to perspire and she didn't want to show up wilted. After a few deep breaths she realized why she was so thrilled about this new interest. It had come about because of the shows, which meant it wasn't just Lynne making things happen, it was Swan, too.

A young couple with two small children was heading toward Swan, perhaps on their way to the hotel. Pulling around the corner just behind them, a black car with tinted windows came to a halt and waited for them to pass. It waited for Swan to scurry by, too, then accelerated down the street and pulled into the same strip mall where she was headed.

Swan checked her watch. Less than ten minutes had passed since she'd left the room, but it felt much longer. She thought she saw the black car disappear into an alley at the opposite end of the mall from the restaurant, but she was preoccupied with trying to find a walkway into the mall itself. By the time she did, she was perspiring and there was nothing she could do about it as she began to jog toward the restaurant. Better wilted than late.

She dodged a couple of cars and grazed a man she hadn't seen coming. "Sorry!" she said, and tried to keep going, but something whipped her around like a ball on the end of a tether. It took Swan a dizzying moment to figure out what had happened. The man had snagged the purse that was looped around her neck and nearly knocked her off her feet.

"Your purse or your head, lady," he snarled.

Swan instantly realized this was no accident. She grabbed the straps of her purse and tugged back—a reflex action. But the guy who'd accosted her was a brute. His head was shaved clean and his burly arms were tattooed like a wrestler's. No way would she win this tug of war.

"Gimme the purse or I'll rip your head off," he hissed.

Swan fought with all her might as he dragged her across the parking lot, pulling her along by her own bag. He was heading into the alley, and once he had her out of sight, he would probably beat her senseless and take the purse. No one was going to rescue her, she realized. Everyone around her was going about their business as if they weren't aware of the drama in the midst. Her arms were on fire and her shoulders felt as if they were being pulled out of their sockets. If she ran toward him, she might be able to throw him off balance and break free. It was a crazy plan, but it was probably the only chance she had.

"FBI. Freeze, you son of a bitch!"

The shout came from somewhere behind Swan. She couldn't see who it was, but it sounded like Rob. Swan's assailant grabbed for her arm. He was going to drag her into the alley one way or the other. Swan sprang toward him, and they both hit the pavement tumbling. She rolled away from him and was yanked back, her purse straps pulling tight as a vise around her neck. Searing pain nearly cut off her breathing. She was going to strangle!

She ended up on her back, being dragged, and all she could see was Rob running full-tilt toward her from the other side of the lot, his face contorted in a grimace of primitive fury. Even if she didn't regain consciousness, she would never forget that look. It was more savage than anything she'd ever seen.

What happened after that was fuzzy, but the pressure on Swan's throat was abruptly gone, and so was the wrestler. He sprinted through a gathering crowd of pedestrians and vanished into the alley. Rob came to a halt, his gun drawn. He was clearly torn between staying with Swan and pursuing her attacker. He stayed with Swan.

"Are you all right?" he asked, holstering his weapon. He knelt down to touch her face and to peer deeply into her eyes. He didn't move her, but he began to check her out as a paramedic would—a finger to the pulse in her throat, a penlight directed at her pupils. His touch was surprisingly gentle and Swan was happy to lie there and let him do it. Except for a mildly sore throat, she felt fine, but she could very well be in shock.

When he was satisfied that she hadn't been badly injured, he helped her to her feet, supporting her with an arm around her shoulders. "How do you feel?"

He was strong and steady and warm, she realized. It felt good.

"I'm all right," she said. "A bit shaken."

"Where's Joe?"

Well, there it was, the question she'd been dreading—and the end of any more tender loving care from Rob Gaines. When she told him the truth, he was going to be furious, but he would find out eventually anyway.

"I don't know," she said. "He's probably back at the hotel."

"What?" The only emotion that registered on his face was shock. "He let you come out here by yourself?"

"He doesn't know I'm out here."

"What does that mean?"

He'd already released her to stand on her own and his voice was taking on the kind of coldness she didn't want to hear. He would never understand, but she did her best to explain anyway. She told him about the call from the buyer, the offer she'd made and the urgency involved in their getting together. "I couldn't wait for Joe, or I might have missed her, so I left."

The look in Rob's eyes made her wonder if she wouldn't have been safer with the thug who'd just assaulted her. He bowed his head in disbelief, shaking it. After a moment of considering his options, he took her by the arm.

"Are you strong enough to walk?" he asked.

"I think so. Where are we going?"

"To meet your buyer."

Swan wasn't quite sure what he had in mind, but she knew if Stella Diamont was still inside, Swan could kiss Stella's interest—and perhaps her own career—goodbye. Rob was probably going to question the buyer and perhaps even accuse her of something terrible, and as much as Swan wanted to beg him not to, she didn't dare.

"Do you know this woman?" he asked.

"Stella Diamont? I know of her. Everybody knows of her. She works for Sebastiani."

"What does she look like?"

"She said she'd be wearing a white linen blazer and navy slacks."

Rob opened the restaurant door and ushered Swan in. "I was in this place," he told her as they stopped at the hostess stand. "I was having coffee when one of the waitresses shouted that someone was being mugged outside.

That's how I got to you before the guy beheaded you. I didn't see anyone inside who could have passed for a fashion buyer, but maybe you'll spot her.''

It wasn't a very big place and what few patrons there were had gathered at the windows to watch the excitement. Swan and Rob walked the length of the restaurant and back again. Swan didn't see anyone wearing the outfit that Diamont had described, nor did any of the customers look like refugees from the rarefied world of fashion.

"Maybe I was tricked," she said when they were outside again. She felt incredibly foolish, and Rob said nothing, which made her feel worse. If he'd upbraided her, she probably could have mustered up some indignation in her own defense.

They walked back to the hotel in silence. Swan was aware of Rob's vigilance in checking out their surroundings, and she didn't want to distract him with questions. It wasn't until they'd nearly reached the hotel entrance that the shock and reality of what had just happened sank in. Her hands began to tremble, and the awful lightness in her stomach was close to nausea.

"Do you think the woman who called me was in on this?"

"It's possible," he said. "Otherwise, why wasn't she waiting for you in the coffee shop?"

"She might have been concerned about the police showing up. If she was meeting me on the sly, she wouldn't want her name in the papers."

Swan was still trying to reason her way out of this mess. She didn't want to believe she was in real danger any more than she wanted to believe that some woman, posing as an important buyer, had set her up. "Maybe he wasn't after the check. Did you ever think about that? Maybe he was just a garden-variety purse snatcher."

Rob seemed to have noticed her trembling and he

slowed his pace. "He wasn't a purse snatcher," he said evenly. "I've seen him before."

"Where?" The way the word dropped out of her mouth Swan was surprised she couldn't hear it hit the ground.

"The last show. He was in the crowd." He looked her over and hesitated. "Are you sure you're all right? You look a little pale."

"Why didn't you tell me you saw something suspicious at the last show? I have a right to know that sort of thing, don't I?"

"There was nothing to tell. I tried to get close to him, but I lost him in the crowd."

"My God," she whispered. "He might have killed me."

"Now you're beginning to understand what's at stake here." His expression was grim. "From now on, you're under my personal watch. I can't trust you, and as much as I hate to say it, I can't trust Joe, either."

"Don't be angry with Joe. I sent him out for some medicine. This was my fault, Rob. Please, don't get him into trouble. He was just trying to be kind." She wasn't sure he was listening to her, so she grabbed his arm. "Please, Rob."

He stopped so suddenly that she was two steps ahead of him before she knew it. "You would've done the same thing," she told him. "You know you would. The only thing Joe is guilty of is trusting me."

Something she'd said had hit home with him. The tightness in his jaw loosened and the steely glaze of his eyes softened. It wasn't a big change, but it was enough. "All right," he said, "I won't report this, but from now on you're mine. Do you understand? You belong to me."

"Yeah…okay." *Of course, he meant professionally. Of course, he did.* "And thanks for not taking it out on Joe."

"I wouldn't thank me just yet if I were you." He cocked his head toward the hotel. "Let's go find my partner, shall we?"

JOE WAS IN THE ROOM when they got there. He'd just returned from searching the hotel. Gerard was with him, and Swan could tell that he was nearly sick with fear, which made her regret her hastiness even more. She apologized to both of them and was instantly forgiven by Gerard, who gave her a fierce hug and then chastised her for giving him such a scare.

Joe handed her the medication he'd gone out for. "Looks like you need this more than ever," he said.

Everyone seemed subdued by the strong possibility that someone was not only after Swan, but willing to use violence to get what he or she wanted. This changed the fundamental order of things, and they all knew it, but neither Rob nor Joe brought it up directly. Swan had the feeling they didn't want to frighten her or Gerard any more than they already had.

Rob ordered in pizza and beer for the four of them, but all Swan wanted to do was to take a shower and lie down with another ice pack. Her headache was back.

By eight-thirty that evening, the men had eaten their fill of pizza, and Joe and Gerard had retired to the other room. An hour later, they could both be heard snoring deeply, but Rob seemed restless, and Swan wondered if she would ever feel safe enough to sleep again.

Now Rob was standing by the window, looking out through an opening in the curtains.

"I didn't thank you for what you did today," Swan said. "You saved—"

"It's part of the job," he said quietly, still looking out the window.

He'd cut her off, and she wondered why. Did thanking

him for saving her life imply something he didn't want to deal with? He was constantly trying to impress upon her how serious this was, and she was just trying to acknowledge that. Was he afraid she would become emotional?

Swan was sitting on the bed, her hands in her lap. She actually felt hurt. How were they supposed to communicate if he wouldn't even let her thank him? Men, she thought. Too many of them tended toward emotional retardation anyway, and lawmen were probably the worst of the lot. Yes, she was painting an entire gender with the same brush, but that hardly bothered her conscience after the day she'd had. In her opinion, it was the nature of the male animal to be tough and to guard their tender parts with their lives, only they thought those tender parts were their balls. They kept forgetting they had hearts.

Some of them, anyway. Present company not excepted.

Moments later the lawman gave up his post at the window and walked to the closet door. He took off his rustling black windbreaker and hung it on a hook inside the closet.

"Do you have to do that sort of thing often?" she asked. "Save damsels in distress, I mean?"

"Every now and then."

"And does that make you feel good?"

"What? Saving women?" He kicked off his shoes and removed his tie. His shirt probably would have followed, except that he suddenly seemed to remember she was there. He left it on, unbuttoned and hanging open.

He indicated the faint stripes of cammy paint that were still in evidence on his chest and abs. "It would make me feel good to get this damn stuff off my body," he said.

"Soap and hot water will do it. Try a shower."

"Sounds like a plan." With a shrug, he headed for the door that led to the adjoining room.

She sat up. "Where are you going?"

"I'm going to wake Joe. He can baby-sit while I take a shower."

"He's tired, and I'm certainly not going anywhere in this T-shirt."

"Like you couldn't throw on some clothes and leave while I was in the shower? No way, McKenna. I'm getting Joe up."

"No, wait! I'll go with you! Into the bathroom, I mean. What's wrong with me staying in there while you're showering?"

He planted his hands on his hips. "And if you decide to take off, I'm supposed to run after you, dripping wet and naked?"

She had to grin at that visual. "I suppose I could get in the shower with you," she suggested innocently. "Then we'd both be wet and naked."

"Wet, naked and running after each other in the shower? Someone might slip and get hurt."

She spotted his wallet, badge and handcuffs where he'd left them on the desk. It took her no time at all to get there. "How about these then?" she said, dangling the cuffs.

He folded his arms as though that wasn't a bad idea, although she had the feeling he wasn't thinking what she was thinking. And sure enough, he wasn't. Mere moments later, she was handcuffed to the towel rack and sitting on the toilet, and he was inside the shower stall, tossing clothes over the door.

"Heads up," he said. His slacks came flying over the top of the stall and landed in her lap. Two black socks followed. She didn't expect to see a pair of underwear and none appeared. "I can't believe I'm doing this. Just don't watch me, all right?" he asked as he reached for the water faucets.

Swan could see what he was doing but not clearly. It

was possible to make out his form and most of his movements because the warm gold of his skin contrasted nicely with the white tile inside the shower, but that was about it. Just enough to make her crazy to see more.

"I won't," she fibbed as she watched him turn on the faucet and adjust the overhead stream. The water pouring out of the showerhead quickly brought a familiar sense of urgency to Swan. Fortunately she was wearing nothing more than a T-shirt, and she was already sitting on the commode. She got the lid up without a problem and moments later her business was done, including the flushing. She felt quite proud of herself.

Warm condensation was filling the room, misting the bathroom mirror and the stainless steel fixtures. If she'd been able to move, she would have turned on the bathroom fan. As it was, she could do nothing but wait for him to finish. Wait and pretend not to watch.

But the enveloping steam only enhanced the natural grace of his movements, and soon Swan wasn't even pretending. Her eyes were glued to the shower stall as if it was a movie screen and the first feature had just started. An adventure movie, to be sure. The steamy fog made her think of jungles and rain forests—and Rob Gaines in the Huntsman piece she'd designed. The male prowess he'd exuded on the runway was just a glimpse into the man and what he could do. What he *had* done today. She'd never had anyone run to her rescue like that. He'd been fast and ferocious, and had he caught her attacker she was certain there would have been a bloody battle.

Ten thousand years ago she would have been the spoils of that battle, and the winner would have taken rightful possession. Rob would have claimed her as his woman. His mate. And the words "you belong to me" would have meant exactly that.

Swan felt her breath come short. For a second she

didn't think she was going to be able to breathe at all. A sharp sensation in the pit of her stomach could have been pleasure. The response caught her by surprise, but this wasn't the first time she'd realized that he could have this effect on her. As hard as it was for her to admit, there was something exhilarating, even thrilling, about the way he'd marched into her life and taken it over. She couldn't imagine any other man daring to do such a·thing. Swan McKenna didn't have time for men. She was much too efficient and driven…when all she really wanted was to be reckless and free, like Lynne.

Maybe the steam was getting to her. She tested the cuffs and found them securely locked. She wasn't going anywhere until he decided to release her, which made her think of the way he'd cornered her in the dressing room and undone her top with the tip of his riding crop. He'd taken obvious pleasure in tormenting her with that crop, but what she recalled most was the heat that had ignited in his blue eyes as he'd circled her. It was the look of a man about to cross a line.

The sound of splashing water made her glance up. He was washing his hair now. She could just make out the way the black waves clung to the back of his neck. With his arms raised high, his muscles were as pronounced as dark hills.

He turned to rinse his hair and she could see the front of his thighs and the unmistakable outline of his penis. That forced her to concentrate on her breathing again. The entire day had been filled with too much stimulation. It was no wonder that she was damp and quivering inside and feeling something she hadn't felt in a very long time. *Physical desire.*

She heard him shut off the water and cleared her throat to remind him that she was still out there. A towel hung near the shower door and seeing it gave her an idea. Warring impulses made her hesitate, but they didn't stop her altogether. Before he could open the shower door, she snatched the towel and tossed it to the other side of the bathroom, out of his reach.

Why she'd done it, she didn't know. Or maybe she did know. But did she really need to see Rob Gaines totally naked? She'd been inches from his private parts on a couple of occasions, and she'd swatted his bare behind with a riding crop. Did she really need to see his whole body naked?

That was a big *yes*.

She suppressed a giggle as the shower door opened and he reached out to snag the missing towel. His forearm dripped with clear, glistening water that molded his dark hair to the powerful cords beneath it. The rest of his body would be sleek and glistening, too, she imagined. Hot from the shower. Wet, with wisps of steam rising from his flesh.

"What happened to my towel?" he asked. When she didn't answer, he said, "Toss me one, will you?"

"I can't reach a towel. I'm currently in bondage, if you recall." Swan bit down on her trembling lower lip, trying not to laugh. Unless he wanted to sleep in the shower stall, he was going to have to come out of there. Naked. Naked and wet. She could hardly wait. Her heart was thumping so hard, she was afraid it might give out.

The shower door slid open and she saw a leg emerge first. It was streaming with water just like his arm, and quite impressive. There should have been one more exiting, along with the rest of him, but he had a little surprise for her. He stepped out of the shower and shook his head like a big dog just out of a stream.

Swan ducked as a shower of droplets came her way. She couldn't see a thing, and that was probably what he intended. It was a smart move, but not smart enough. She grabbed some toilet paper and stole a look at him as she blotted her face.

Seeing bits and pieces of him naked didn't begin to compare with the total picture. The man was built. He had the shoulders and arms of a spear thrower, and a river of muscles rippled from his chest all the way down to the dark nest that crowned his thighs. The rest of him wasn't bad, either, but then she knew that.

Maybe the fashion show had released the inner exhibitionist in Rob Gaines. He didn't seem at all embarrassed by his nakedness, and he even cast her a challenging look.

"I know there was a towel there a few minutes ago," he said. "I'm tired but I'm not *that* tired."

Swan shrugged innocently and jangled the cuffs around her wrist. "Don't look at me. I'm helpless, remember?"

"Helpless, my butt."

He passed her on his way to retrieving his missing towel, and Swan got a chance to examine the butt in question. His bend from the waist gave her a view she'd never had before. It only lasted a minute, but what a minute that was. She was stricken with a desire to touch him. What would it be like to run her fingers down his satiny skin and feel those taut muscles work?

Speaking of taut muscles, she could feel knots of pleasure forming in the pit of her stomach, and it was becoming difficult to sit still on the commode. But she had to. Any obvious squirming would have given him too much satisfaction, and this was supposed to be her revenge, not his.

Once he had the towel wrapped around his waist, he turned to face her. Swan was almost relieved not to be getting the full frontal she'd imagined. Her vital signs weren't up to it.

"Wasn't very smart tossing my pants over here," he said as he picked them up from the floor and dug in the pocket. "The key is right here." He pulled out a metallic ring and showed her an odd-looking key. It only took him a moment to free her.

"What now?" she asked, rubbing her wrist.

"It's bedtime. I'm exhausted and I can't imagine you aren't, as well."

"Bedtime?" Swan felt the word click in her throat. "Together?"

"Up to you," he said, already on his way out the door. "You could always sleep in a locked closet. I'm fine either way."

9

BEING HANDCUFFED to a handsome bodyguard on a hotel bed might have been a very hot fantasy, unless the goal was to get some sleep. Swan knew she was in for a long, sleepless night.

"Is this really necessary?" Swan asked as Rob cuffed his right wrist to her left.

"No, I could cuff you to the bed and sack out on the couch, but this way I *know* you're not going anywhere, and I'll sleep a lot better. I'm beat."

"At least one of us will sleep well." Swan was exhausted, too, but his bright idea of holding her wrist hostage was presenting problems. They were standing at the foot of the bed, and she couldn't figure out how they were supposed to get on the bed, unless he intended for them to sleep on their stomachs, which she'd never been able to do without half smothering herself. The other option would be to turn around and fling themselves onto their backs.

"I can't sleep on my back," she said. "I need to be on my side and preferably my left side. I've been sleeping that way since I was a kid."

"Whatever works," he said. "I don't care how you sleep as long as you follow the rules. I want one foot of space between us at all times."

"That is so silly," she scoffed. "Like I'm going to molest you or something."

"You have molested me, woman, several times."

"And you loved it!"

He blushed, which she found delightful. Finally, it wasn't her turning pink, it was him. If this wasn't evidence of divine existence, what was?

"Come on," he said, climbing onto the bed on his hands and knees and tugging her with him. He was wearing pajama bottoms only, very loosely tied at the hips, and she was wearing the oversize V-necked T-shirt she'd put on after her shower, so neither one of them was exactly dressed for this little adventure.

She tugged back, but he just kept going, like a very determined bear in search of his cave. "This isn't going to work," she pointed out as she scrambled to keep up with him. "How am I supposed to lie on my side?"

"When we get to the pillows, you can skooch onto your side, facing me, and we'll drape our wrists between us."

"'Skooch'?" She gave him a look. "That would put me on my right side. I need to sleep on my left."

"Oh, yeah. Hang on while I fix that." He sort of rolled beneath her, which caused Swan to lose her balance and topple onto his freshly scrubbed chest, and all the rest of him, as well. He smelled good. Like Junior mints. She loved Junior mints. He felt good, too, all the way up and down. There wasn't an inch of her that wasn't touching him. Even her toes were nestled against something that belonged to him. Probably his shins. He was tall.

"How does this keep a foot of space between us?" she wondered, staring directly into his blue eyes. She could feel the string tie of his pajamas poking through the fabric of her T-shirt and she was being welcomed a few inches south of that, as well. Was someone wearing a number two tonight?

"We're not done," he said. "This move requires one more crocodile roll. Hold on."

He was sounding a little breathless and, more significantly, he didn't do anything for a full moment except stare back at her until she thought her heart was going to kickbox its way out of her chest. Her gaze kept drifting to his lips and she could almost taste them. His eyes were darkening so rapidly that she knew he was feeling it, too, but there was no way he was going to allow anything to happen, so she could imagine to her heart's content.

Would he kiss hard or soft? Would there be tongue? she wondered, and instantly regretted it. Her lips tingled in anticipation and heat flooded her face.

"Do you ever think about kissing?" she asked.

"Incessantly," he admitted, and hastily rolled them both over.

Once they'd accomplished the feat of changing places, Swan managed to wriggle and push her way onto her left side, where she collapsed with a heavy sigh. He was on his back, and their wrists were linked between them. Fortunately the lamp was on his side. She couldn't have turned it off and rearranged herself again without seriously straining something.

"'Night," he said as he stretched for the light. Since she was facing him she saw all the muscles involved in that move, and it was a miracle of nature. He had a lovely rib cage, and the tufts under his arms looked as dark as the waves on his head. She liked hair in sexy places.

She also gave his behind the once-over, since she had the opportunity. It was impossible not to remember what she'd seen after his shower. He had a bit of fabric covering him now, but the thin cotton bottoms clung to his firm flesh and had even insinuated their way into the tight seam. Deliciously erotic, was the thought that came to Swan's mind. The sound that caught in her throat was a tight little squeak of pleasure and her poor stomach lifted and dropped like an elevator.

Good thing she was so darn tired. Otherwise she'd be

figuring out how to molest him from a foot away. She was almost too tired to close her eyes, but once she did it felt as if every muscle in her body would melt into the bed. She'd never known such exhaustion.

LAWMEN ON DUTY rarely slept hard, and Rob was no exception. He drifted in and out of consciousness all night, but his exhaustion was profound enough that he thought he must be dreaming when he heard a voice murmur something about measuring tapes and pincushions. That was the first awareness he had that there was anything going on in the hotel room besides sleeping.

He gave some thought to rousing himself, but not much. This was one of those dreams you never wanted to wake up from. He had rolled onto his side, or maybe he hadn't, but in the dream he was turned that way and his knees were bumping something—or someone. A gentle feminine voice was whispering in his ear and, even though he couldn't see her, he knew this must be a visitation from an angel of mercy because of the way she was tenderly ministering to his needs.

Her fingers were like dandelion fluff—if it was fingers she was using—and they were stroking, touching and caressing him as if he were a lump of clay she intended to fashion into a huge golden sword. Sword? Where had that image come from?

She wasn't a shy angel, either, because it was only a certain part of his anatomy that she seemed to be involved with. A certain ultrasensitive part of his anatomy. God, he could let her touch his sword that way all day.

"Down, boy," she said languidly. "How'm I suppose to measure you when you keep going up and down like a..."

Her soft voice trailed off, but Rob began to sense something familiar about this dream. The fluff tickled his belly and he smiled. But her touch was a little firmer now and the quality of it had changed, more like massaging than caressing. He felt something slide down the entire length of his sword and then gently cup him and squeeze. He gave out a little moan of pleasure. Why hadn't this angel ever visited his dreams before?

"Lesstriiissonf'size," she said, running the words together.

Her voice was growing huskier and he could now feel her breath on his chest. Her fingers were wrapped around him like a silk sheath.

This was one hot angel of mercy, unless...

"Such a nice big crotch stuffer," she said, giggling. "Biggest one I've ever seen. Warm, too."

...unless this was no dream.

Rob slowly opened his eyes, trying to get his bearings. Except for the moonlight that spilled through the window blinds, the hotel room was dark.

Somewhere in the night, he had turned toward Swan, and she was now cuddled close to him, her face mere inches from his collarbone. Her left hand, the one that he had cuffed, lay atop his right wrist on the bed. Exactly where it should have been. Her right hand, however, was not where it was supposed to be. It was involved with his pajama bottoms. Intimately involved.

That's what had brought him to. She had somehow freed him from the fly front of his pajamas, or he'd freed himself with her help, and he was fully erect. Stiff as a sword, to be more precise. Even more interesting was the way she held on to him as though he were a pull toy, her hot little fingers wrapped tightly around his shaft.

She appeared to be sound asleep, but he wasn't sure he should wake her. Hell. For one thing, she might stop. On the other hand, if she didn't stop, there was going to be a christening of sorts. He didn't know how long she'd been at it, but from the pressure building up inside the pipeline, it was plenty long enough. Every male part he had down there was hot and swollen, including the ones she wasn't playing with. The urge to release was rampant, a steady thrust of fire in his groin.

God, it felt good—and bad—at the same time. One foot in heaven, the other in hell. This was what lawmen fantasized about on stakeouts. It was what all men fantasized about all the time—having a beautiful woman awaken you with her tender fondling of your shaft. He wasn't sure how much longer he could control the force of his arousal, though, especially with her fingers gliding up and down him as though she was priming a pump. Literally. Each little pull brought him closer.

Waking her up now would only complicate things, and complicated things took longer, and the longer his member got, the less time he had. *Move, Gaines.*

As carefully as possible, he took hold of her wrist. When he tried to lift it, Swan shook her head, mumbled something, and tightened her grip. Her entire body wriggled as she sought to get closer to him. It was like trying to take a toy from the clutches of a sleeping child.

"Hold still," she said on an exhaled breath. "I need to alter this."

Okay, this was getting serious. He was taking his mighty golden sword back, thank you. It had been in her evil clutches long enough. Using both of his hands, he managed to pry her fingers open, one by one. But as he was removing himself, he realized the key to the hand-cuffs was over on the desk with his gun and his badge. It had never occurred to him that he would be the one desperate to get out of the cuffs.

A soft moan slipped through her lips as she lost possession of her toy.

"Oh, did I prick you?" she whispered breathlessly.

The pieces suddenly began falling into place. Measure, size, alter, prick? Maybe he wasn't the one who'd been dreaming tonight. Maybe the underwear lady did alterations in her sleep.

Swan *was* dreaming. In color and with sound effects. She was back in the fitting room, reliving every moment of the morning she'd sized Special Agent Gaines for her skimpiest designs. It was a challenge to work with a man who responded with such unbridled virility to a woman's touch. Most of the models didn't, thank goodness. But she had to admit that this one inspired her. She felt feverish with excitement and suddenly she was in the grip of a burst of creative energy the likes of which she'd never experienced before. He was giving her underwear ideas! There were Wonderbras. Why not Wonder Jocks? Maybe she would design one with stars and stripes, and then every part of him could salute at once.

She would have to work on a skit for that.

A THICK CLOUD OF STEAM followed Swan out of the bathroom as she towel-dried her hair. She was wrapped in one of the hotel's terry robes, and she'd hoped that the long hot shower might snap her senses back into working order this morning, but she hadn't experienced much progress so far.

Normally she didn't remember her dreams, but the one she'd had last night was a ringing exception. Not only was it lingering, it was lingering in excruciating detail. Every touch, every moan, every hot little squeeze of her fingers seemed to want to play itself over and over again in her mind. Thank God it was only a dream. He would be accusing her of molesting her again.

"Hungry?" Rob had accepted delivery of a room service cart laden with breakfast goodies. It was just the two of them this morning. Joe was paying a courtesy visit to the local field office, and Gerard was catching an early flight to Seattle to set up the next show.

"I'm starving," she said.

He grinned at her with a certain mischievous glint in his eyes. "I'll bet you are."

"Why would you say that?" She gave him a searching look and then realized he couldn't possibly have meant anything by it. Feeling a little paranoid, Swan? Maybe a serving of guilt to go with it? He'd arisen before her and was already dressed. As he went about the business of pouring coffee for them, Swan pulled some clothes from her suitcase. This was a travel day. She chose jeans, sneakers and a cotton V-necked top. No sense being uncomfortable on a long road trip.

"No reason," Rob said. "You've been busy lately. You know, having your hands full and all."

Swan was bent over the side of the bed, smoothing her clothes out, but there was something in his tone of voice that made her glance back at him. He refused to look at her and she knew he was doing it deliberately as he dished out scrambled eggs and bacon. That knowing smile was still loitering in the vicinity of his lips, too. Even a mother wouldn't have trusted that smile.

She finished with her clothes and walked over to the table he'd set. He was humming something to himself as he picked through a bowl of fruit. He chose a large banana and as he began to slowly unpeel it, he looked straight at her. "Care for one of these? Nice and firm."

The blush that raced across her face was sudden and fierce. "No, thank you," she said, pulling out her chair. She sat down and all but whipped her napkin from the table. He shrugged and bit into the banana.

"How'd you sleep last night?" he asked.

"Like a log, thank you. How about you?" Swan primly adjusted her napkin in her lap and took a sip of coffee.

She wasn't going to play this game. He knew something. It wasn't as if she could prove it in a court of law, but he knew something, all right.

"Funny you should mention it," he said. "I slept like a log, too. Only the log I slept like kept me awake most of the night."

She buttered a piece of toast. "You're not suggesting that I had anything to do with that. Your log, I mean."

"Actually, you did."

"Oh?" She bit into the toast.

He nodded as he reached for the pepper shaker. "Seems you talk in your sleep, McKenna."

Swan swallowed wrong and nearly choked. She held her hand up to signal that she was all right, and when she was able, took a quick drink of orange juice. "I do not," she got out.

"Really, that's strange." Very solicitously he leaned over to refill her orange juice glass. "Well, maybe I was having a dream," he said, "but I could have sworn you said something about a wonder jock. I figured you meant an athlete, but then you said how great I'd look in one. You were incredibly busy for an unconscious, handcuffed woman. It was awesome."

"I think you must have been having a dream," she said firmly.

"Yeah, maybe. By the way, in my dream you broke the one-foot rule."

She picked up her toast and set it down again. "I can't very well be held responsible for what I do in *your* dream."

"Good thing because you were rooting around in my pajamas and talking about altering my sword."

"That's not true." Her expression questioned his intelligence. "I was talking about altering the thong you were wearing."

"You know," he said, "it sounds like you and I had the very same dream."

His loitering smile made a sudden reappearance.

She rose from the table in a huff. "It meant nothing, Gaines. Just the way your erections mean nothing whenever I get within touching distance—or so you claim."

"You don't touch, McKenna. You help yourself. You dive for pearls."

She spun on her heel and went to finish her packing. "In your dreams," she said, wishing she hadn't used that particular reference as she marched into the bathroom and scooped up an armful of toiletries.

He could be heard chuckling in the other room, and that annoyed her to no end. She *should* have altered the great big smart aleck. Maybe next time she would.

SWAN WAS ZIPPING UP her suitcase when there came a sharp knock at the hotel door. She sensed trouble immediately. "Who is it?"

"It's me, Joe. Open up."

Rob went to let his partner in. He quickly shut and bolted the door after Joe, and the two men exchanged a look.

"Bad news," Joe said as he tossed his morning copy of the newspaper on the table. He poured himself a cup of coffee.

"Well, are we supposed to guess or what?" Rob asked.

Joe glanced at Swan, and she knew this bad news had to do with her.

"I called Erskine, like you asked," he told Rob. "He wants us to bring Swan back. Says it's time to cut our losses and pull the plug on this sting."

"Who's Erskine?" Swan asked.

Joe answered. "He's the acting Special Agent in Charge. In other words, our boss."

"What about Art Long? Still not talking?" Rob asked.

"Nothing," Joe said, blowing on his coffee to cool it. "He hasn't said a word and Erskine is convinced Long's accomplice has gone underground, meaning he or she won't risk coming after the money."

"Did you tell him there was an attempt on Swan last night?"

Joe nodded. "He thinks it was a coincidence, a standard mugging."

Swan felt as if she were in a state of shock. They were talking about Art Long and this sting of theirs, but what about her company? If they forced her to return to Los Angeles it meant that the last show—the finale of the tour—would have to be canceled.

"Can't we ask for another day or two?" Swan said. "What could it possibly hurt? I *have* to be in Seattle for that last show, Rob. You know how important this is. You both do."

Rob hadn't said a word, but his expression was telling. The firm set to his jaw and the focused concentration she saw in his eyes made her fear that he wasn't about to bend any more rules for her. If she was reading his expression right, she was destined to be on a plane this afternoon.

Desperate, she glanced at Joe, who was now doctoring his coffee with several packets of sugar. "Haven't either one of you guys had a dream?" she asked him. "Something you wanted so badly you were willing to give up everything for it?"

Joe nodded. "Tell me about it," he said finally. "I've been dreaming for years of owning a little bar on some sunny tropical island. That's where I'm heading when I retire."

She turned to Rob, hopeful, but he obviously had had

no such dream. He was in a world of his own, staring moodily at the floor, his arms folded.

Swan didn't know what else to do. She'd already begged and pleaded to no avail, and she didn't think getting hysterical would be any more effective in getting through to Rob Gaines, Joe Harris or the bureaucracy that was about to crush her.

The silence that filled the room seemed to have a weight all its own as Swan continued to look expectantly from one agent to the other. At last, Joe spoke, but it was only to excuse himself. "I guess I need to pack," he said, and started for the other room.

"Hold on, Joe." Rob moved toward his partner, meeting him halfway between the bed and the adjoining door. "We're not taking her back. Not yet, anyway. I'm going to put her in a safe place and fly back to L.A. and talk to Erskine myself."

He wasn't taking her back? Swan waited for him to realize what he'd said and correct himself. But he didn't.

"What do you mean, a safe place?" Joe's brows furrowed. He didn't seem to like what he was hearing.

"Don't ask. You're not involved in this, okay? There could be trouble with Erskine, and it'll be better for you if you don't know where she is. I'm going to try and persuade him to give us a few more days. That's all we need."

Rob glanced back at Swan. "There's too much at stake here for Erskine to screw it up by being impatient."

He was talking to Joe, Swan knew, but he was looking at her. Too much at stake? Was he referring to her and the possible loss of her business, or was this all about Art Long and the case? If they'd been alone together she might have come right out and asked him, but right now she was too weak with relief. He'd bought them some time. It didn't matter why. That was what she told herself.

"Do you think he'll listen to you?" she asked Rob. "What are the odds that he'll give us the extra time?"

"All we can do is ask. If he doesn't…" Rob shrugged, "we'll do something else."

"What?"

"One hurdle at a time, okay?" He exhaled deeply. "Let's all get packed as quickly as possible. There's a chance the local office might send a couple of agents here to pick Swan up. We need to be out of here before that happens. I'll be back in a minute," he said, snapping his windbreaker from the closet. "I need to make a call from the lobby."

Swan didn't have to be told twice. She was packing before he got to the door.

10

————

ROB HAD FORGOTTEN how dark it could be in the redwood forest that led to Jack Mathias's cabin. He and Swan were on a stretch of road where almost no light penetrated. The towering trees soared so high they'd formed a vaulted ceiling that was beautiful, but eerie.

"Are we lost?" Swan asked. For several miles she'd said nothing, quietly looking out of the window of the passenger seat.

"No, we're fine," Rob said. "Almost there."

He was driving the Bureau car. Whoever was after Swan would be looking for an SUV so they'd left the Ford Bronco and the U-Haul trailer with Joe, who would find a secure site to lock up both while he and Rob were in L.A.

Rob had been watching the road behind them to be sure they weren't being followed. It would have been easy to spot someone tailing them to a location this remote, which was one of the reasons his old friend Jack Mathias had built the cabin.

It was Jack who Rob had called from the lobby of the hotel. He had been Rob's first training officer and mentor at the Bureau, and the men had become friends, despite the difference in their ages. Jack had become obsessive about privacy since he'd retired, and over the years, had had all kinds of high-tech security devices installed in the cabin. This included an alarm, which if triggered, would alert another retired buddy, a former county sheriff, who lived not far away.

Rob had known Swan would be safe there, but he sensed she wasn't feeling safe, and he could hardly blame her. The location alone was enough to make her uneasy. They were only about ninety minutes north of San Francisco, but it looked as if they were lost in the dark heart of a Tolkien wilderness.

Moments later they rounded a bend and the forest broke open, revealing a breathtaking view of the coast. On their right, majestic redwoods soared skyward, and on their left, the Pacific Ocean rolled at the bottom of a craggy bluff, the waves exploding into white mist against the rocks.

Swan seemed to perk up a little. "This is breathtaking," she said. "I've never stayed in a cabin. Will your friend be there?"

"No, he's rarely around since his wife Grace died. He meant for it to be their retirement nest, but with her gone, he's spending more time in Southern California with his grandkids. He doesn't come here much anymore. Too many memories, I guess."

Rob turned the steering wheel sharply to make a tight turn onto a gravel road. "I think you're going to enjoy roughing it," he told her. "I helped Jack build this place. It was quite a project."

He made another sharp turn, this one to the right, and drove down a narrow, dirt access road. They were flanked by stands of poplars, ash and evergreen trees, and dappled patterns of sunlight played through the leafy canopy. One more turn and they reached the clearing where Jack's cabin was situated.

Swan immediately decided that the word "cabin" was being used very loosely here. The home was a huge A-frame and it *was* constructed of rounded logs, but that's where the similarities stopped. She spotted at least three large decks, one jutting out over the bluff, with a view that promised to be spectacular. Huge, single-sheet windowpanes greeted them in the front of the house. A row of flowering bushes flanked the walkway leading to the door.

"It's beautiful," Swan said.

The doors and windows were secured with combination locks, but Jack had given Rob the latest security code when they'd talked. The master panel was on the wall next to the front door. Rob opened the panel and tapped in the combination. Only then was he able to use the spare door key he carried.

"This place is Fort Knox," he told Swan. "Once I take you through the drill, you'll feel safer here than you do in your own home."

"That would be impossible," Swan replied with a quick shrug. "I've never had my own home."

Rob heard the wistfulness in her tone. He knew she lived and worked out of her partner's home. The Bureau's background check had shown that Swan's mother had been the Carmichael's live-in housekeeper, and Swan had grown up in whatever mansion the Carmichaels were calling home at the time. He wondered if that was an issue for Swan. He understood the loneliness of feeling like a displaced person. He'd felt that way most of his adult life, but it was largely by his own choice.

He let Swan into the cabin while he went back to the car to unload their luggage. He brought in his duffel, as well as her suitcase, and set the bags in the living room. He couldn't stay long, but he wanted her to know that he was coming back. Once he had his business done, he would be on the first plane back from L.A.

Before he left, he took Swan on a quick tour of the cabin. Jack's taste in furnishings ran to the masculine with lots of rich, dark leather and webbed rattan tables. It was beautiful, but definitely lacking a woman's touch. In fact, Jack had taken most of Grace's things with him to Southern California, so there were very few knickknacks around and no houseplants at all.

"There's a guest room right down the hall," Rob told her. "I'll take your bag down there."

When he came back, he explained the cabin's security system. The exterior was protected by motion detectors, but she could trigger the alarms herself with a remote that he instructed she should keep with her at all times. All the windows and doors were shatterproof glass, and there was even a panic room in the basement that could be accessed by pressing a particular button on the remote.

Jack had a case of guns, too, but Rob left them locked up. Swan had no training with weapons, and the risk of her hurting herself was too great. He took a few moments to show her how to use a stun gun instead.

By the time he'd finished showing her the ropes, he realized he didn't like the idea of leaving her alone, no matter how secure the place was. But there was no way to say that without frightening her and perhaps implying things he didn't want to imply. He wasn't sure either of them had recovered from her nocturnal "alterations," and he was trying to avoid misunderstandings, not create more.

"I won't be gone long," he said. "You'll be fine here."

"Of course," she agreed. "I'll be fine."

On the trip up, she'd thanked him repeatedly for helping her, but she was unusually quiet now. He could only imagine that she was visualizing her life going down the tubes. He wondered if she was feeling as reluctant for him to leave as he was. On the other hand, maybe she couldn't wait for him to get out of her hair. It hadn't exactly been comfortable between them.

"I guess I'd better get going," he said, feeling awkward. "Joe's taking a shuttle and meeting me at the airport. There are plenty of canned goods in the cupboard and the freezer is stocked, as well. I'll try to get back tonight, but it'll be late. No sense waiting up."

She looked up at him suddenly, with large wounded eyes. "You think I could sleep not knowing if I'll be in jail tomorrow morning? Not likely."

Rob wished he could promise her that wasn't going to happen, but he wasn't exactly optimistic himself. He couldn't lie to her or give her false hope, knowing he might have to let her down. Any number of things could happen in the next twenty-four hours, which included his being charged with obstruction of justice, if Erskine wanted to take it that far.

He had a fleeting vision of taking Swan into his arms and comforting her, which all too swiftly turned into a fleeting vision of racing hearts and deep, anguished kisses and clothes melting away in the raging fires of their need.

Maybe you'd better just talk to her, Lover Boy.

"I know you're worried," he said, "but let's not borrow trouble, okay? Let me see what I can do before you start hearing cell block doors close."

She nodded, but something was sparkling in her eyes and it might have been tears. "Why are you doing this?" she asked him. "Why are you taking such a chance on me? This could blow up in your face, couldn't it?"

Little did she know. There was no love lost between him and his boss, especially since Rob was one of the candidates for the position that Erskine now held in an acting capacity. Even without that complication, Erskine wasn't going to be happy when he learned that Rob had hidden a suspect without authorization and disobeyed a direct order to bring her back to Los Angeles.

Rob was torn, but he couldn't tell Swan what was going

through his mind and then stroll out of here and leave her to sweat it out alone. Besides, he wasn't doing this just for her—or at least that's what he'd been telling himself. God knew he wanted to believe it was the truth. Otherwise he should hand in his badge and his gun. He had no business carrying either.

He walked to the window that looked out over the cliffs and the blue seas beyond. It was a beautiful view but, at the moment, there wasn't a ship on the horizon or a bird in flight, and that made him feel inexpressibly lonely.

"I've been after Art Long for five years," he said, "and I want to put him in jail for at least ten times that long, but I need his accomplice to make it stick."

Swan brushed the wetness from her cheeks and squinted at him as if the glare from the window was hurting her eyes. "So this *is* about Art Long?"

The right answer to that was yes, but he couldn't bring himself to say it. "What else would it be about?" he said, hating himself.

"Me. You," she insisted. "Something more than this case."

"It can't be about me or you, Swan. At the very least you're going to be a material witness for this case, and I can't go there."

"You mean, you can't go there again."

The hair on the back of his neck stood up. "Why did you say that?" he asked her. "What do you mean *again?*"

She had the sense to look faintly nervous about going any further with this line of discussion. Her hands were stuck in the pockets of her jeans. She pulled them out, but didn't seem quite sure what to do with them, so she stuck them back in again.

"I know about Paula Warren," she said after another moment of fumbling. "I know what happened to her and that you blame yourself for her death. You took responsibility for it.''

Rob approached her in disbelief. ''Did Joe tell you that? He had no business discussing that with you—or with anyone.''

''Don't blame Joe for being honest,'' she said, standing her ground. ''He was trying to help me understand why you're so difficult. I'm sure he didn't tell me anything that wasn't true. And besides—''

''Besides what?''

''How am I supposed to find out anything about you unless I ask someone else? You sure as hell aren't very forthcoming.''

''What do you want to know?''

''Well, about us, for one thing—and don't tell me there's nothing to talk about. There is!''

''There's probably plenty to talk about, but what good would it do us? You've seen what happens every time I get near you, McKenna. What else needs to be said?''

''But is that all it is, Rob? Just physical arousal? Is there anything deeper than that?''

Rob had once thought of her as light against the dark and been embarrassed at his sentimentality. But here she was doing it again. She wanted to get to the truth, the light. She wanted him to open up and share his feelings with her. But how could he? That night in the gardens he'd stayed in the shadows, watching her, hidden from view. Now he felt as if he had no choice but to keep his emotions in the shadows, too. The very thought of opening up his inner world to her, of letting her know what went on inside him, was terrifying in some way he didn't begin to understand. He had to shut her down, and he had to do that now.

The view from the windows seemed even more bleak as he looked out.

"I don't know what Joe told you," he said, "but here's the truth. It was my job to keep Paula Warren alive. It was my job to keep her safe until she could testify. I didn't fall in love with her or do any of the things she accused me of, but I had feelings for her, feelings I shouldn't have had. I let my guard down, I did lose focus, and I *did* fail her. When she needed me most, I wasn't there and she paid the price. That is *not* going to happen again."

Swan was awfully quiet behind him, but Rob didn't look at her. He needed to get through this.

"You want to talk about feelings?" he said. "Of course, I have feelings for you, but I have a responsibility to you, as well, and that has to take priority over my emotions. If you could get that through your head, we'd get along a lot better. Now leave it alone, all right?"

He didn't like using his past as a weapon to push her away, but she was unbelievably tenacious. She didn't seem to know when to stop.

Rob turned to her, not sure what to expect, maybe more tears. Instead he faced a woman with her arms crossed and her brows puckered in a frown. He felt like groaning. She was going to take a stand.

"What do you mean, of course you have feelings for me?" she asked. "What kind of feelings?"

"Oh, my God, McKenna, please—"

"That's not a hard question, Gaines."

Rob raked his hands through his hair. "Am I talking to the wind? I just asked you to leave it alone, didn't I?"

"No. I can't," she said in a voice that was as soft as it was firm. "I don't want to. This is where it gets real, Rob. I want to know if your attraction to me is purely physical or if there's something else there, as well. And if there is, I want to know what it is."

She closed the remaining distance between them. When she was no more than six inches in front of him, she looked him directly in the eyes. "It won't kill you to answer the question."

"No, but it might get you killed."

Swan shook her head. "You're wrong. You've been carrying that guilt for so long now it's become a part of you. How long are you going to blame yourself for something that you had so little control over? I know that Paula was deeply unstable and probably obsessed with you. But what were you supposed to do, Rob, put her in your pocket and carry her around with you twenty-four hours a day? I'm sorry about what happened to her, but you've got a life—a life of your own—a life that you're not living."

For the first time in half a decade, Rob felt as if some of the weight of that godawful episode had been lifted from his shoulders. And what amazed him most was that he had never been able to do it for himself. She had done it, by being annoying and tenacious and by backing him to the wall.

"I felt things for her that I shouldn't have felt," he persisted.

"So what? Aren't you the FBI agent who told me that it's okay to have feelings, as long as you don't act on them?"

His rueful smile was an admission, but she didn't delight in her victory. Her gaze turned sparkly again and she whispered, "What am I supposed to do if you don't come back, Gaines?"

Rob brushed a strand of hair from her cheek. Her hair was always flying around her face, and he'd always wanted to do that. A million other things went through his mind that he wanted to do, but this would have to hold him. This and the tear that was rolling down her cheek.

"I have to go," he told her. "You'll be safe here."

Swan placed her hand on his chest. She did it tentatively, as if she were afraid he might pull away at her touch. Rob wasn't about to pull away. If anything, he wanted to pull her into his arms and never let go. But that, too, was against the rules.

IT WAS AFTER 5:00 p.m. when Tom Erskine called Rob Gaines and Joe Harris into his meticulously neat office. Erskine was a short, stubby man, rumored to be only a quarter of an inch taller than the FBI's minimum height requirement. He kept his graying hair cropped close to his almost perfectly square head, and his shoulders were lined up at right angles to his thick neck.

The unfortunate image it brought to mind was of a walking fireplug, but Rob had always respected the man. Erskine might be a bureaucrat now, but he'd spent years on the street and had worked some of the toughest cases on record. He and Rob had actually worked together on the Warren case, and when Internal Affairs investigated Rob, Erskine spoke up on his behalf. Rob would never know what went on behind those closed-door sessions, but he was certain Erskine's support had helped save his ass.

"Sit down and tell me why I'm looking at two people instead of three," Erskine barked, waving Rob and Joe toward the pair of vinyl chairs in front of his desk. "Where's the suspect?"

Rob and Joe had already agreed that Rob would do the talking.

"Before we get into the details," Rob said, "I want you to know that Joe had nothing to do with this. It was my decision not to bring Ms. McKenna in, and I'm acting alone on that."

Erskine cast a questioning glance at Joe, who shrugged slightly.

"She's in a safe place," Rob added.

"You left a suspect alone?" Erskine's bushy gray eyebrows raised like twin feather dusters. "Tell me I didn't hear that right."

"She's not a flight risk," Rob stated flatly.

"Enlighten me as to how you know that." Erskine leaned forward and folded his hands on his desk blotter.

"She's never been in trouble before, not even a parking ticket. She's a long-term resident of her community and a respected businesswoman who's completely committed to her fashion design company. We're not talking about a criminal here, Tom. We're talking about a victim, another in a long line of Art Long's patsies. He used her, and probably her partner, too. But that isn't why I didn't bring her back."

Erskine was silent, so Rob continued. "There's been one attempt on her already. A serious attempt. I should have caught the guy, but I didn't, and he's going to try again. I'm certain of it, and I want another shot."

"You think this guy was the accomplice?" Erskine asked.

A red blotch had begun to crawl up the man's neck and Rob sensed that Erskine was doing everything possible to keep his impatience in check. For some reason, he wanted this case shut down.

"No, I think the accomplice is a woman," Rob explained. "That's how Art Long works. He preys on women, but this time he found one as larcenous as he is. She's also someone high enough to authorize electronic transfers of large amounts of money, and she's hired a thug to steal that money back."

Joe offered his two cents. "The accomplice doesn't know Art Long's in custody, so she probably thinks he's double-crossed her, and she's trying to get to the money before he does."

"She's going to try again," Rob said with low force. "We need a little more time—one more show—and we've got her, or whoever is doing her dirty work. Meanwhile, you could be running checks on First National Heritage's women bank execs, anyone high enough to authorize the transfer of five million.''

Erskine looked as if he'd chomped down on something sour. ''Apparently you boys are having a great old time on this road trip of yours, but the fun is over. You're not getting one more second of government per diem out of me.''

Rob was already shaking his head.

''Let me finish!'' Erskine bellowed. ''I want her back here tonight, and I'm giving you exactly forty-eight hours to wrap up this case. If you don't have the accomplice by then, we'll proceed with the evidence we have, and that means your underwear lady is as much a suspect as Art Long.''

''Bringing her back here will send the wrong signals,'' Rob said. ''It would force her to call off her tour, which would look suspicious. The accomplice will back off.''

The red blotch now covered Erskine's throat. ''I should have both of you brought up on charges—that's what I should do.'' His fingers drummed against his desk pad. ''Consider yourselves confined to this building until further notice. I'll have someone from the San Francisco office pick up the suspect and bring her back, and I don't want any arguments.''

''That's not going to happen, Tom.'' Rob spoke in a tone of utter finality. ''You were wrong about the accomplice not following us to San Francisco. We were followed. There was a legitimate attempt to steal the phony check from Ms. McKenna, and it was an attack that could have gotten her killed. What I can't figure out is why you're so anxious to shut down this case, but if it has anything to do with the rumors about my being up for your job, you can relax. I don't want the job. I wouldn't take it if it were offered to me.''

Joe gaped at Rob in shock, and Erskine acted quickly. ''Joe, I'd like to talk to Rob in private,'' he said. ''Would you mind stepping out?''

On his way out of the office, Joe shot Rob a hang-in-there-buddy look, which Rob wasn't expecting. His partner was due to retire in a couple years. He should have been covering his own butt, not worrying about Rob's.

When they were alone, Erskine leaned back in his chair until it creaked. His voice and manner were now oddly calm. ''I'm not sure what's going on here, Rob, but I'm not at all comfortable with how you're handling any of this. It's bringing back bad memories.''

Erskine was referring to the Warren case, and Rob could hardly blame him for that. There were similarities.

''I think you're too close on this one, Rob. It's just a gut feeling, but it's a strong one. Are you? Too close?''

More than either of us knows, Rob thought. ''I have a gut feeling, too, and it says I can crack this case wide open.''

''You didn't answer the question. Are you getting too close?''

Had it not been for the angry blotch on his neck, Erskine would have made a master poker player. His expression revealed nothing of what was going on inside him at that moment. ''I'm pulling you off this case,'' he said. ''I'll have you reassigned to something else by morning, but don't think you're getting a pass. Disciplinary action is a distinct possibility.''

Rob stood up. ''I'm sorry you feel that way.'' He pulled his gun from his holster, released the magazine from the grip and laid both on Erskine's desk. His badge and ID followed. ''I'll save you the trouble of disciplinary action,'' he said. ''I took this job to enforce the law, not to run roughshod over people's lives. If it's true that I'm too close to the suspect, then I agree that's a problem, but what you're proposing we do to her is worse. It's an abuse of power, and I won't be a part of it.''

Rob didn't wait for Erskine's response. He'd made his decision and there was no backing out now. Swan McKenna needed him—needed him as much as Paula Warren had needed him—and he wasn't going to let Swan down the way he had Paula. If it meant his career, if it meant jail time, so be it.

"I could have you brought up on charges!" Erskine sputtered as Rob walked to the door.

Rob turned back. "Yeah, you could."

Erskine's red blotch had turned crimson. "Get the hell out of here. Tell Harris to get in here."

"Tell him yourself," Rob said as he shut the door behind him.

ROB STARED at his empty cup of coffee and the slab of untouched razzleberry pie in front of him. He'd lost count of the number of cups he'd drunk, but he could feel the caffeine buzzing in his temples and the heavy thud of his heart.

Where the hell was Joe? Before the meeting with Erskine, Joe had made Rob promise to meet him at a coffee shop afterward, if things went badly. Things couldn't have gone worse, and Rob had figured Joe would show up as planned, but he was more than an hour late.

Rob checked his watch. He'd already missed his flight back to San Francisco, but he'd checked the schedule and there was one more out tonight. He would have to take his chances with standby. With a heavy sigh, he left a ten on the table and headed for the coffee shop door.

His gut was churning, and it wasn't just the acid from the coffee. He was on the outside now, maybe one of the bad guys in Erskine's view, and Rob had no idea what to expect. Erskine might even send some agents out to apprehend him. Rob didn't want to compromise either himself or Joe with a phone call. He had no idea what his former partner was being subjected to now that Rob had turned in his badge, and he didn't want to add any heat to a pot that was already boiling.

Moments later Rob was standing on a street corner, watching a steady stream of taxis go by. He was supposed to be hailing one of them to take him to LAX, but he hadn't even lifted his arm. Something had stopped him. It was the sight of the federal building several streets down. The setting sun was reflected in the windowpanes of the lofty structure, giving the impression of a raging fire within. Rob wondered if it was a sign.

The Bureau had been a huge part of his life for nearly twelve years now. Swan had implied that it *was* his life, and maybe she was right. He hadn't realized the extent to which it had structured his thinking and dominated his decisions, even the personal ones. That fiery citadel was the closest thing he'd had to a home and a family. As he stared at it now, he felt as if he'd landed on an alien planet where he had no idea what the rules were or how civilians were supposed to conduct themselves. Meanwhile, two questions were spinning like moons orbiting his head.

What the hell had he done? And what was he going to do next?

SWAN HAD TO DO SOMETHING. She couldn't just sit and wait for Rob to return. Staying busy would keep her mind off everything that could go wrong, and at the moment, she couldn't imagine anything going right.

Jack Mathias was a meticulous housekeeper. Try as she might, Swan couldn't find a single thing that needed cleaning. Mathias might not spend much time here any-

more, but it was obvious to Swan that the cabin and surrounding property had once been his pride and joy. For a
few minutes, she actually contemplated rearranging the
furniture just for the hell of it and then putting it back the
way it was.

That's whacked, McKenna. That's just whacked.

She headed for the kitchen, where she found a box of
her favorite ginger peach herbal tea. As she put the kettle
on the stove, she glanced at the wall clock. Rob had been
gone for a little more than an hour. It was going to be
one long day and night.

A short time later she was out on the front deck with
a steaming mug of tea, her cell phone and the panic button
remote tucked in her jeans' pocket. She wasn't sure how
much the remote would help outside, but if she had to use
it, at least the alarms would make a lot of noise. She
needed the fresh air and the sound of the ocean for her
sanity.

On impulse, Swan set down her tea and dialed Lynne's
cell. A message in the display told her the signal was too
weak. It was just as well, she decided. There was no way
to hide her anxiety from Lynne, and why upset her when
there was nothing Lynne could do? Nothing anyone could
do, for that matter. Swan couldn't remember ever feeling
quite this helpless—or so dependent on the whims of one
person.

Would Rob come back?

How many times today would she have to ask herself
that question? Maybe she was trying to prepare herself,
but she really wasn't sure what she would do if he didn't
return, and that wasn't like her. Swan McKenna always
had a plan. Her mother had instilled the need to be ready
for the worst and so, of course, Swan had come to expect
the worst, especially where men were concerned.

She'd already decided that if Rob didn't show up, she

would turn herself in to the authorities. That might make it easier for him if he'd been detained in L.A. for not bringing her in. Of course there was the problem of how she would get back to civilization. Maybe she would set off the alarms and someone would come, Jack's retired friend or the security company.

A strange sensation shivered through her and in its wake a startling idea was born. Maybe she should hope for the best for once. Did she dare let herself believe that things might work out, that Rob might come back and tell her that he had approval for her to continue the tour? Was it possible that the world wasn't coming to an end tonight, that she ought to be hopeful and believe that everything she touched wasn't doomed?

What an outlandish concept that was. Still, she felt the need to cling to it. It was all she had. Quickly gathering up her things, she went back to the kitchen with a whole different plan in mind. Jack Mathias had enough food stocked away in the cabin to feed a small army for a month. Unfortunately, it was all canned goods. There were no fresh vegetables, milk or eggs, but Swan found two thick steaks and some lush broccoli crowns in the freezer section of his refrigerator, and there were some potatoes rolling around in his vegetable bin. An unopened wedge of cheddar cheese and a jar of mushrooms, tucked in the shelves of the fridge door, made her sigh with delight.

She could work with this. Now she had to figure out what to do with herself.

He'd put her bag in the guest room. She pulled nearly everything out of it, trying to decide. Clothes were strewn all over the bed, but nothing struck Swan as right. The sexy blue mini that made her legs look like toothpicks, but in a good way. No, it was too sexy. He might not have reached his teasing threshold, but she had. It was becoming painful. She didn't want to tease him, she wanted to be *with* him. Desperately, in fact. She ached with wanting that. But they couldn't, so she wouldn't.

She would greet him chastely, and they would follow all the rules, and everything they did and felt would be on the list of acceptable responses. They would be good.

If he came back.

No, no, no, he *was* coming back. He was.

Finally she picked out a sheer linen blouse, cropped at the waist, and a linen skirt that buttoned up the front. The floral print had always made her think of barefoot walks in lush green meadows. Okay it was a little sexy, but nothing that shouted *Take me, take me now,* which was how she really felt.

Once she'd released her hair from its ponytail and brushed it out thoroughly, there was nothing to do but wait. Wait and practice an emotion with which Swan Mc-Kenna had very little personal experience. Hope.

11

SWAN HAD NO IDEA how many hours she'd been sitting on the couch in the living room, waiting. It felt as if she'd entered into a trancelike state. Her knees were drawn up to her chest and she'd draped her arms around them and hugged herself, but other than the rise and fall of her breathing, she hadn't moved.

She'd been sitting so long she was numb. Her feet had fallen asleep and there was an odd prickle creeping up the back of her legs, but it felt safer to stay this way, in suspended animation, where nothing could touch her. A fragile cocoon surrounded her that held off the doubts and fears and the forecast doom of her mother's voice.

She had long ago realized that he wasn't coming back, but there had been that brief and terribly sweet span of time when she'd allowed herself to believe that he would, and she didn't want to let go of the feeling. Everything would come crashing down if she did.

She would have to set off the alarms and wait for someone to arrive. There would be the horror of turning herself in and having to watch the impact it had on others— Lynne and Gerard and the La Bomba people who'd given them their first break. It would undoubtedly hit the papers, and their families would find out. Her mother, of course, would feel vindicated in believing that the universe conspired to trip people up and steal their dreams...so why bother to have dreams?

If Swan never moved, could she stop all that from happening?

She had begun to lose the feeling in her hands when she heard something outside. It was faint, but it sounded like tires on gravel. A car? She couldn't get up and look. She was frozen, but her heart was pounding and the blood was flowing again. Time seemed to slow down and screech to a halt as she listened for any other signs of life out there. Feelings flooded back into her awareness that were almost too sharp to bear.

Was it Rob? Had he really come back?

She nearly screamed when she heard a key slip into the lock and the tumbler click over. The door swung wide and when Swan tried to get off the couch, she came close to toppling to the floor. Only a squeak came out of her, which meant her voice wasn't working, either.

"Rob?" she finally said, her throat tightening on a sob.

He stood in the doorway with a bewildered expression, watching her try to get her hands to work and her legs unbent.

"Were you expecting someone else?" he asked.

Swan was dimly aware that she was gaping at him in amazement as she tried to shake the life back into her limbs. He looked bad. He looked weary and beaten up, like a knight who'd been through the Crusades and seen a lot of carnage. But he'd survived. And he *had* come back.

She seemed to be having some trouble believing it, and so did he. Or maybe it was her physical predicament he couldn't believe. She was bent over like a gnome, picking up her feet and setting them down, trying to make them work so that she could run to him the way they did in the movies and throw her arms around him. Even if he'd come back to take her to jail, she wanted to hug him just for showing up.

"Can I help?" he asked, pulling off his windbreaker and throwing it on the nearest chair. "What are you doing, Swan?"

He sounded confused and concerned and totally clueless as to what she'd been going through while he was gone. Dying a nanosecond at a time is what she'd been doing.

"It's my feet," she said. "They're a little numb, but I'm fine." She stopped thumping and shaking herself and looked up at him. "I really am fine. How are you?"

"In need of a drink," he said, heading for an unusually large globe of the world that stood in front of the bookcases. "Can I get you one?" The globe opened up into a well-stocked bar, and he poured a fifth of Scotch.

Swan didn't drink hard liquor, but this seemed like as good a time as any to start. Maybe it would help her circulation. As he walked over to her with a tumbler of Scotch, she noticed that he wasn't wearing his shoulder holster.

"Where's your gun?" she asked.

"Take a sip first," he suggested. "It's not a long story, but it's been a long day."

He sat down next to her on the couch, and she'd taken several sips of the potent stuff, each one going down like liquid fire, before he'd finished telling her what had happened. The only reason she didn't interrupt him was because her voice had stopped working again.

"You turned in your badge?" she got out. "You just set it on his desk and walked out of his office?"

Rob took a swallow of his Scotch and made a hissing sound as it went down. "Look at it this way," he said. "I didn't get arrested."

"Is that why you don't have your gun? They took your gun?" Apparently she'd come to rather like his weapon because that seemed to be bothering her more than the loss of his badge.

He rose from the couch, Scotch firmly in hand, and went to the sliding-glass door that opened onto the deck. "They didn't take the gun, as in throw me to the ground and wrest it from me. I turned it in, too."

Swan hoped her feet were working now because she needed to use them. She left her glass on the coffee table and walked right over to him, but all she could do when she got there was stand in front of him and shake her head.

"Rob," she said. "Rob, my God, what have you done?"

"Don't make a big deal out of it—"

"A big deal? A big *deal?* You loved that job. Maybe you didn't say it in so many words, but the Bureau was your life."

He was shaking his head and trying to fend her off. "Could we let it go?" he pleaded. "It's better this way, and that's all you need to know, Swan. It's all *I* need to know."

"You did this for me?" she asked him in a whisper.

"Well, there were other reas—" He heaved a sigh. "I really didn't have much choice. Erskine backed me into a corner."

"Oh…of course, I see. He gave you no choice." Her voice was throaty and full. She was inching toward him again, closing that mere foot of space between them. She was about to shatter the one foot rule as if he'd made it to be broken.

"Can he get away with that?" she asked, her voice getting fuller and throatier by the minute. "Surely some-one will see what a mistake he's made, and they'll come after you, begging you to take the job back."

"Swan—"

"Rob," she whispered.

"Swan, don't."

"You did it for me," she said, her eyes beginning to swim. "You did, Rob, and I can hardly believe it. No one's ever stood up for me like that. They've never— n-never—"

She couldn't get the rest of it out, and the tears had begun to burn like fire.

"Never what?" he asked.

"N-never believed in me like that."

She meant every shaky word of it, and while she blinked away the wetness, she stared at him as if he surely had to be a figment of her imagination. Eventually she realized that it might be a good idea to touch him, just to rule that out. His jaw felt like heavy-grade sandpaper, and his mouth was hot, dry, under her fingers. He was real, all right, and this was probably as far as he would want her to go. But the second she felt the heavy pulse beating in his throat, she knew she had to take it further.

She began to unbutton his shirt.

She was unsteady but determined. The first button was nearly undone before he caught on. He was a little slow. So many of them were.

"What are you doing?" he asked.

"I just wanted you to be more comfortable." She did. She wanted him to be much more comfortable. She wanted him to be all but naked and kissing her deeply, that's how comfortable she wanted him to be.

He didn't exactly stop her from her task, but she had the feeling he was debating what to do. His gaze seemed to be fastened to her face. She didn't blush for once, and she didn't retreat. She might be shaking a little, but who wouldn't be under the circumstances? She was no stranger to the intimate details of the male physique. After all, she designed the things they wore next to their skin. But this wasn't like that. This was personal.

He had just given away everything for her. He had nothing to gain and everything to lose. She might have been wrong about why he did it—only he could answer that question—but she refused to believe that this was about catching Art Long. It was a matter of honor and integrity. And perhaps…love?

"Careful, Swan," he said, his voice thick with emotion. "I'm not a cop anymore. Those rules about not kissing you don't apply now."

"I know," she said. It surprised her that her own voice felt so heavy. "I never liked those rules anyway." A tiny shiver of delight ran up her spine as she fingered open the front of his shirt.

Bare skin shone through the opening and his stomach muscles clenched as if he was anticipating her touch. She felt an answering tightness that crept all the way down to her thighs. The next step was obvious. She was supposed to slide his shirt off his shoulders and let it fall in a graceful heap to the floor. But she'd just realized what she was doing.

"I'm taking off a man's shirt," she said in a hushed voice. "I've wanted to do that my whole life." The fact that it was *his* shirt, Rob's shirt, just blew her mind. She slipped her hand inside the broadcloth material and felt the heat and satin smoothness that was Rob Gaines.

A ripple of movement beneath her fingers made her look up at him. His eyes were dark with desire. He wanted this as much as she did, but something was holding him back. Maybe in his heart he would always be an agent who thought of her as off-limits. And yet, this was the man who had responded like lightning to her touch—and she couldn't help but wonder what condition he was in now. She couldn't look, but there were other ways to find out.

"I'm your first shirt?" he asked.

"You're my first everything. I'm not counting that dreadful experience when I was sixteen."

"Nothing counts but this," he said.

She slipped both her hands inside his shirt, and he swept her close, into the radiant heat of his embrace. "Christ," he whispered, enfolding her as if she were both breakable and the only thing that could keep him from expiring right there on the spot. She burrowed her head into the hollow of his shoulder, and a ragged sigh slipped out of her, or maybe it was a sob. She still couldn't believe he was here.

"I didn't think you were coming back," she said.

"Of course, I came back. Why wouldn't I?"

"I don't know." She looked up into his face cautiously, perhaps thinking she might see something there she feared. But he seemed genuinely perplexed.

He brushed his thumb pad across her eyebrow and then down her cheek. Like a kitten being petted, she raised her head and moaned softly. His touch was wonderful. Gentle and generous at the same time.

"I want to be touched just like that," she whimpered, *"everywhere."*

It surprised her that she could be this open and vulnerable with him, and maybe it surprised him, too. But then, look what he'd done. Her only thought at that moment was to be closer to him, as close as possible, but she could see that he was studying her.

"Maybe we shouldn't do this," he said. "Maybe it's too soon."

Swan narrowed her eyes at his concern. "But I want to do this. Are you still trying to protect me?"

His fingers slid into her hair. "I guess I am," he said.

"Well, don't. I can take care of myself tonight."

He pulled her head back and gazed at her mouth as if it was the most succulent delicacy he'd ever seen—and he was a man with an appetite.

"Don't be so sure, Swan McKenna. Don't be so sure."

She melted against him as if there wasn't a bone in her body. Her breasts pillowed against his chest and her hips nestled wantonly into his. She pressed herself against him everywhere it was possible to make contact with his long, hard body, and gloried in how ardently he pressed back. He wasn't just aroused. He was as rigid as the gun he'd left behind.

His hands dropped down to cup her bottom and Swan felt a deep clutching need. He moved against her, locking them into the rhythm of sex.

"Do it," she said in the pleading that had taken control of her voice. "Whatever you want to do with me, do it."

His mouth pressed to hers. Then she felt a sharp sensation and cried out in surprise. He had nipped her lip, the inner edge where it was plump and tender.

"You taste like Scotch," he whispered. "Scotch and sex and deep, shuddering sighs. I want to drink you to the last drop."

He tasted like sex, too. Powerful male-on-the-hunt sex. It was intoxicating.

His hands began sliding down her back as his lips found the side of her neck. Instinctively he seemed to know the sweet spot between the base of her neck and her shoulder. Hot kisses there made her arch her back and moan as she rocked against his pelvis. The hard flesh encased in his jeans caused her to sigh deeply. She had freed him from that prison before, and she knew how exhilarating that could be.

"We can still stop," he told her. "It's not too late."

Stop? Swan had never heard anything more ridiculous

in her life. She slid her hands straight into his back pockets and took possession with a squeeze of her fingers. It surprised both of them. His muscles flexed powerfully and a sound of satisfaction rumbled in his throat. Swan now knew what it felt like to be weak at the knees. A small galaxy of stars sparkled brightly in her belly and her thighs began to quiver.

"If you stop, I'll evaporate," she told him. "There'll be nothing left of me but Scotch, sex and sighs."

Rob was nuzzling the tender flesh behind her ear and causing sensations that threatened to liquefy her all over again. Her hands had migrated to his hips and her thumbs were curled into the deep pelvic grooves. And she could hardly breathe it was all so hot and sensual.

"If you want to talk about rules," he said, "we'd better talk about them now."

Rules? There was only one rule she could think of at the moment, and he was never going to go for it.

"You're not allowed to say no," she murmured.

He broke the kiss with a little groan. "No, as in 'No, you can't do that'?" His expression was quizzical.

"That's right."

He glanced down at his open shirt and slacks. "I'm supposed to give you total access?"

"That's *right.*"

"Let you do anything you want? Take advantage? Run amuck?"

"That's right."

He smiled at her, his eyes glimmering. "Deal."

"Excellent," she said, hardly able to believe it. She eyed his belt buckle and her fingers must have been heading there because he stayed them with his hand.

"Not so fast," he said. "I have a rule or two of my own."

"Really? And what are your rules?"

"Well, the first one sounds like *no* but it's spelled a little differently: *k-n-o-w*."

She perked with interest. "As in biblical knowledge?"

"As in I want to get to *know* you in every way possible, and the more intimately the better."

That might be the best rule she'd ever heard—and she'd heard a few. She met his gaze, aware that he was studying her eyes and her lips and her auburn hair very intently. This was what it felt like to be the only thing in the world on a man's mind, she realized.

"And your second rule?" she asked.

"Let's save that one for later." He inclined his head as if to say go ahead, run amuck.

She toyed with his belt buckle. "I can do anything I want?"

"That's right."

"And you won't say no, even if I ask you to make love to me?"

"Any particular way?" he inquired.

The breath she sucked in left her without a voice. And it wasn't just his question, although that was reason enough. His belt was undone and she'd realized something. There wasn't going to be anything under these slacks but male nakedness, fully blown, so to speak.

"I'm only familiar with one way," she admitted, as offhandedly as she could be about such a thing. "In the back seat of a car."

"Well, we need to change that, don't we?"

He whispered a kiss over her lips and left her standing there, ever so slightly woozy, as he went over to start a fire in the fireplace. When he had one burning, he brought her over and slowly warmed her up in his arms. The flames licked high, enveloping them in a silk screen of red and gold. Rob buried his hands in the thick waves of her hair. He eased her head back, exposing her neck, and the pulse that fluttered there.

Swan's heart was thrumming. But hers wasn't the only one. She stole inside his shirt and discovered that his heart was beating as wildly as hers. His thumbs stroked her jaw, as light as air. How could that be when his body was so big and hard? The urge to return his caresses was strong, but Swan resisted it. He'd said he wanted to spend time getting to know her, and that was fine with her. Besides, it was one of the rules.

He was studying her again, she realized, as someone might step back to look at a painting. It wasn't scrutiny exactly; it was something else.

"What are you thinking?" she asked him.

His gaze drifted to her breasts, which were straining against the fabric of her blouse. The tiny pearl buttons looked ready to pop.

His voice was husky. "This may be the first and last time, Swan. I want us both to remember it."

"It doesn't have to be the last," she said, but she knew what he meant. He was referring to the possibility that they might be separated by jail cells in the very near future.

His arms brushed maddeningly over her breasts as he undid the top button of her blouse. One by one, the pearl discs opened up and, one by one, Swan's inhibitions began to surface. Something had changed now that he was doing the undressing. She felt out of control, and that was thrilling, too. But would he find her attractive? It had been so long she didn't know if any man would. And would he feel differently about her afterward? Would this change their relationship?

Did they have a relationship?

He didn't seem concerned about any of those things as he peeled the blouse off her shoulders and let it fall to the

floor. And with the clothing went most of her fears. Some
risks were worth taking, she told herself. Some fears were
destined to be faced head-on. She wanted Rob to take her
into his arms, to take her into his heart and to love her.
If he broke her heart tomorrow, so be it. They would still
have tonight.

His pace was deliberately slow as he took in her trembling body. Her breasts were swollen with longing, and
the demi-bra she wore begged to be taken off. He'd said
his quest was to know her intimately, and time was not a
factor. But his dark, smoldering eyes confessed the
truth—that he was fighting back his own need to simply
take her and make her his own.

Rob unbuttoned her skirt just enough to slide the material down her thighs. She placed her hands on his shoulders as he knelt down to help her step out of the skirt.
His face was now only inches from her womanhood. She
could feel his warm breath on the coppery curls. His hands
glided smoothly along her hips and then around back,
where he gently cupped her buttocks. Swan slipped her
fingers into his hair and arched her back as he pressed a
lingering kiss against the juncture of her legs. She was
wet and throbbing for more, and he hadn't even taken her
panties off yet!

Her breathing turned shallow as he lifted his mouth
from her parted legs. A frustrated sigh escaped her. Why
had he stopped? It felt so exquisite.

Rob eased his fingers into the band of her panties and
coaxed them down her legs. The silk was cool in contrast
to his warm fingers, and she could feel both sensations
caressing and teasing her skin. She was shaking by the
time she stepped out of the panties.

"Sit down," he said.

There was an overstuffed chair just behind her, and
Swan assumed that was what he meant. He was still kneel-

ing in front of her and didn't seem to have any intention of standing or joining her in the chair. Swan sat on the edge and when she tried primly to close her legs, he conveniently got in the way.

His voice was almost harsh as he said, ''Lie back.''

Swan sank back into the pillowy cushions. She was lost in the big chair, and she'd never felt more vulnerable as he spread her legs wide and began planting hot, lingering kisses along the inside of her thighs. His fingers stroked her pubic area, and the sensations were maddening. He used the very tip of his tongue to trace warm lines up her thighs, and she knew where he was heading. He was in no hurry, though, which made her quiver with anticipation.

She was so caught up in the feathery movement of his mouth that she could barely give a thought to the defenseless position she was in. She desperately, insanely, wanted more of the same, and she had never been like this in her life. She was not hot-blooded by nature. She was cautious and practical and moderate in her needs. Even her sexual responses were timid, like stars twinkling in some faraway galaxy. But there was nothing moderate about the stars that were bursting inside her now. The twinkling galaxy was ablaze.

Finally his mouth whispered along her slit and Swan thought she might scream. As if undoing the ribbons of a satin bow, he spread her labia and began kissing her there. When his tongue entered her, Swan clutched a fistful of velvety cushion and gave herself over to the incredible things that were happening to her. The stars were flying every which way, spiraling and streaking. She had never actually seen a comet shower, but this was what she imagined it must be like.

''Let it go, Swan,'' he whispered. ''My other rule is

don't hold back. I don't want either of us to hold anything back."

She had no choice but to follow that rule. Her first orgasm rocked through her body, causing her to arch her back and press herself shamelessly against his mouth. Small, desperate cries came out of her throat. Like a string of pearls, one bead of pleasure after another rolled through her body.

Rob watched her in silent wonder. She clutched his hand fiercely as she was taken by a series of tremors. It was beautiful, like watching a woman turn into an undulating ocean wave. Her head rolled from side to side and her eyelashes fluttered, but she never let go of his hand.

She called his name and he dropped alongside her into the chair. Her flushed face cried out to be caressed, and when he did, she curled into him, trembling, murmuring sweet things that he couldn't quite hear. He had never wanted a woman more in his life. His body was rigid, throbbing. He could hardly manage breathing without pain, but she wasn't ready for him, and she might not be, he realized. This might be all she could handle.

"How's that for obeying rules?" she whispered, nuzzling her cheek against the back of his hand.

"You're way beyond rules," he said. "You're in a category all its own."

She lifted her lips to his throat and her wet little kitten kisses did nothing to help him relax. She was worming and squirming her way closer to him, and she finally managed to press her naked body along the entire length of his. Sounds of throaty contentment came out of her, but they turned to surprise as her cool soft flesh came into contact with his hot hard flesh.

It was all he could do not to groan in pain.

"You're very hard," she said under her breath.

The woman had a talent for pointing out the obvious. "I'm fine," he insisted, but she clearly didn't believe him. She pulled back and gazed down with great interest. His erection was prominent and pressing so hard against his fly that flesh was grazing metal.

He flinched as she reached for his zipper. "I don't think you should—"

"Someone has to," she said. "You could hurt yourself in there."

Rob's laughter was closer to a moan of despair. "Nobody's going to get me out of these pants until I stand up." He leveraged himself out of the chair with his arms and got to his feet. His hands were on his belt buckle, but not for long.

"Let me," Swan said, but she was still a little shaky, and it took her a while to work open the belt and unsnap the clasp at his waistline. Rob slipped his feet out of his loafers and kicked them to the side. With him standing and her sitting on the edge of the chair, there was no way for her to miss the profound effect she'd had on his body. No one could have missed it. Nor could they have missed the fact that she was naked and trembling with anticipation.

Carefully, she inched down his zipper and tugged at his slacks until they fell to his feet. He stepped out of them, a little embarrassed at how outrageously aroused he was. No way to hide his desire for this woman…or her power over him. She seemed slightly taken aback, too, although she'd certainly had plenty of prior experience with that part of him. Maybe it was because he was less than three inches from her beautiful face?

"Can I touch?" she asked, adding, "Rule number one?"

Touch? *God help him.* Rob's head fell back as she brought her hands up and captured his shaft between her palms. Her touch was like silk, like water sliding over stones. He wouldn't have thought it possible to get any harder, but he did, and she didn't even seem aware of his anguish. He had taken his own sweet time with her, and it was only fair that she get equal time, even if it forced him to have the mind control of a Ninja.

She spent the next few moments gently exploring him with her fingertips, but he was certain that his touch couldn't have given her a fraction of the pleasure—or pain—that she was giving him. It was sweetly torturous. When she seemed to have satisfied herself, she nuzzled him lightly with her cheek, her eyelashes fluttering.

He knew from experience that she was enjoying herself when her eyelashes fluttered. He didn't know that her tongue could flutter, too. She pressed her lips to the side of his shaft and lightly ran them up and down the hot and fiery length of him, breathing her hot breath on him more than kissing him. God, her mouth was heaven. Any minute now it was going to engulf him and deliver him from this bondage. Any minute!

Little purring sounds came from her throat and her tongue was like a kitten's—tiny, quick and pink as it darted over his engorged flesh. The fluttering sensations were the least of it, he realized. The real pleasure came from watching what she was doing to him. She was luminous and beautiful, and utterly absorbed in her task.

Finally she moved back and took him in her mouth, and as her warm lips rolled over him, he groaned in relief. His body's reaction was instantaneous. His gluts clenched like fists, and his thighs began to quiver. It felt as if his entire being was shaking. He buried his hands in her hair, guiding her gently. By now he was too large for her to take him completely, so he didn't thrust deeply. Instead he let her love him and pleasure him in her own way.

But he was swelling and tightening with each stroke.

He could feel it happening inside her mouth, and every muscle in his body clenched, trying to prevent it. Instead of slowing, she began to move faster, gliding up and down his shaft in a sweet little frenzy, and finally he couldn't take it anymore.

"You have to stop," he said. "I don't want to come like this. I want to be inside you."

Swan felt the pressure of his hands. She heard the grip in his voice, but some wild rhythm had taken her over and it wouldn't let go. She loved the radiating heat and the sheer size of him, but he clearly wanted her to stop. He held her face gently and withdrew himself with a tight groan. She swallowed thickly.

"I'm sorry," she said, still slightly dazed.

He gazed into her eyes, his hands caressing her face. "Rule number…four, I think. Never apologize for driving a man out of his mind with need. It's all good."

They fell back into the chair in a tangle of arms and legs and heated kisses. It seemed impossible for them to touch or to kiss or to be close enough to each other. His penis pressed into her thigh, riding its softness as he embraced her tightly. They both writhed with heat and desire as he moved up, rocking in the valley of her pelvis.

All Swan wanted in the entire world was for him to be inside her, and she tried to tell him, but his mouth covered hers, capturing her soft, whispering cries. He moved between her legs, and as his cock began to slide into her, spreading her walls, she pushed upward, taking as much of him as possible. He obviously knew exactly what she wanted, and she tightened with every one of his powerful thrusts. The tension built exquisitely until that moment when she felt herself opening like a cloverleaf at the first hint of light.

The orgasm that followed ripped a cry from somewhere deep within her. It was a sound she'd never heard before, full of the sweet anguish of surrender. Rob clasped her buttocks, holding her firmly until she finished. His hands squeezed her rhythmically as he kept going, and the frenzy of completion took him over, as well. He thrust deeply several times before he allowed his own shuddering release.

Rule number three…don't hold anything back.

Perhaps Swan even said it out loud as she clung to him afterward. She never wanted to let him go, but as their breathing quieted, she realized that he seemed as hesitant to pull out of her as she was for him to go. She noticed that he was still erect, too. Not quite as large as before, but firm and hard.

"Are you done?" she asked. She brushed her fingers along his cheek and saw his jaw flex. "Do you need more?"

His breath was hot against her face and breasts.

"No," he said. "I just don't want to be alone again."

Her eyes misted as she felt the deep sadness of what he'd admitted. He *was* alone. And this might be the first thing he'd said to her that had come straight from his heart. He'd just given her a glimpse of who he really was and why he kept himself so guarded. His heart had been broken, and now that he'd pieced it back together, he couldn't trust anyone with it again.

"You don't have to be alone," she said. "I'm here."

Rob brushed his lips against hers and then gently kissed her. His fingers traced small, tender lines along her cheeks and chin. Swan smiled up at him as she ran her fingers through his hair.

"I don't want to hurt you," he said. "I don't want to hurt you in any way."

"How would you hurt me?" she asked.

His voice was low and passionate, but he was clearly bemused by what he'd just said. "I don't know where that came from.'' He gathered her close, holding her. "But I couldn't handle it if any harm came to you. I'm not going to let that happen, Swan."

She settled into his arms with a sigh. A part of her wanted desperately to know what he'd meant, and where this was heading, but this wasn't the time to go into it. Tonight had been special and wonderful, and they both needed to bask in those feelings for a while. Whatever had to be said could wait until tomorrow.

But she knew he had been wrong about her in one way. She wasn't beyond rules or in a category by herself. She was a normal woman with all the normal doubts and fears, and she had just given everything she had and everything she was to this man. She had surrendered completely to the moment, but she wanted more than a moment with him. Much more.

12

Swan awoke to the tantalizing aroma of ham being grilled and coffee being brewed. Her stomach growled loudly, announcing what she already knew. She was starving. She was also alone. Rob was no longer next to her and she wondered when he'd slipped out of bed and gone to the kitchen. Last night, after making love in the chair, they'd gone down the hall to the master bedroom. The minute they'd climbed under the covers, they'd been at it again. That second session must have sedated her as effectively as knockout drops.

But a man who could cook? She rolled over and stretched luxuriously beneath the goose-down comforter. How perfect was that?

As she savored a feeling of deep contentment, she could almost hear her mother's voice telling her that nothing was perfect and she was tempting fate even thinking in those terms. That was the thing about negative thinking, Swan realized. It was seductive because it was safe. If you always assumed the worst, you could never be disappointed. But Swan didn't want to be closed up in that box anymore. She would take her chances, no matter how scary. And they were scary. Very.

Of course, she could always start by going down to breakfast naked.

She peeked under the comforter and scrutinized the body that she'd neglected so shamefully over the past couple of years. Rob hadn't seemed to mind the tummy pooch or her less-than-firm muscle tone, but last night they'd been making love by the light of a fireplace. Morning sun could be brutal. Braving it naked wouldn't be taking a chance. It would be positively reckless.

She threw off the bulky comforter and gathered up the top sheet, pulling it around her to use as a wrap. As she rolled to the side of the bed and sat up, she realized she was smiling. It felt as if she might have been smiling all night, and with every part of her body. Was this the glow she'd heard other women talk about?

She glanced at the bedside clock. Nearly nine-thirty? That was late for her. Normally she was up by seven at the latest. Years of habit prompted her to run through her mental "to do" list. The Seattle show wasn't scheduled until tomorrow afternoon, but it was a fourteen-hour drive, and they were leaving tonight. She and Rob would have today, at least. She'd left Gerard a message letting him know that everything was okay and they would see him in Seattle as planned. He'd agreed to handle the preliminaries for this last show, and there was little doubt that he could do it. He'd proven that time after time in the past few days.

She left the bed and headed for the bathroom to take a quick shower. The sheet fell to the floor as she adjusted the knobs and the water began to flow. While she waited for it to run hot, watching the steam begin to rise, she thought about last night, about the urgency of their love-making, and how it had opened Rob up. There really had been no rules to stop them, and neither one of them had held anything back...until the very end.

He'd said he would never hurt her—she only wished she could believe it. But he had touched her to her soul. He had opened her up, too, and it was going to be in-credibly difficult to protect herself from him in any way, maybe impossible. How could she, after what had happened between them? She hadn't been taken, she'd given herself, and yet it was ravishment of the most shattering kind. With the simple act of opening her legs, she had plunged to the depths and soared to the heights with him, and it had left her changed.

Opened. Naked. And needing more. She hadn't a clue about any of the practical things: Did they have a future? Were they even compatible? And there didn't seem much point in thinking about them now. She couldn't be sure that either of them was going to be alive from one day to the next. But she knew it would tear her apart to be without him. She would be bereft because he had given her such a precious gift—an entirely new dimension of herself.

Getting involved with Rob Gaines felt like a bigger risk than anything she'd ever contemplated. Bigger than the stalker who might threaten her life. Bigger than going to jail. Bigger than the precarious state of her business. She didn't even know if he wanted to get involved with her. As she stepped into the shower, she realized that was the question she had to ask. And she wasn't sure she could.

ROB HAD THE CABIN'S kitchen smelling like a truck stop in the early morning hours. In other words, good. He'd found some ham slices and a packet of hash browns in the freezer, and there was a loaf of raisin bread stashed in there, too. Some thawed steaks were sitting in the fridge that had probably been intended for last night's dinner. He left those in reserve in case either he or Swan was still hungry after breakfast.

What he needed now was caffeine. Jack had an old-fashioned percolator, and at the rate it was going, they'd have coffee any day now. Rob wasn't a morning person, but he'd been up since eight. Like a good ex-agent, his first thought had been of putting together a plan of action for the next show. His second had been of the woman lying next to him, which was probably why he was an *ex-*agent.

He'd found himself silently watching her sleep and wondering at the power she had to turn a simple flesh-and-blood man into something that resembled the tower leg of a suspension bridge. She wasn't your run-of-the-mill seductress. She actually looked childlike with her head resting peacefully on the pillow and her chin tilted toward him. Maybe it was the hand she'd curled into the softness of her breast that finally made him aware of the word he was looking for, the right word to describe her.

Angelic.

With her brow relaxed and her auburn hair splayed over the crisp white pillowcase, she appeared angelic. His own angel lying next to him, spent from their night of passion. If he'd wanted, he could have leaned over and kissed her mouth. That thought had echoed in his groin with the brightness of a highway flare, but he'd decided against disturbing her. She'd been through hell the past few days and she needed her rest.

That's what he'd been thinking as he'd watched her sleep.

Was he in trouble. Men didn't think about women in those terms unless they were emotionally involved. Deeply emotionally involved. Falling in love. Or already there. Flat on their silly, grinning faces.

No way, he told himself. It hadn't gone that far. He wouldn't have let it go that far without reining himself in. Nothing could sneak up on him that stealthily and do that much damage without him knowing about it. *No way*.

He set about flipping the hash browns when Swan walked in the room.

The angel was awake? And wearing a toga?

She'd wrapped a huge white sheet around herself that

made her look more like an angel than ever. He was definitely in trouble. His heart was going a mile a minute, and she looked a little unsure of herself, too.

"You've been busy," she said softly.

Once again, she was an astute observer of the obvious. He had every appliance in the kitchen hopping except the dishwasher. That would come later.

"Have a seat," he said, gesturing to the table, which had already been set with colorful earthenware plates and shiny stainless-steel flatware.

He flipped the sizzling ham, popped two pieces of raisin bread in the toaster and put a lid on the hash browns to keep them moist. She was still standing in the doorway when he looked around, and it occurred to him that she might need a little more encouragement after last night.

He abandoned his post at the stove and held out a hand to her. "I'm hungry," he said, "but I won't bite."

Swan was in his arms in about two seconds flat, clinging to him, laughing and telling him how hungry she was, too. "Starving," she exclaimed. "I could eat the skillet you're cooking that ham in!"

Rob laughed as if that was the cutest thing he'd ever heard.

It was worse than he'd thought. He had been sneaked upon and the damage was bad. How had that happened? He'd obviously needed one more rule last night. *No falling in love, genius!*

Moments later, he proudly set a plate in front of her that was so heaped with ham and potatoes, the steaming food was spilling over the side. He went back to get them both a slow-perked cup of coffee, and then he returned with his own plate and sat down kitty-corner from her.

Eating took all their concentration at first, and neither said much except to comment on how delicious the food was. Rob managed to clean his plate before she did and go to the stove for seconds, but he didn't beat her by much. She could eat, and even that struck him as adorable. An angel in a toga who eats like a horse.

Oh, somebody put me out of my misery.

It hadn't occurred to him that it might be her who dispatched him, but clearly he was destined to be wrong about that. By the time he'd cleared the table of their plates and refilled their coffees, Swan was looking rather serious. Even bathed in the golden rays that had begun to stream through the windows, she seemed suddenly focused and determined.

"Rob, about last night—"

Here it comes. This was where we talk about what it all means and where it's going.

She pursed her lips, as if reconsidering her words. Finally she leveled a slightly desperate look at him and blurted it out. "Are you afraid you're going to hurt me because of what happened to Paula Warren?"

The surprise must have shown on his face. They weren't the words he was expecting, but perhaps it was good that she'd said them. "I guess that could be it," he admitted. "I screwed up pretty badly with her. I couldn't handle it if I let that happen again."

"And that's why you're afraid to give another relationship a chance?"

She had been doing some thinking, hadn't she? Women were prone to that, analyzing everything up and down, inside and out, which was why they were always several steps ahead of any guy dumb enough to try to keep pace.

"It wasn't just Paula," he said, "although that was bad enough."

He forced himself to go on. Swan really did need to know this stuff. She needed to know who he was, and then maybe she wouldn't be so hot to talk about relationships. "Once the Bureau decided Paula wasn't witness material, they cut her loose and yanked me off the case. They said I was too close to her, and they ordered me to stay away from her. Maybe I could have accepted that if they'd provided her with protection, but they didn't. We'd subpoenaed her and forced her to testify. We had a responsibility to keep her safe.''

''But you weren't able to?'' Swan asked. ''And she died?''

Rob hated how that sounded, but it was true. ''Three days after they pulled me off the job, she was found dead of a gunshot wound to the head. It was ruled a suicide.'' The word still left a foul taste in his mouth. ''You could argue that the Bureau failed her, but I didn't agree with what they were doing, and I went along with it anyway. Was my job more important than her life? I don't think so.''

He went quiet, studying his coffee cup, and Swan posed another question. ''*Was* it suicide?''

''Probably not. There were discrepancies in the forensics reports, and even the gunpowder residue indicated that she might have been murdered. But she left a note, blaming it all on me, actually.''

A note that Art Long had forced her to write, he thought with a bitterness that still ran so deep it surprised him. And then the bastard killed her. Rob couldn't prove it, but that's what he believed.

Swan was standing now, apologizing and pulling that silly toga around her. ''I wish I didn't have to ask these things,'' she said. ''I know it's hard for you.''

And she wasn't done. He knew that.

''You said that Paula was part of what soured you on relationships. Was the other part your fiancée? I'm not being nosy, Rob. I need to understand what I'm—''

What I'm getting into? Was that what she'd started to say? Whether she was getting into anything or not, she had a right to know what she was dealing with. He wanted her to know. Maybe she'd have the sense to back away when she found out that it wasn't just Paula, although that was the most recent disaster. He had quite an impressive history of letting women down.

"It wasn't my fiancée," he told her. "She'd already decided she didn't like the idea of being an agent's wife before the Paula Warren mess. She actually stuck around until things were resolved, and I owe her for that. The other disaster was my mother. She died of alcohol poisoning when I was a teenager."

"And you feel as if you failed her in some way?"

He shook his head. "You can't force people to stop abusing. I know that now, but I didn't know it then. My little sister grew up watching her mother self-destruct, and I suppose I was trying to shield her and create some kind of a normal family. Our father had walked out years before because of the drinking, which left me the man of the house. If anyone was going to do anything, it had to be me."

He was still sitting at the table, and the burning sun that hit his back told him it was going to be a scorcher today. Still, he felt cold in the small room. Even Swan had clasped her arms.

"But you said your little sister went into the military, that she was all right."

"She is, thank God."

"Then you must have done a pretty good job with her. You raised her, right?"

He nodded, fully aware of where she was heading. She was trying to get him to see that he had done everything he could for two people who had chosen their own fate when they started abusing. It was even possible he'd been drawn to Paula because of his failed need to save his mother. And maybe he already knew all of this on some level, but it hadn't stopped him from being gun-shy with women…except with this one.

As he studied the coffee cup he held in both hands, he realized the extent to which Swan McKenna had touched him. And not only with her lips and fingertips. Somehow she'd slipped under the electrified fence he'd built around his heart and stolen her way inside. It must have been a pretty dark journey, he imagined. He rarely had the courage to brave that place himself. But she had. And once there, she could easily have taken advantage of his male weaknesses and flaws. But instead she'd begun mending his wounds. She was doing that now by forcing him to talk.

He looked up at her, not at all sure what to say. He wasn't good at emotional tugs-of-war, especially when he was the rope.

A series of soft beeps saved him from the awkward moment. He dug in his pants' pocket and pulled out his cell phone. The message light was blinking and the digital display told him the message had come in last night. Rob hadn't checked his cell in a while. He'd had other things on his mind.

He typed in his pass code and held the phone to his ear. "It's from Joe," he told Swan as he listened to his ex-partner's hushed voice.

By the time he'd clicked off, Swan was right next to him, waiting anxiously. "What did he say?"

"He said Erksine asked for your show schedule, and Joe gave him an old itinerary, one that says the last show will be in Portland. Erskine thinks that's where we're going next. Joe's given us some time."

"That sounds like good news," she said.

"It is, but I'm a little concerned that Joe would stick his neck out like that. I've been trying not to involve him. On the other hand, I'm not sure we could pull this off without him.'' Lost in thought, he got up to refill his coffee cup and brought the pot back to the table.

''We're going to need a plan,'' Swan said, holding out her cup for a warm-up.

''A plan would be good.''

''Have you got anything in mind?''

Plenty, actually. The Seattle show would be Rob's last opportunity to close this case, nail Art Long and clear Swan's name. Despite Joe's help in covering their tracks, there was always the possibility the Bureau would do their own intelligence and have agents at the show, waiting for them. It could get tricky. He and Swan would have to handle this alone, with no backup except Gerard. At the same time, they'd have to avoid apprehension themselves.

How did he tell her all that without scaring her? If he owed her anything at all, he realized, it was to stay focused on this case and to do whatever was necessary to get her safely through the next twenty-four hours. That much he could promise her, but that was all.

''We'll talk about it over coffee,'' he said. ''Let's go out on the deck.'' Determined to lighten the mood, he added, ''And when we're finished strategizing, I have something to show you.''

''What's that?''

He'd already decided not to give her any clues, especially since this was something he had never imagined himself showing to anyone. ''Just a little surprise. You'll like it.''

He could see by her knitted brow that she was harboring some suspicions about this surprise, and it felt good to laugh. ''Sorry to disappoint you,'' he said, ''but it has nothing to do with handcuffs or cutting off your underwear.''

She pretended to be greatly deflated. ''What a shame.''

"WELL? WHAT DO YOU THINK?" Rob gestured toward the gaping hole in the solid rock cliff, his gaze fixed on Swan.

It was pure pleasure watching her reaction to his surprise. She'd stopped, staring in silent awe the moment she'd seen the natural opening to the sea cave. He'd discovered the place years ago while helping Jack build the cabin, and this afternoon he and Swan had picked their way down some fifty feet of sheer cliff on a stone path etched out of solid granite. When they'd hit the sandy beach, their walk to the cave had taken another five minutes, and they were still a little breathless.

"It's magnificent," she said, moving closer for a look.

The mouth of the cave led to a grottolike hideaway that was a place of many natural wonders. Rob had been captivated the moment he'd laid eyes on it.

"How did you happen to find it?" she asked.

"It was back in the days when I was suspended from the Bureau and I came out here to help Jack build the cabin—and to get away. I was taking long walks on the beach in those days, searching for answers, probably. I was so preoccupied that I passed by the cave several times without noticing it, but then one day I turned my head and there it was."

There were some jagged rocks hidden in the sand drifts and he took her hand to lead her inside. "When I showed this place to Jack, he named it Big Hole in the Rock, and then, damned if he didn't give it to me. Wrote it right into the deed that this cave—Big Hitter, he called it because of the acronym Big H-I-T-R—belonged to me."

Big Hitter was a cavernous opening in an outstretched finger of the cliffs. Eons of water erosion had carved an entrance the size of a large truck on one side and a nearly perfectly matched opening on the other. In between lay fifty yards of pristine sand, illuminated, in places, by brilliant shafts of sunshine that poured in through small odd-shaped openings in the high, vaulted ceiling.

"It really is magnificent," Swan said.

"You haven't seen anything yet," Rob told her. As they entered the cathedral-like enclosure, they were immediately bathed in cool, tangy air. The outside temperature was over eighty degrees, but in here it was closer to sixty-five. A low, soft murmur seemed to fill the open space—the muffled sound of the waves crashing outside, deadened by thick stone walls.

Swan pulled up short, yanking his hand back with her. "Do you hear that? It sounds like water running."

Rob picked up the excitement in her voice and in her sparkling eyes. She was like a kid on a treasure hunt. "Ah, that's the *real* surprise!"

He tugged her hand and she followed, exclaiming at the lush vines and fernlike plants that grew out of niches in the rock walls and ceiling. Lacy green moss covered the huge boulders that jutted from the sandy floor, and a blue mist hung in the air, feeding the rampant foliage.

Other than Jack, Rob had not shown this place to anyone. He'd always thought of it as his own personal health spa, but it felt good sharing it with Swan. He could almost go as far as to say it felt right. At any rate, he was pleased that she appreciated it, too.

"This way," he said, indicating a gleaming stone wall just ahead of them that acted like a huge ornamental screen, hiding what lay beyond. Rob took her around the wall and into a serene grotto at the very back of the cave. A pool of glistening water lay before them, fed by a small waterfall. Bright, hot sunlight shot down from an opening, landing squarely on the surface of the pool. Rob tugged on her hand again and they walked to the edge.

"Take off your clothes," he said.

Swan's eyes widened. "What?"

"Strip. Quick! We don't have much time."

Rob didn't wait for her. He had a feeling she might follow his lead. He'd put on fresh jeans and a black T-shirt before they'd left the cabin. He pulled the T-shirt over his head and tossed it aside. Next he shimmied out of the jeans and left them on the sandy bank. When he glanced over at Swan, he found her standing there, watching him as if he'd gone crazy.

"Come on," he said as he waded into the water. "You're going to miss it."

"Miss what?" She held her waist and shivered. "Isn't that cold?"

"No, it's like bathwater. There's something about the concentration of sunlight that heats it up fast. Right now it's warmer than the air, but that won't last forever. If you want to experience this, get with it, girl."

Swan's skeptical smile said she wasn't sure this wasn't some kind of trick. "All right," she conceded, "but turn around."

"I've seen your body, Swan. I've seen every last inch of it."

She blushed. He loved it when she blushed. Her whole face lit up.

"Yeah, well, just turn around anyway," she said.

Rob did as he was told. He could hear the soft ruffle of material as her clothing came off, and his imagination went into overdrive, reminding him exactly how she'd looked and felt, inside and out. It was almost too much detail to handle, particularly for a man who *wasn't* emotionally involved. Lucky he was up to his chest in water, or she'd have thought the pond was inhabited by a water snake.

When the pool's surface began to ripple around him, he knew she'd entered. "Can I turn around?"

"Yes," she said, flashing a shy smile at him over the surface of the water.

That same water just covered her pink nipples, which were tightly budded. He'd wondered if she would find it cold, but as it turned out, he didn't have to ask. She must have seen him noticing.

"The water is invigorating," she told him in a droll tone. As she moved toward him, rippling the surface, he was reminded of the graceful creature she was named for, and nothing could have been more right. It was as if she belonged here, had always belonged here. Loving this woman would be the easiest thing in the world, he thought. Living with her might be a challenge, given his track record, but loving her would be a snap.

"You're just one surprise after another," Swan said. "I would never have guessed you to be the secret-hideaway type."

"Agents don't have secret hideaways?"

"Lovers have secret—"

That was all she got out when the walls around them began to rumble. In the distance there was a low roar, like an oncoming train.

"What's that?" she asked, looking around. "What's happening?"

There wasn't time for Rob to explain. "Let's go," he called to her over the noise. "It's time to get out!"

He was halfway out of the pool before he realized she hadn't moved. She seemed mesmerized by all the rumbling and shaking. But she had no idea what was causing it, and how dangerous it was. He waded back in and swept her into his arms, carrying her up the bank of the lagoon just moments before the massive blast of water hit.

Breathing hard, they stood by the stone wall and watched the tiny waterfall above the pond become a roaring Niagara Falls. A wall of river water poured over the huge granite shelf.

"That's the other reason Jack called this place the Big Hitter," he told her. "The waterfall is fed by a river that spills into a natural reservoir, and when that reservoir overflows, this is what happens. It can be pretty dramatic."

"Could we have drown?" she asked, looking at him.

"No," he said emphatically, "I would never have let you drown."

They were both still naked and dripping wet. Maybe it was the brush with death, but something happened as they stood there looking at each other. It was as sharp and startling as a collision, and the impact brought them together with a wild clash of feeling.

A mist rose from the waterfall, enveloping them as Rob cupped Swan's face in his hands and brought his lips down to hers. It wasn't a feverishly hot kiss, like so many had been the night before. This one was almost desperate. Rob's heart began to pound as he felt her hands slip around his neck. She was kissing him back. Accepting him.

"I need to make love to you," he said.

Swan nodded, fighting to get the words out. "I need that, too." A frenzy to connect with him had overtaken her, and her arms tightened around his neck as he lifted her into the air. She wrapped her legs around his waist and groaned with the wildness of her need to have him inside her. It was a primitive urge. A beautiful, wild call to the senses.

He turned her to the wall and pinned her there, his hands gripping her waist as he guided her to the head of his shaft. Swan was a sweet, aching void, and every cell of her attention was riveted by the hard flesh that pressed into her. There was a moment of pressure, of demand and acceptance, and he slid into her as if she had been made expressly to sheathe him and him alone.

Swan moaned softly into his ear. She clung to him, rocking her hips back and forth with his thrusts. The ease with which they joined and moved together enthralled her. It was as natural, and yet as magical, as the cave.

He clasped her buttocks to thrust deeper. "Hold me tight," he said as he rocked and bucked.

Swan's nails dug into his shoulders and she felt a jolt of deep, shuddering pleasure. It was followed by another and another. Jolts of such intensity that she was quickly spent and nothing could register on her senses except the rhythmic quivering of her muscles and the thrumming of her nerves. She fell against his chest, letting herself be tossed and buffeted by the sudden savagery of his release. And when a hot, streaming sensation flooded the barrier of her womb, she knew that it was him.

Swan rested her head on his shoulder for a moment as she tried to catch her breath. His chest was rising and falling, too. It seemed neither of them could stop trembling. Finally her legs slid down his legs and she found her footing.

"Are you all right?" he asked, holding her close and trying to warm her.

She told him she was, but the trembling inside her had overtaken her whole body and suddenly she was chilled and frightened. She'd fallen in love with him, but she had no idea what he wanted. At breakfast it had seemed as if he was intent on scaring her off, but then he'd made love to her again, like this, so fiercely that it felt as if he could turn her inside out with a touch, a kiss.

But he had never answered her question, she realized. Was he capable of a relationship? Did he even want one? A powerful sexual attraction just wasn't enough for her. But she couldn't deny that anything else with this man felt too dangerous.

13

ROB GLANCED at the digital clock imbedded in the dashboard of Swan's SUV. Green, luminous numbers told him it was a quarter after four in the morning. Swan was sleeping next to him, the back of her seat as far down as it would go. Occasionally she would shift or sigh, and he could tell she wasn't resting comfortably. That didn't surprise him with the ordeal they were facing. And the odds were it would get worse before it got better. *If* it got better.

But he had a hunch that wasn't what was bothering her. She'd been quiet and withdrawn since their interlude in the cave, and when he'd tried to get her to talk about it, she'd said she didn't want to, not until all this was over. She, who wanted to talk about everything, had suddenly gone mute on him.

Well, it would all be over soon. Twelve hours from now the tour would be history and so would the sting. Whether they pulled it off or not, the Bureau would have caught up with them by then. And then what?

Rob's plan was simple, but it was simplicity based on desperation. He was betting that Long's accomplice felt the same urgency he did. This was the last show and the last chance to recover the money. The accomplice had managed to move millions of dollars nearly undetected and without revealing his or her identity. Someone that resourceful wouldn't give up easily.

It was another hunch, but this one had the back of Rob's neck tingling the way it did when he was onto something significant. The rats were crawling out of the sewer. He could feel it. And if he was wrong, it was all over, too. Hiding Swan was not an option. Sooner or later, the Bureau would catch up to them and there would be a whole host of charges to face, including unlawful flight to avoid prosecution.

He could not let that happen.

The road ahead of him was as dark as a train tunnel. He flicked the lights to bright and stared hard at the bleak, mind-numbing view. It wasn't himself he was worried about. He'd made his own decisions, including the one to quit the Bureau. Swan, however, had never had a choice in this mess. It had been dumped in her lap by Long and compounded by Erskine, but it was Rob himself who'd come up with the sting operation and coerced her into participating. He'd gotten her into this. He had to get her out.

Swan moaned and rolled to her side, facing him. Listlessly she reached out as if to touch him and murmured his name. Rob nearly went off the road. Her eyes were still closed and those fluttery eyelashes told him she was dreaming. All day she'd been pulling away from him at the speed of light, and he figured it was pretty much what he deserved. After all, he had cut a vein and told her everything. Couldn't have been very pretty.

He'd also made love to her twice, and it had gotten pretty wild. He'd known better both times, especially the second, but the forces of nature in that cave had seemed to compel them together. He hadn't been able to fight it any more than she had. She was fighting it now, though. And winning. Of course, she was right. He wouldn't have wished himself on any woman, much less her. He actually *cared* about her.

A freeway sign told him they were about three hours out of Portland. They were making good time. Better than halfway there, he thought. When he was closer to Seattle, he'd find a motel on the outskirts of the city where he and Swan could shower, change and maybe catch a short nap. Part of his plan was to dress like a store security guard to mix more easily with the crowd and to help avoid detection. A nice and simple plan. Desperately simple.

A semi passed him on the left. The wind from the big rig rocked the SUV and the trailer Rob was pulling, making him realize how fast he was going. Rob eased his foot off the accelerator a little and settled back for the rest of the journey. It would all be over soon.

"WE CAN TALK back here," Gerard whispered as he herded Rob and Swan into a narrow space between several racks of Brief Encounters clothing. Once they were safely out of sight, Gerard gave Swan's hand a squeeze. "As far as the show goes," he assured her, "everything is taken care of."

"I knew it would be," Swan said. It was perhaps the *only* thing she knew with any certainty. Emotion welled unexpectedly. It was so good to see Gerard, she could have cried. And surrounded by her designs it almost felt as if life had returned to normal again. This was her tour, her first big break. Of course, that was an illusion, but she couldn't think about that. Today of all days she had to hold it together. She couldn't cry. She couldn't freak out in any way.

She took a deep breath and asked Gerard about the models.

"Rehearsed *and* paid for." He slipped a credit card from his shirt pocket. "Don't leave home without it."

"You're a gem, Gerard. I'll make sure you get it back." She glanced over at Rob, whose head was clearly elsewhere. He'd already cased the store and checked out the audience for the show. Now he was peering through a space in the hanging garments, scrutinizing the crew and the models that Gerard had recruited.

He'd found no agents lurking around, which was good news, but he also hadn't spotted anything suspicious, which, ironically, was bad.

Rob turned back to them and looked at his watch. "The show starts in a few minutes. Let's go over everything one more time, all right? Gerard, you're the backstage security. Consider anyone you don't recognize suspicious, whether male or female, but don't try and apprehend them. Signal me with this."

Rob had rigged a remote security device from materials he'd found in Jack's cabin, and it could be triggered by the panic buttons he'd made for both Gerard and Swan. The device actually vibrated rather than beeped or rang, so no one but Rob would hear it.

"The one thing we don't want is to give ourselves away prematurely," he warned them. "We need to catch the accomplice in the act of stealing the money. Otherwise, we have no grounds for arrest."

Rob's gaze shifted to Swan. "For you, it's business as usual except that you'll keep the beeper in your hand at all times, and if something doesn't look right, hit the panic button to alert me. There are a couple of hundred witnesses out there, so you should be safe enough on stage. The attempt is most likely to happen right after the show, and we want to give the accomplice some time. But if you haven't been approached in say, thirty minutes, we go to Plan B."

Plan B required Swan to leave the organizer in plain sight while Rob kept it under surveillance to see who might pick it up. Of course, anyone might be tempted to walk away with an expensive leather organizer, and there was always the chance some Good Samaritan would pick it up with the goal of returning it to its owner. Swan considered Plan B flawed, and hoped she was approached directly, although it seemed crazy to be wishing someone would mug her.

"Any questions?" Rob asked them both.

Swan had a few questions, but she didn't dare voice them. *Could you hold me for a moment? Can you make all of this go away? Can you kiss me—for perhaps the last time?*

The lump in her throat had to be visible. For a split second, emotion threatened to overwhelm her again, but she quelled it and answered his question with a shake of her head. *No, sir, no questions, sir.* Lord, how she wished he wasn't so perfectly in control and agentlike today. They'd hardly spoken since they left the cabin except to discuss the plans for today, but maybe that was for the best. It had stopped her from dwelling on what was going on between them. He seemed to have no trouble putting his mind on other things.

His gaze, which never rested in one place for more than a few seconds, reminded her of hammered steel. She had once compared the color of his eyes to a winter morning, and it was more apt than ever today, considering the frost. He was somewhere else, somewhere cold and dangerous. Such determination and concentration should have comforted her—she couldn't have asked for a better bodyguard—yet she felt no comfort. Only dread.

"I need to get out front," Rob said. "Are we okay back here?"

Swan managed a nod without actually looking at him. She just wanted him to go so that she could regain her composure. It didn't seem possible that she'd let herself get closer to him than she'd been to anyone else in her life, and now she was being frozen out of his existence.

Once he'd disappeared from view, she began to fuss with her clothing to calm her nerves and distract herself.

She'd chosen a bright fuchsia wraparound dress and ac-
cessorized it with sexy black sandals with low heels. Better for running, Rob had pointed out when she'd originally
put on stilettos. She'd also worn her hair up, thinking she
needed the lift, but of course the whole look seemed
wrong now.

When she glanced up, Gerard was staring at her with
a worried expression. "You look awful, Ducks," he said.
"I mean you look beautiful, but you look *awful*. Are you
sure you're up to this?"

"Of course," she assured him in a voice as heavy as
her heart. "Aren't I always up to it?"

He flashed a doleful look in the direction Rob had gone.
"It's that man-beast, isn't it? I told you he'd break your
heart."

"I wish it were that simple, Gerard. Come on," she
said, determined to ward off any further sympathizing on
his part. "Let's see what you've done with the models."

The men were all costumed, lined up near the stage
curtain, and ready to go. Swan stopped by to greet each
one and wish him well, and when her intro music started,
she realized that their nervousness had actually helped
her. She'd encouraged them with pep talks, and some of
it must have worn off because by the time Gerard tapped
his watch and gave her a gentle push through the curtain,
she was ready to go—or as ready as she would ever be
on a day like this.

Bring it on, muggers, she thought. *Do your worst!*

ROB HAD WORKED A LOT of cases and put in a lot of
surveillance duty, but never had he been as stone-cold
focused as he was at this moment. Swan had taken the
podium nearly thirty minutes ago, and the show was well
on its way, but she'd stumbled getting started, and his
heart had stumbled, too, watching her. He'd thought she

was going to break down, and it had been all he could do not to kidnap her off that stage and get her the hell out of this place.

Stupid heroics, of course. There was only one way he could help her, and he was doing that. He felt almost telepathically connected to her right now. It was a vibe so strong he could almost hear the heartbeat in her voice. If a threat existed in this room, he would know it before anyone got near her.

He checked the vibrator in the breast pocket of his shirt. The navy-blue, security-guard gear had been a good idea, too. It had allowed him to walk the perimeter of the room and scan the crowd repeatedly. So far he hadn't seen anything that aroused his suspicions, but he hadn't expected to. The first attempt had been too obvious. This time the attacker would try to blend in, and what better way than to be another laughing, cheering woman in the crowd? It might just be the accomplice herself.

As Swan began the last series of skits, he took another walk around the perimeter. If he timed it right, he could make the circuit and be back by the stage steps as she finished. As he walked, the crowd jumped to their feet, applauding something that had happened on stage, and Rob stopped to look around. He saw nothing unusual, but the hairs at the back of his neck had begun to stand on end.

He visually scanned all the exits and confirmed that they were clear. No one had just entered or left, but that didn't stop the tingling sensation. And the message it conveyed was clear. Whoever was after her was here. In this room.

SWAN HAD THE CROWD with her now, and she was grateful for that. When she'd taken the podium, she'd frozen up briefly. With the spotlight on her, as well as every eye in the audience, she'd felt like the center of a bull's-eye. But the show had progressed with no major blunders, and about halfway through, she'd realized one of the reasons. She was getting good at winging it. Since meeting Rob Gaines in her bathroom that night, her life had been one improvisational performance after another. She'd had plenty of practice.

From the corner of her eye, she saw Rob surveying the audience with an intensity that could be felt all the way to the podium. He hadn't given her any kind of signal, but she had the feeling he'd picked up on something—or someone. She couldn't let herself think about that now, however. She had to get through the rest of the show. Still, almost reflexively, she ran her thumb over the red button on the remote he'd given her, preparing herself to use it.

As the last model left the stage, Swan turned to the audience. They were clapping and cheering, but their applause sounded distant. Even the popping flashbulbs weren't registering on her nervous system. All the stress and excitement had been too much, she realized. She'd gone numb inside. She could feel nothing but the burning lump in her throat that had formed before the show.

Rob had come back around and was now standing about ten feet from the steps that would take her down to floor level. His face betrayed nothing of what he felt inside, but she wondered if he was as strangely detached as she was. Swan thanked the audience one last time, picked up the dreaded organizer and made her way down into a gathering of press people and well-wishers.

There were the usual questions. Where did she get her inspiration for the line? Who were her fashion influences? How did she start the company? What was next? She answered as many as possible, but she was only going through the motions. Some defense mechanism within her had been unleashed cutting her off from her feelings. She was on the brink of losing everything that meant anything to her—her business, her freedom, possibly even her life…and him. She met Rob's steely gaze in the milling crowd. It was too much to take in and her nervous system had shut down to protect her.

As the crowd around her thinned, Rob finally stepped over to her. "Did you lose something, Ms. McKenna? Security sent me over."

"Only my mind," she said under her breath.

He took her by the arm and led her out of earshot. "Pretend you're reporting a lost cell phone," he said. "If anyone is watching, they'll think that's what we're talking about."

Swan went into a discourse about losing her cell and how she couldn't do business without it. He took out a pad of paper and pretended to be taking notes. It was a good enough ruse to keep people away, and it gave her a chance to ask him what was going on.

"I wanted to touch base," he said. His gaze softened as he studied her. "How're you holding up?"

"I'm all right." But the defenses that had protected her for the past hour or so began to crumble. She was too close to him, and when she saw the depth of his concern, her heart twisted. "Rob, is this going to work?"

He reached out as if to touch her but caught himself.

The burning lump in Swan's throat wouldn't let her speak. She couldn't even swallow, but as he pulled his hand back, she realized something. She *needed* Rob Gaines. She needed him in her life, in her heart and in her arms.

"Rob—"

"It's all right," he said. "We'll get through this."

There was a catch of passion in his voice, and it actually thrilled her. Did he know what was going on in her head right now? In her heart? Did he know how crazy she was to be thinking of him this way when their very lives could be at stake?

"We're changing the strategy," he said. "I want to go to Plan B now."

"Why? We haven't given this enough time. Let me circulate a little more, talk to the crowd, maybe go off by myself. I have the panic button."

"You're not going off by yourself."

Swan could tell by the gravity in his tone that something was up. Maybe he'd decided it was too risky for her to be involved, but she didn't agree. They weren't going to catch their thief without some risk.

"What's going on?" she said. "I can tell something's wrong."

"It's just a hunch, but it's a strong one. I think our mark may be on the premises."

"All the more reason for me to hang on to the organizer." She held the leather notebook to her chest and felt a twinge of pressure down below. The sensation surprised her. She hadn't had to make any emergency trips to the loo in days. "You're not going to like this," she said.

He frowned as if he'd read her mind. "Don't tell me you have to pee."

She gave him a helpless look that said, *what can I do?*

Rob knew better than to ask her to hold it. That would be like asking the sun not to rise. He glanced around in search of a new plan. "Okay, there's a ladies' room in the hallway by the back exit door," he told her. "You head over that way, but take your time. Stop and talk here and there. I'll be around when you get there. And before you go in, open the door and take a good look inside. If it's empty, go in, but don't take more than five minutes to get your business done, or I'm coming in after you."

Rob gave her a nod and went on his way, as if their

discussion was over. Gradually he made his way to a vantage point that would give him a clear view of the ladies'
room. Meanwhile, Swan did exactly as she'd been instructed, chatting with customers who were buying her
garments, and at one point stopping a clerk, apparently to
ask directions to the ladies' room. When she reached the
room, she opened the door and then bent down suddenly,
adjusting one of her sandals.

Rob hoped she'd used that move to take a look at the
stalls and scan for feet. When she disappeared inside, he
glanced at his watch. *Good girl,* he thought.

Rob turned his attention to the store customers. They
were ninety percent women, with a few reluctant males
who appeared to be significant others. What single guys
there were looked as though they might be friends of Gerard's, which was why Rob almost immediately spotted
the heavyset man with the gray fedora, who was coming
out of the men's room. He was wearing a suit, but it
wasn't much of a disguise. Rob would have recognized
his thin-lipped sneer anywhere.

This was the thug who'd attacked Swan, sans beard and
black leather.

Three things occurred to Rob in the span of a split
second: the man was on the other side of the store, and
he was looking straight at Rob. From the expression on
his face, he'd recognized Rob, too. More important, he'd
just glanced at the front door as if he was about to make
a run for it.

Rob took off like a shot, nearly bowling an elderly lady
over in his wake.

He wasn't going to lose this bastard a third time.

THERE WERE THREE STALLS in the rest room. One had an
Out Of Order sign taped to the door, and the other two
appeared to be empty. Swan hadn't seen any feet when

she'd bent down, and there was no one else in the small room, so she really was alone. The urgency she'd experienced was mysteriously gone now, which made her wonder at the mind-numbing absurdity of it all. If her condition had actually been cured, that would be the first good news she'd had in days.

She stopped at one of the sinks and peered at herself in the mirror. It wasn't fear she saw in her face, it was some mix of horror and resignation that must have been building inside her for days. What frightened her was how beaten down she looked. Her mouth drooped with fatigue and her brows were tightly knotted with tension, even dread.

She set the organizer on the countertop, dropped the remote Rob had given her into the pocket of her dress and turned on the faucet. Her hand hadn't been steady in so long she could hardly remember what steadiness felt like. Maybe some cold water would help.

Before Swan could get the towel she'd dampened to her face, an elderly woman burst into the room and glanced around hurriedly, as if checking the place out. Swan picked up the organizer, as if to move it out of the way. The woman reached in her shopping bag, probably for a makeup case or a pack of tissues. She sensed the woman's urgency, but was stunned when she saw the gun in her hand.

The black nine millimeter handgun looked terrifyingly real—and so did the crazy glint in the woman's eyes as she turned the weapon on Swan. Her voice was little more than a grainy whisper, but Swan heard the threat distinctly.

"Don't make a sound or I'll kill you," the woman said. "I swear to *God* I'll kill you."

Swan froze where she was. Her hand squeezed shut reflexively, but the panic button was gone. She'd dropped it into the pocket of her dress, and she didn't dare try to get it now. But Rob must be outside the door. He must have seen this woman come in and within minutes he would realize Swan was in trouble.

Swan told herself to be calm. No one was going to shoot anyone. The woman's face had contorted into a terrifying grimace. She looked insane, but it could be fear. If Swan could stall, even for a few moments, Rob would figure this out. But how did she do that? How did she buy herself enough time?

ROB WAS CLOSING the distance between himself and his prey quickly. Surprisingly quickly. The small-frame .38 caliber revolver he'd borrowed from Jack's private arsenal was strapped to his right calf in an ankle holster. No way to get to it without stopping, and Rob wasn't about to do that, even though the guy wasn't nearly as fast as he looked as if he should be. Anyway, the last thing he needed was to cause a panic in the store by brandishing a pistol in clear view.

The biker was just going to make it to the front entrance before Rob could get to him. But then the man suddenly stopped and doubled back. Rob came to a near halt and threw a quick glance at the doors. Had some uniformed cops entered? A security guard perhaps?

There was no one there. Not even a customer.

Rob quickly found his suspect again. The man was hidden behind a circular rack of clothing, but he'd just peeked out at Rob. What the hell was going on? Within seconds, Rob would be close enough to pull a gun on this guy, but again something stopped him.

What was wrong with this picture? Rob's mind flicked back to the moment he'd first seen the biker, and he remembered what else had happened in that split second. He'd nearly flattened an old lady. This was the third of

Swan's shows that he'd staked out and he'd seen lots of women, but there hadn't been any little old ladies with stooped backs and big shopping bags.

And now this biker punk was playing cat and mouse with him.

It was a setup. The biker was a decoy, and Rob had fallen for it hook, line and sinker. Rob cursed under his breath and slid to a stop on the waxed linoleum floor. Without giving the thug another thought, he whirled around and raced back to the rest room.

SWAN KNEW SEVERAL THINGS at once. The woman holding her at gunpoint was disguised to look like an older person, and Swan had never seen her before. The blunt, fleshy facial features brought no sense of recognition, and yet who could she be but Art's coconspirator at the bank? Rob had been right. The accomplice wasn't male.

"Give me the organizer," the woman said. Her voice was low, but Swan detected a strong undercurrent of fear and desperation. She was on the edge, and edgy people could kill.

Swan's trembling was gone, replaced by a burst of adrenaline. The attempt they'd planned for was actually happening. The woman knew about the organizer, and she was making her move. She'd come after the check, but somehow she had to be apprehended before she got away. Swan couldn't let her leave this bathroom!

God, where was Rob?

Swan had the organizer curled into the crook of her right arm. She reminded herself that the accomplice didn't know Art was in custody. She probably thought he'd double-crossed her and skipped. Maybe Swan could stall for time, even create a bond with the woman.

"Art Long put you up to this, right?" Swan stepped toward her. "He's been using you. He used me, too."

"I don't care who the bastard's been using. I want the organizer. Now!"

The woman raised the gun, and Swan heard the click of something metallic. It was the most terrifying sound she'd ever heard—the hammer of a pistol being pulled back and locked into place.

Rob, where are you?

"Wait," Swan said. "I'll give you the org—"

The rest room door swung open viciously, and the metal handle crashed into the tiled wall behind, breaking out a large chunk of it. As the tile hit the floor and shattered, the woman screamed and made a dash for Swan. She dragged Swan in front of her and pressed the gun to the back of Swan's head.

At the same instant Rob burst into the rest room, his weapon trained on the two women.

"FBI. Freeze! Drop the weapon and step away from her." His voice was harsh and commanding, but there was little he could do. It was a standoff.

"Get out!" the woman warned. "Get out or I'll shoot!"

Rob's gaze flicked down to Swan's right arm and Swan knew what he wanted. It was terribly dangerous, but she had to trust him. For days now they'd communicated this way, a glance here, a nod there, each with its own meaning. They could have created their own silent language.

Swan threw the organizer to him, and Rob caught it in his free hand. "This is what you want," he told the accomplice. "Let her go and I'll give it to you. Hurt her and I'll shoot you where you stand."

Swan could feel the woman behind her trembling. This wasn't a career criminal. She was frightened, trapped, and way out of her league. That could work in Swan's favor or it could be the worst thing imaginable. Anything might happen.

Finally the woman spoke. "Show me the check."

"Fair enough," Rob said. "But first point that gun barrel somewhere other than her head. You're making me nervous."

Swan felt the cold barrel drop to her shoulder blade. Now if it went off accidentally, it would only sever her spinal cord and paralyze her, not kill her. She guessed that was the lesser of evils. Her sense of proportion was seriously off, to say the least.

Rob fished out his penknife and cut open the back of the organizer. He pulled out the check and held it up. "See it? Let her go and I'll give it to you."

At that moment, a man's voice rang from the last stall.

"Actually, why don't you give it to me?" Joe Harris opened the door and stepped out, a gun in his hand. It was aimed directly at Rob.

Swan wasn't sure who was more surprised—her, Rob or the woman behind her. The accomplice spoke up. "Who the hell are you?" she asked.

"Joe Harris," he said, glancing at the woman. "Who the hell are *you*?"

"Joe?" It was all Rob seemed to be able to say. The confusion on his face was evident. "What are you doing here?"

"Waiting for Swan to make a bathroom run," he said. "I knew she'd be in here sooner or later. I wasn't expecting such a crowd, though."

Rob shook his head, still not understanding.

"The check, Rob. I never switched them. The counterfeit one is in the evidence locker. That's the real one— and I'm taking it with me."

"This is a joke, right?" Rob asked.

"I wish it was." Joe went on, explaining as if he wanted Rob to understand. "I got a shot at an IPO a couple of months ago," he said. "I put my entire savings into it, and it crashed. I'm wiped out, Rob, and I'm not a young man anymore. This is my last chance at the kind of life I've always wanted. Twenty-five years my old man worked as a beat cop and he died broke, without realizing even one of his dreams. I won't do that, buddy.''

"But, Joe, you don't want to spend the rest of your life looking over your shoulder, do you? You know they'll come after you. They'll make your life a living hell.''

"My life is hell now, Rob. I was never meant to be a cop. I only joined the Bureau because my whole damn family's in law enforcement.''

"That's right, Joe, they are. And your nephew's about to join the Bureau. If you won't think about yourself, think about what this will do to him.''

Swan didn't imagine it would help, but she chimed in, too. "Rob is right, Joe. What good is a dream if you have to steal it from others? You'll never have that peace of mind you talk about, not this way.''

Her voice had a warmth that surprised her under the circumstances, and when Joe glanced at her, she thought she saw a softening in his features. Maybe it was wishful thinking, but they had to get through to him some way.

"It's not too late, Joe,'' Rob said. "Put the gun away. You haven't done anything yet. We can still fix this.''

The accomplice backed around to get a look at Joe, pulling Swan with her. "Don't listen to these Pollyannas,'' she told him. "They're lying to you! What do they know about you and your life? What do they care?''

"And you *do* care?'' Joe said, glancing her way.

"I can help you get what you've always wanted,'' she told him. "Take the check and we'll split it. I have the contacts we need to get it cashed and get out of the country. I have a private jet chartered. If you can get us safely to the airport, I'll take care of everything else.''

Joe was clearly listening, and she immediately upped

the stakes. "This is your dream, right? I'll give you more than half. Three million dollars! I'm offering you enough money to live comfortably for the rest of your life. Take it!"

All eyes were on Joe now. His gun hand wavered as he glanced from Rob to Swan.

"Make up your mind!" she shrilled at Joe, and then turned her fury on Rob. "Hand over the money or I'll put a bullet through her head."

Joe broke in, his tone hard and unyielding. "Let me see that check, Rob," he demanded.

Swan was heartsick. Joe was going to do it. He was going to take the money. She didn't expect Rob to co-operate, but he actually held the check out as if he were going to give it to Joe. The two men locked gazes for a moment, the tension palpable. Then something passed between them and Rob gave a slight nod. More of his sign language.

Rob thrust the check out at arm's length, holding it by a corner. Then Joe unexpectedly took aim, fired his pistol and put a bullet through the center of the heavy gauge paper, leaving a nice, neat hole. The five-million-dollar cashier's check was now essentially worthless.

The accomplice howled with rage. She shoved Swan against the countertop, apparently crazy enough to try to fight her way out. Swan fell back, but managed to grab the woman's gun as she passed. She held her arm away with one hand and with the other punched her squarely on the chin. The accomplice hit the floor like a sack of rocks.

"Damn," Rob whispered in awe. "Remind me to practice ducking."

Swan shook her hand vigorously. Her knuckles stung like fire. She'd never actually punched anyone like that before, and it wasn't something she wanted to do again.

Harris had already holstered his weapon and taken out his cuffs, as if he were about to make the arrest. He had the unconscious woman's hands behind her back and her ID out of her coat pocket, apparently before he realized what he was doing.

"Sorry," he said, glancing at the ID before handing the woman's wallet to Rob. "She's an insider, all right."

Rob whistled as he scanned the ID and read the name for Swan's benefit. "Janet Marlow, president of the bank. Looks like we caught a pretty big fish."

Joe had picked up Marlow's weapon, too, and as he gave it to Rob, said, "I guess I should be giving you mine, as well. Am I under arrest?"

Rob clearly had a decision to make and Swan couldn't imagine how he was going to handle it.

At last Rob shook his head. "I'm not the cop here, remember?" he told Joe. "You are. Maybe you should take her in. And return the check while you're at it, big guy."

"Thanks, man," Joe said, kneeling over the suspect. Marlow was slowly coming around, but she looked dizzy and confused as Joe helped her to her feet. "The room service isn't great where you're going," he told her, "but maybe we can arrange for you and Art Long to have adjoining rooms."

As Joe hustled the stunned woman toward the door, Rob slipped his own weapon in his back pocket and went over to Swan.

"Are you okay?" he asked her. "Anything hurt?"

She had to smile at that one. "Nothing important."

"Thank God," Rob breathed, tugging her into his arms. "It would have been hell if I couldn't have hugged you."

She laughed and gave herself over to the warmth of his arms and the amazing strength of his character. He was tough and guarded and difficult to deal with, but he was the best man she'd ever met, and even though she had no idea what their future was or what he wanted, she did know one thing. She was sticking with him...or maybe she should say he was stuck with her.

"Is it over?" she asked him, her voice muffled by the soft material of his shirt. "Is it really over?"

Rob buried his hands in her hair and brought her even closer. "Yeah, it's over, and I've never been so scared in my life," he admitted. "The thought of you being harmed was more than I could handle."

Swan was deeply touched. Fighting back tears, she tilted her head up to kiss him and was surprised to find him studying her. He looked as if he'd never seen her before, and suddenly she found herself being held at arm's length.

"I don't think I can live without you, McKenna. I know I'm a lousy risk, but would you take a chance on me anyway?"

"A chance?" Her heart began to pound as she saw the kindling desire in his blue eyes, and she wondered if he could possibly be saying what he thought she was saying.

"A chance on the future," he said. "It looks like I'm going to be needing a partner and—"

"Rob Gaines, is this some kind of proposal?"

When he nodded, she let out a gasp.

"Oh, no! Not that. Not now!"

"I guess that's a no?" he said uncertainly.

She broke away from him and raced into one of the stalls, slamming and bolting the door behind her. "Don't go away!" she said. "I'll be right back."

Rob stood there, watching in confusion until he heard the rustling of her scrambling out of her hose and panties, then a tinkling sound and a sigh of relief.

He was already laughing when she called out to him.

"If you were serious about that proposal," she said, "the answer is yes!"

14

Four months later...

LYNNE CARMICHAEL tapped a silver spoon against a crystal goblet, causing the cheerful voices that surrounded Rob Gaines to fall silent. Swan sat next to Rob, cradling his hand lovingly in her lap. An emerald-cut, blue-white diamond sparkled on her ring finger, and he felt a familiar sensation as he glanced at it. The burning lump in his throat wasn't on the list of acceptable emotions for strong, silent types, but it was pretty much his lot in life these days. *She* was his lot in life, thank God, and everything that came with her, including burning lumps in his throat.

Reluctantly he turned away from Swan and took in the smiling faces of everyone at the table. On this balmy Saturday afternoon in mid-December, the guests had assembled in the most beautiful part of the Carmichael villa gardens. Gerard, party planner extraordinaire, was on Rob's left, and directly across from Rob sat Rob's sister, Beth, followed by Swan's mother and Jack Mathias. As the party's official hostess, Lynne was at the head of the table.

When she had everyone's attention, she rose and cleared her throat.

"Thank you all for coming," she said, introducing herself all around.

Rob had met the infamous Lynne for the first time when she'd testified at Art Long's trial, and it hadn't been easy to get her back to L.A. in time for that. She was having too much fun "negotiating" with Gvon, who, as it turned out, was interested in more than dressing women. He rather liked undressing them, too. Currently he and Lynne were dating, whatever that meant.

Maybe the riot of blond curls and the flamboyant mini Lynne had worn to court shouldn't have surprised Rob, given what he knew about her, but he had probably blinked once or twice. Maybe even winced. Today her summer outfit reminded him of a tightly wrapped floral shower curtain, but he kept it to himself. He had learned a few things in the past apocalyptic few months. Mostly that he knew nothing about fashion, but also that it was Lynne's energy, generous spirit and wide-open heart that counted.

"I'm so glad that you could join us," she said, "to celebrate Swan and Rob's upcoming nuptials—in just *two* weeks. I also want to thank our very own Gerard for putting this party together," she said. "He has to be one of the most talented event planners on planet earth, as well as a friend who is loyal to a fault."

"It's nothing," Gerard said dismissively, adding, "when someone else foots the bill." He raised his goblet of wine to salute Lynne, who returned the gesture.

Rob now lived in a Marina del Rey condo that would be his and Swan's home after they were married. He'd started his own executive security agency, and Swan still put in long days at the villa. But their nights and weekends were spent together.

They had both been surprised when they'd arrived today. Unlike the big bash Gerard put together for the Brief Encounters launch party this was an intimate affair that conveyed a warm, embracing essence. The table was covered in crisp white linen. The centerpiece was an ice sculpture of intertwined wedding bands with a heart-shaped base. Platters of finger food filled the table—iced shrimp, hot wings, sushi and fire-roasted artichokes, along with marble slabs bearing exotic patés and cheeses, bowls heaped with fresh-cut fruit, several bottles of champagne and vintage wines.

But as lovely as the table and surrounding gardens were, there was one thing conspicuously out of place. A tarp-covered object as large as a small monument sat mysteriously in the center of the garden, waiting to be unveiled. When Swan had earlier tried to sneak a peek under the canvas, Gerard had threatened her with dismemberment.

"When Swan told me she was marrying the FBI agent who'd busted her," Lynne continued, "I was speechless—and I'm *never* speechless. Then I met Rob and, well…I almost wished he'd busted me."

She grinned and raised her glass to Swan. "Good work, partner. Never again will I think of you as lacking in the spirit of adventure. And never again will I love you more or owe you more than I do at this moment. It's because of you—well, Rob and Gerard helped, too—that Brief Encounters is still in business. A thriving business, I might add. It's also because of you that yours truly isn't in some smelly jail somewhere, awaiting trial. And, finally, it's because of you that the Carmichael estate is *still* the Carmichael estate.

"What I owe you, my dear friend, is beyond words." She blinked away the threat of tears and spoke to the others. "And now that she's proven herself so valiant and brave, this lawman is going to take her away! Can you believe it?" She raised her glass a notch higher. "Here's to Rob and Swan!"

Wineglasses shot up, joining Lynne in the toast. Rob felt his heart clutch as his little sister stood to say a few words. Her silver and brass medals and service ribbons caught the sun and glinted like stars on her blue dress uniform. It was still impossible for him not to get choked up with pride and admiration for her. She'd joined the army right out of high school, pursued a college degree and made it into Officer's Candidate School, finishing in the top ten percent of her class. She was a first lieutenant now, but he'd learned today as they'd spoken privately that she was on the captain's list. There didn't seem to be any stopping her now. All despite her teen years, which had been touch and go. Back then, she'd seemed determined to prove that she was her mother's daughter.

His only regret today was that their mother wasn't there to see how her kids had turned out. She might even have been proud. He was.

"I just met Swan," Beth said to the group, "but I have a bit of sisterly advice for her. He's going to be a handful, Swan. I suspect you already know that. What I can tell you with total conviction is that he's worth the trouble. He will put you first over everything else, even his own life, and he will love you and protect you and take care of you to his last breath. I'm living proof of the strength of his love."

Swan's fingers tightened on Rob's arm, and he placed his hand over hers. Beth had just expressed some of the things he deeply felt but would never have been able to say in that way.

As Beth sat down, Mrs. McKenna stood up. Swan went very still, and Rob sensed that, even after all she'd been through, Swan was still nervous about what her mother might say. She was getting married, and apparently she needed her mother's approval. Rob hoped she got it.

Pat McKenna was tall and slim and had a reserve about her that could have been mistaken for aloofness. But from what Swan had told him, her mother was a prisoner of her own high standards, not unkind or uncaring. Still, she had an imposing look about her, and Rob could imagine that she was an intimidating figure to a small child. Her hair was short, but expertly cut. She wore a teal-blue sheath and matching jacket with three-quarter sleeves, along with white gloves, which she'd reluctantly removed to sample the finger foods.

Now she held those gloves tightly in her hands.

"I hope you know how proud I am of you, Swan," she said. "I never dreamed that you could accomplish such things," she took a moment to swallow, "but maybe I should have. If I didn't encourage you enough, it was only because I was trying to protect you and spare you as much pain as I could. It isn't always safe to wrap your heart and dreams in a blanket of hope. Like all blankets, hope can unravel and leave you exposed and unprepared for the dangers out there. I wanted you to be safe, and I really believed that if you risked nothing, you lost nothing."

Rob glanced over at Swan, who was looking directly at her mother. Swan managed a little smile, apparently trying to remain composed.

"But you know something, my daughter?" Pat said, "I'm glad you didn't listen to me. You found your own way despite my fears and concerns, and I'm very grateful you did. If I could ask one thing of you now, it would be this. I'd like you to listen just this once because you're about to take the most important step of your life. You're marrying a good man, Swan. Be sure you risk loving him with all your heart."

That's all it took to get the tears brimming in Swan's eyes to overflow. As she struggled to thank her mother, Pat reached across the table and took her hand. Both of them were crying openly, and Rob was honestly at a loss. He pulled out his handkerchief, but of course it was Gerard who saved the day.

"All right, you two," Gerard said, "enough with the

tears. There'll be plenty of time for that at the wedding. Jack, speak up, man.''

Jack Mathias was well over six feet tall, and even in his mid-sixties, he was blessed with the craggy good looks of a much younger Clint Eastwood. Under other circumstances, Jack would probably have been as cool and collected as Clint, too, but a man could only take so much, and the sentiment flowing back and forth seemed to have gotten to him.

"Rob, Swan," he said gruffly, "I have only one thing worth saying. Don't ever take your love for granted and don't ever take *time* for granted. Spend each and every day loving each other as if it were your last. It might be.''

He nodded and sat down. Rob gave him an answering nod, which was all either one of them could handle at that moment.

Again, Gerard broke in. "Oooookay, time for a change of pace.''

He rose with a great flourish and picked up his wineglass, but instead of toasting the guests of honor, he pretended to use it as a microphone. "May I just say that I had a very long and moving speech prepared for this occasion, but between the bunch of you, you've stolen *all* my material. There's nothing moving left to say, and, besides, I think it's time for some waterworks of a different kind, don't you? So, without further ado, my tribute to the perfect couple.''

He excused himself from the table and walked to the tentlike object, which had been the focus of everyone's intense curiosity all afternoon.

"What have you got under there?" Lynne asked. "A giant marital aid?''

There were chuckles all around the table and Gerard's reaction was an innocent shrug. "Could be," he admitted.

"Swan and Rob," he said, "knowing the strength of

your passion for each other and the weakness of Swan's plumbing, I believe this is something you will never want to be without.''

He did a passing imitation of a drum roll and then yanked on a rope that whisked away the tarp and unveiled the tribute. As the object was revealed, the entire table gasped with delight. Spontaneous applause broke out, and even Swan and Rob joined in.

Gerard's gift was a brand-new, royal-blue portable toilet, mounted on wheels and sporting a trailer hitch. The decal on the door was a white swan.

"KIND SIR," Swan murmured, "whatever would I have done if you hadn't kidnapped me and dragged me off to your cabin in the woods?"

She seemed determined to show her appreciation as Rob pulled the car off the main drag and turned onto the access road that led to Jack's cabin. Cuddled up next to him on the car seat, she batted her eyelashes, indulging in a little shameless flirting as she quite brazenly stroked his thigh.

Rob's smile was only slightly lascivious. "You're welcome, m'lady. Glad I could be of service."

Actually, he couldn't wait to be of service. It had been a full week since the engagement party and Rob had only seen Swan sporadically during that time. She, Lynne, Beth and Swan's mother had been flitting all over L.A. in their quest to put the finishing touches on the wedding plans. Rob had begun to wonder if he would *ever* get Swan alone again, so he'd kidnapped her, to use her word. And he intended to give "m'lady" plenty of opportunity to show her gratefulness.

In fairness, he had to admit that he'd been busy, as well. His agency was growing at warp speed. He'd already hired two retired police officers and would need another two or three in the coming months just to keep pace with the work pouring in.

As they neared the cabin, Swan grew quiet.

"Regretting your abduction already?" he asked. "Kind Sir has something special in mind for M'lady, and he predicts she's going to like it."

She laughed softly. "I'm not regretting anything. I'm just remembering the first time I was here. I have to admit that I'm not sorry Art Long got twenty years in a high-security federal prison. I almost wish Janet Marlow *was* in an adjoining cell, although I suspect she was conned just like the rest of us."

"True, and she did the right thing testifying against Long. Plus, it's her first offense. She'll be out in five years if she behaves herself. It could have been a lot worse."

Swan continued to stroke his thigh and send shivers along his nerve endings. "You haven't heard from Joe in nearly a month," she said. "I hope he's surviving in his island paradise."

"Frankly, I'm more worried about paradise surviving." Just as Rob had predicted, Joe had gotten off light. He'd been disciplined by the Bureau, suspended without pay and ordered into stress counseling, after which he'd been given an opportunity to retire early. Naturally he'd jumped at that, which was probably a good thing for all concerned.

"I got a letter postmarked Barbados two days ago," he told her, "but I haven't had a chance to tell you about it. Joe bought a little beachside bar on credit and he's decided to offer a ladies' night with male waiters in thongs. He also said something about an all-male revue. I'm going to write back and tell him that Gerard is on his way."

Swan's laughter was quick and infectious. It was still resonating like cheerful music as they neared the turnoff to the cabin. Rob eased his foot off the gas pedal and slowed just enough to press a kiss to her waiting lips. It was amazing how she could anticipate him, but he doubted she knew what was coming next.

"Remember those special plans Kind Sir has for M'lady?" he said. "If she closes her beautiful blue eyes, he'll share one of them."

"I always close my eyes when you kiss me," she pointed out.

"Well, this time keep them closed until I tell you to open them, or Kind Sir will be forced to make use of the riding crop he keeps in the console just for such purposes."

She let out a little squeak of protest, but did what she was told like a good captive. As far as he could tell, she wasn't peeking as he drove the last hundred yards to the cabin.

"Can I open my eyes?" she asked when they stopped.

"Not yet." Rob left the car door hanging open as he came around to let her out. When she had her feet firmly planted on the ground, he said, "Now you can look."

Her eyes blinked open and her hands flew to her mouth. She stepped back, teetering as he thought she might. He steadied her with a hand to the small of her back, giving her time to take it all in.

The cabin was wrapped up like a gargantuan Christmas present with a foot-wide red ribbon wound around the entire structure and a huge bow attached to the front door.

"What does this mean?" she whispered through her fingers. She seemed frozen in place, afraid to move, to breathe, to do anything, maybe for fear it would all disappear.

"It means exactly what you think it means," Rob assured her. He put his arms around her and pulled her close, but a moment later she walked right out of them, a woman on a mission. There was a white envelope taped underneath the bow on the door, and she was heading for it.

Rob followed, smiling as she hurried up the steps to the front porch.

Despite her shaking hands, Swan didn't waste a minute freeing the card from the envelope and devouring the words. She was expecting a note from Rob, but she was in for another surprise.

Make it a home, Swan. It deserves that much and so do you and Rob.

> Best wishes forever,
> Jack.

"Oh, my God," she whispered. "He's given us the cabin."

She turned to Rob in utter shock. This was too much. There was no way she could make herself believe it, even as she watched Rob reach into his jacket to pull out what looked like legal papers.

"Yes, he's given us the cabin. It's a wedding present, and he knows we'll be making it a home—our second home—and that we'll be up here every chance we get."

Swan's chin began to tremble and the tip of her nose was fiery hot. "I don't think you know what this means to me, Rob," she said, her voice wavering. "I've never lived in any place that I could call my own."

"That's why I had him make out the deed to you and you alone. It's my wedding gift to you."

He handed her the papers, and she crushed them to her chest without the slightest awareness of what she was doing. Her entire mind was focused on two things: that he had just given her the one thing she'd waited her whole life for, and that she could do the same thing for him.

He'd told her what he wanted the first time they were at the cabin, just moments after they'd made love.

"Rob Gaines," she said softly, "you *are* my home. You are my heart. I promise you will never be alone as long as there is breath left in me. And I plan to keep breathing for a very long time."

His chin looked as though it might be a little wobbly, too, his nose a little red.

"Come here," he said. He held out his arms, and she rushed into them, never wanting to be anywhere else.

Is your man too good to be true?

Hot, gorgeous AND romantic?
If so, he could be a Harlequin® Blaze™ series cover model!

Our grand-prize winners will receive a trip for two to New York City to
shoot the cover of a Blaze novel, and will stay at the luxurious Plaza Hotel.
Plus, they'll receive $500 U.S. spending money!
The runner-up winners will receive $200 U.S.
to spend on a romantic dinner for two.

It's easy to enter!

In 100 words or less, tell us what makes your boyfriend or spouse a true romantic
and the perfect candidate for the cover of a Blaze novel, and include in your submission
two photos of this potential cover model.

All entries must include the written submission of the contest entrant, two photographs of the model
candidate and the Official Entry Form and Publicity Release forms completed in full and signed by
both the model candidate and the contest entrant. Harlequin, along with the experts at
Elite Model Management, will select a winner.

For photo and complete Contest details, please refer to the Official Rules on the next page. All entries
will become the property of Harlequin Enterprises Ltd. and are not returnable.

Please visit www.blazecovermodel.com to download a copy of the Official Entry Form and
Publicity Release Form or send a request to one of the addresses below.

Please mail your entry to: **Harlequin Blaze Cover Model Search**

In U.S.A.
P.O. Box 9069
Buffalo, NY
14269-9069

In Canada
P.O. Box 637
Fort Erie, ON
L2A 5X3

No purchase necessary. Contest open to Canadian and U.S. residents who are 18 and over.
Void where prohibited. Contest closes September 30, 2003.

HBCVRMODEL1

HARLEQUIN BLAZE COVER MODEL SEARCH CONTEST 3569 OFFICIAL RULES
NO PURCHASE NECESSARY TO ENTER

1. To enter, submit two (2) 4" x 6" photographs of a boyfriend or spouse (who must be 18 years of age or older) taken no later than three (3) months from the time of entry: a close-up, waist up, shirtless photograph; and a fully clothed, full-length photograph, then, tell us, in 100 words or fewer, why he should be a Harlequin Blaze cover model and how he is romantic. Your complete "entry" must include: (i) your essay, (ii) the Official Entry Form and Publicity Release Form printed below completed and signed by you (as "Entrant"), (iii) the photographs (with your hand-written name, address and phone number, and your model's name, address and phone number on the back of each photograph), and (iv) the Publicity Release Form and Photograph Representation Form printed below completed and signed by your model (as "Model"), and should be sent via first-class mail to either: Harlequin Blaze Cover Model Search Contest 3569, P.O. Box 9069, Buffalo, NY, 14269-9069, or Harlequin Blaze Cover Model Search Contest 3569, P.O. Box 637, Fort Erie, Ontario L2A 5X3. All submissions must be in English and be received no later than September 30, 2003. Limit: one entry per person, household or organization. **Purchase or acceptance of a product offer does not improve your chances of winning.** All entry requirements must be strictly adhered to for eligibility and to ensure fairness among entries.

2. Ten (10) Finalist submissions (photographs and essays) will be selected by a panel of judges consisting of members of the Harlequin editorial, marketing and public relations staff, as well as a representative from Elite Model Management (Toronto) Inc., based on the following criteria:

Aptness/Appropriateness of submitted photographs for a Harlequin Blaze cover—70%
Originality of Essay—20%
Sincerity of Essay—10%

In the event of a tie, duplicate finalists will be selected. The photographs submitted by finalists will be posted on the Harlequin website no later than November 15, 2003 (at www.blazecovermodel.com), and viewers may vote, in rank order, on their favorite(s) to assist in the panel of judges' final determination of the Grand Prize and Runner-up winning entries based on the above judging criteria. All decisions of the judges are final.

3. All entries become the property of Harlequin Enterprises Ltd. and none will be returned. Any entry may be used for future promotional purposes. Elite Model Management (Toronto) Inc. and/or its partners, subsidiaries and affiliates operating as "Elite Model Management" will have access to all entries including all personal information, and may contact any Entrant and/or Model in its sole discretion for their own business purposes. Harlequin and Elite Model Management (Toronto) Inc. are separate entities with no legal association or partnership whatsoever having no power to bind or obligate the other or create any expressed or implied obligation or responsibility on behalf of the other, such that Harlequin shall not be responsible in any way for any acts or omissions of Elite Model Management (Toronto) Inc. or its partners, subsidiaries and affiliates in connection with the Contest or otherwise and Elite Model Management shall not be responsible in any way for any acts or omissions of Harlequin or its partners, subsidiaries and affiliates in connection with the contest or otherwise.

4. All Entrants and Models must be residents of the U.S. or Canada, be 18 years of age or older, and have no prior criminal convictions. The contest is not open to any Model that is a professional model and/or actor in any capacity at the time of the entry. Contest void wherever prohibited by law; all applicable laws and regulations apply. Any litigation within the Province of Quebec regarding the conduct or organization of a publicity contest may be submitted to the Régie des alcools, des courses et des jeux for a ruling, and any litigation regarding the awarding of a prize may be submitted to the Régie only for the purpose of helping the parties reach a settlement. Employees and immediate family members of Harlequin Enterprises Ltd., D.L. Blair, Inc., Elite Model Management (Toronto) Inc. and their parents, affiliates, subsidiaries and all other agencies, entities and persons connected with the use, marketing or conduct of this Contest are not eligible to enter. Acceptance of any prize offered constitutes permission to use Entrants' and Models' names, essay submissions, photographs or other likenesses for the purposes of advertising, trade, publication and promotion on behalf of Harlequin Enterprises Ltd., its parent, affiliates, subsidiaries, assigns and other authorized entities involved in the judging and promotion of the contest without further compensation to any Entrant or Model, unless prohibited by law.

5. Finalists will be determined no later than October 30, 2003. Prize Winners will be determined no later than January 31, 2004. Grand Prize Winners (consisting of winning Entrant and Model) will be required to sign and return Affidavit of Eligibility/Release of Liability and Model Release forms within thirty (30) days of notification. Non-compliance with this requirement and within the specified time period will result in disqualification and an alternate will be selected. Any prize notification returned as undeliverable will result in the awarding of the prize to an alternate set of winners. All travelers (or parent/legal guardian of a minor) must execute the Affidavit of Eligibility/Release of Liability prior to ticketing and must possess required travel documents (e.g. valid photo ID) where applicable. Travel dates specified by Sponsor must be after May 30, 2004.

6. Prizes: One (1) Grand Prize—the opportunity for the Model to appear on the cover of a paperback book from the Harlequin Blaze series, and a 3 day/2 night trip for two (Entrant and Model) to New York, NY for the photo shoot of Model which includes round-trip coach air transportation from the commercial airport nearest the winning Entrant's home to New York, NY, (or, in lieu of air transportation, $100 cash payable to Entrant and Model, if the winning Entrant's home is within 250 miles of New York, NY), hotel accommodations (double occupancy) at the Plaza Hotel and $500 cash spending money payable to Entrant and Model, (approximate prize value: $8,000), and one (1) Runner-up Prize of $200 cash payable to Entrant and Model for a romantic dinner for two (approximate prize value: $200). Prizes are valued in U.S. currency. Prizes consist of only those items listed as part of the prize. No substitution of prize(s) permitted by winners. All prizes are awarded jointly to the Entrant and Model of the winning entries, and are not severable - prizes and obligations may not be assigned or transferred. Any change to the Entrant and/or Model of the winning entries will result in disqualification and an alternate will be selected. Taxes on prize are the sole responsibility of winners. Any and all expenses and/or items not specifically described as part of the prize are the sole responsibility of winners. Harlequin Enterprises Ltd. and D.L. Blair, Inc., their parents, affiliates, and subsidiaries are not responsible for errors in printing of Contest entries and/or game pieces. No responsibility is assumed for lost, stolen, late, illegible, incomplete, inaccurate, non-delivered, postage due or misdirected mail or entries. In the event of printing or other errors which may result in unintended prize values or duplication of prizes, all affected game pieces or entries shall be null and void.

7. Winners will be notified by mail. For winners' list (available after March 31, 2004), send a self-addressed, stamped envelope to: Harlequin Blaze Cover Model Search Contest 3569 Winners, P.O. Box 4200, Blair, NE 68009-4200, or refer to the Harlequin website (at www.blazecovermodel.com).

Contest sponsored by Harlequin Enterprises Ltd., P.O. Box 9042, Buffalo, NY 14269-9042.

If you enjoyed what you just read,
then we've got an offer you can't resist!

Take 2 bestselling love stories FREE!
Plus get a FREE surprise gift!

1. As you may know, there are many different lines under the Harlequin and Silhouette brands. Each of the lines is listed below. Please check the box that most represents your reading habit for each line.

Line	Currently read this line	Do not read this line	Not sure if I read this line
Harlequin American Romance	❑	❑	❑
Harlequin Duets	❑	❑	❑
Harlequin Romance	❑	❑	❑
Harlequin Historicals	❑	❑	❑
Harlequin Superromance	❑	❑	❑
Harlequin Intrigue	❑	❑	❑
Harlequin Presents	❑	❑	❑
Harlequin Temptation	❑	❑	❑
Harlequin Blaze	❑	❑	❑
Silhouette Special Edition	❑	❑	❑
Silhouette Romance	❑	❑	❑
Silhouette Intimate Moments	❑	❑	❑
Silhouette Desire	❑	❑	❑

2. Which of the following best describes why you bought *this book?* One answer only, please.

the picture on the cover	❑	the title	❑
the author	❑	the line is one I read often	❑
part of a miniseries	❑	saw an ad in another book	❑
saw an ad in a magazine/newsletter	❑	a friend told me about it	❑
I borrowed/was given this book	❑	other: _____	❑

3. Where did you buy *this book?* One answer only, please.

at Barnes & Noble	❑	at a grocery store	❑
at Waldenbooks	❑	at a drugstore	❑
at Borders	❑	on eHarlequin.com Web site	❑
at another bookstore	❑	from another Web site	❑
at Wal-Mart	❑	Harlequin/Silhouette Reader Service/through the mail	❑
at Target	❑		
at Kmart	❑	used books from anywhere	❑
at another department store or mass merchandiser	❑	I borrowed/was given this book	❑

4. On average, how many Harlequin and Silhouette books do you buy at one time?

I buy _____ books at one time   ❑
I rarely buy a book   ❑

MRQ403HB-1A

5. How many times per month do you shop for any *Harlequin and/or Silhouette* books?
   One answer only, please.

1 or more times a week	❏	a few times per year	❏
1 to 3 times per month	❏	less often than once a year	❏
1 to 2 times every 3 months	❏	never	❏

6. When you think of your ideal heroine, which *one* statement describes her the best?
   One answer only, please.

She's a woman who is strong-willed	❏	She's a desirable woman	❏
She's a woman who is needed by others	❏	She's a powerful woman	❏
She's a woman who is taken care of	❏	She's a passionate woman	❏
She's an adventurous woman	❏	She's a sensitive woman	❏

7. The following statements describe types or genres of books that you may be
   interested in reading. Pick *up to 2 types* of books that you are most interested in.

I like to read about truly romantic relationships	❏
I like to read stories that are sexy romances	❏
I like to read romantic comedies	❏
I like to read a romantic mystery/suspense	❏
I like to read about romantic adventures	❏
I like to read romance stories that involve family	❏
I like to read about a romance in times or places that I have never seen	❏
Other: _____	❏

*The following questions help us to group your answers with those readers who are
similar to you. Your answers will remain confidential.*

8. Please record your year of birth below.
   19 ____

9. What is your marital status?

   single ❏   married ❏   common-law ❏   widowed ❏
   divorced/separated ❏

10. Do you have children 18 years of age or younger currently living at home?
    yes ❏   no ❏

11. Which of the following best describes your employment status?

    employed full-time or part-time ❏   homemaker ❏   student ❏
    retired ❏   unemployed ❏

12. Do you have access to the Internet from either home or work?
    yes ❏   no ❏

13. Have you ever visited eHarlequin.com?
    yes ❏   no ❏

14. What state do you live in?

    _____

15. Are you a member of Harlequin/Silhouette Reader Service?
    yes ❏   Account #_____   no ❏   MRQ403HB-1B

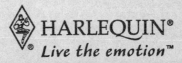

HARLEQUIN®

Blaze™

COMING NEXT MONTH